£2
W

Brought up in Kent and Norfolk, William Ardin was educated at the Royal Grammar School, Worcester and won a scholarship to Oxford. Much of his subsequent career with ICI was spent on Teesside, researching petrochemical markets.

He and his wife now live in a hillside cottage in Galloway, looking down towards the ruins of Sweetheart Abbey which was built by Devorgilla in the thirteenth century.

Light At Midnight

William Ardin

HEADLINE

First published in 1995
by HEADLINE BOOK PUBLISHING

First published in paperback in 1995
by HEADLINE BOOK PUBLISHING

10 9 8 7 6 5 4 3 2 1

ISBN 0 7472 4482 0

Typeset by
Letterpart Limited, Reigate, Surrey

Printed and bound in Great Britain by
Cox & Wyman Ltd, Reading, Berks

HEADLINE BOOK PUBLISHING
A division of Hodder Headline PLC
338 Euston Road
London NW1 3BH

Light At Midnight

Prologue

One wheel of the mobile stretcher was squeaking as they pushed her along the warm well-lit corridor towards the delivery room and it offended her sense of what was proper. One didn't spend what one was spending in this place to be offended by the noise of a squeaking wheel – here in Switzerland in this clinic as safe and secure as a womb itself. Her husband had insisted that she make the journey and he always got his own way, providing so many layers of protection for the life inside her – Switzerland, the clinic, and lastly her own body surrounding it. It was she who had provided that. That was the one that really mattered. Switzerland, she thought contemptuously. There had been absolutely no need to make her come all this way – she would have been looked after just as well at home.

Squeak, squeak the wheel went. There came another bright light in the ceiling of the passageway above her, came and went. Squeak, squeak. She could sense the expectant ladies ranged in their private rooms on either side of the passageway waiting for their time to arrive or congratulating themselves on a job well done surrounded by flowers, messages, books and magazines. Now it was her turn to be the centre of attention. The queen bee, waited on by her attendants.

Would there be congratulations for her in the morning? What would happen to her if she hadn't produced a son? *He* wanted a boy, had demanded a boy and was therefore quite confident that she would give him one. Just as he expected her to run the domestic side of his life with Rolls Royce precision and to give him sexual relief now and then, when he couldn't be bothered to make the effort to go to one of his mistresses. She amended that to 'one of his women', and then again to 'one of his whores'.

She had always disdained to pay him back in his own coin. It was a much more subtle ploy to be the perfect wife, poised and competent – the charming companion disarming him with her acquiescence.

How she detested him – and she hated him even more as another contraction seized her, a spasm like a monthly pain only ten times worse. It was out of her control and she hated that.

'Take a little gas and air,' murmured the voice behind her, and then with more urgency, more like a command, 'Don't push. Don't push. Hold back. It won't be long now.'

As the pain lifted for a moment she prayed that it would be a daughter just for spite and then, remembering *him*, thought better of it . . .

It was a long labour. A lonely uphill fight until through a mist of relief and exhaustion she heard it cry, a vigorous cry – but she was too tired to hold her arms out for it and tactfully they took it away.

'Later,' the nurse said, fussing over her, 'you must have a little rest first.' They wheeled her back to her room to the freshly made bed with its clean sheets and the dozens of roses which her sister had sent her. The sun was already high in the sky and it was lunchtime.

'The baby,' she asked when the auxiliary brought her lunch, 'is it a boy?' The woman smiled to placate her and obviously didn't understand a word.

'Nurse. Find the nurse.'

Nodding her comprehension the woman laid a soothing hand on her arm and went in search of help. The nurse arrived.

'Is it a boy?'

Automatically the nurse leant over to tuck in the straying edge of her top sheet, concentrating on the task, her head bent.

'Yes, you have a boy,' she said. Nothing else.

The new mother didn't know whether to be relieved or angry that she had fulfilled her lord and master's wishes. He always got what he wanted somehow, by luck or sheer willpower, using his money as a bludgeon. This time he had got himself a son. He didn't deserve it.

The nurse straightened up, rearranged the roses, fussed about.

'Can I see him?' The mother in the bed felt much stronger now that she knew where she stood.

'All in good time. You've been through a difficult labour and you really ought to sleep now. That would be much the best.'

When she awoke at six, feeling renewed and full of energy she asked the same question. This time they told her that the baby was asleep and it would be a pity to disturb him. To divert her they brought in a television set but she soon tired of the dancing black and white shadows and she didn't understand German. There was news of some sort of trouble in Cuba – there were pictures of the young and vigorous Fidel Castro haranguing crowds of followers and President Kennedy fending off questions at a news conference – she didn't understand what it was all about. It could have been anything from simple political point scoring to a full-blown international crisis. It was all curiously remote from her and she had the machine turned off. She felt isolated here in this foreign clinic where nobody spoke her language, and she longed to telephone her sister – her far-off voice would have been a comfort – only was reluctant to do so when she had so little to tell her about the baby. She would want to know his exact weight, the colour of his eyes, whom he most resembled. It was frustrating to know none of those things.

After she had breakfasted the next morning the obstetrician was brought to see her. After he had examined her, the nurse left them alone together closing the snow-white door behind her with finality.

Yes, the baby was in good health, he assured her, choosing the phrase as though selecting the scalpel. There was a pause.

'If I am recovered and the baby is well, why has he not been brought to me?' She spoke in English, the only language that they had in common.

There was an uncompromising look in her eye which spoke of power and money and the readiness to use them which she had learnt from her husband. This clinic was no match for either of them.

'I wish to see him now if you please.'

Having reached a decision the specialist pressed the bell beside her bed and when the nurse opened the door – so quickly that she must have been waiting outside – he gave the necessary order, almost under his breath. Then he went to the window and stared out into the woods surrounding the clinic as though he had suddenly developed an interest in silviculture.

The nurse returned with a small bundle in the crook of her arm and bent down to show it to the mother, unwrapping it gradually, reluctantly, making no effort to hand it over – simply exposing it completely, while the doctor seated himself on the bed on her other side and took her hand between his own. This was the kind of sympathy she was paying for.

'A lot can be done these days. These days we can . . .' The sudden spasmodic grip of her hand on his arm silenced him.

She forced herself to look at the baby, detail by detail. Certainly a boy, vigorous and demanding like his father. The legs and toes, the remains of the tied-off umbilical cord, hands and arms with tiny pink nails – all as they should be. But at the other end of the arms, above the shoulders, things were not as they should be.

'It is not my field but I can see that much can be done . . .' his voice faded away as he considered the task facing any plastic surgeon. Keeping her hand in his he began again, 'We were not certain what should be done – what you would wish us to do.'

What did he mean? That this inconvenient little mon-ster should be allowed to fade away discreetly on a diet of water, false affection and nothing else? Wasn't that what they did sometimes? And, of course, it was that kind of consideration for her feelings that she was paying for. That is why she was there – to be protected from inconvenience.

She looked down at the infant again, yowling with his arms and legs outstretched, and all at once felt her first freezing dismay being replaced by a kind of triumph. All her married life she had been a model wife, refusing to pay her husband back in his own coin. Now quite by accident she found herself in a position to level the score. It was he who had fathered this indignant little creature bellowing in front of her; he would not be able to disown it nor would he be able to hide it. She had laid a burden on his shoulders which he would have to carry for the rest of his life and nobody was going to take that achievement away from her.

Withdrawing her hand from the consultant's grasp, she looked him dispassionately in the eye. 'All this child needs is to be fed,' she said. 'See to it.'

Chapter One

'What on earth is this?' asked Charles Ramsay.

'It came for you. I signed for it,' she answered, putting one hand lightly on his shoulder and squeezing past him although she didn't really need to. It was nice of her – she could have gone round the other way.

It stood on the polished surface of the excellent Georgian two-pedestal dining table they had set in the centre of the showroom. A large irregular package about two feet high wrapped in brown paper and string, or rather baler twine – hairy stuff, the kind of thing that farmers used. He gave it a squeeze – soft on the surface and hard underneath. A bit like Julia. No, that wasn't right, not at all. Just one of those silly clever-clever thoughts that came into one's head unbidden.

'Aren't you going to open it?' she said without looking at him. Her gaze was elsewhere, her eyes glancing here and there around the showroom, then down to the clipboard in her hand, checking off the pieces one by one. Her lips moving.

His hands moved over the object, pressing, probing. The top was familiar enough. It felt like a figure of some kind but the base was very odd. It was nothing like the sort of plinth you would expect, being broad and very thin in relation to its area. No more than a quarter of an inch thick.

'I'm trying to guess what it is.'

'Don't waste time, Charles. It's the opening tomorrow night.'

'I'm well aware of that but you don't expect me to wait that long to open this intriguing package surely. I need something with an edge. To cut the string with, you know.'

'In the back. You're not going to open it there are you, for goodness sake? It'll make a mess.'

Picking it up carefully with both hands he shouldered his way through the door marked 'Private' and put it down on the large businesslike desk he had bought himself. A modern executive's desk. Scissors. Where were the scissors?

'By the window.' Sure enough there they were. What a memory Julia had. What would he do without her?

Snip. The blades sheared through the rough twine in a very satisfying way and it fell smartly away. Snip. He brushed it to one side and slowly began to cut through the transparent sticky tape which held the covering together. Delicately he unwrapped it to expose a mass of newspaper – pages of the *Eastern Courant* he noticed, their local newspaper at Bressemer. He peeled each sheet off one at a time and laid it neatly aside. Ah, here was an envelope with his name on it, scrawled in block capitals in bright blue ink. Eager to get to the heart of the matter he laid that aside too and took away the rest of the paper.

Good Lord, it was porcelain. Hastily he inspected it for damage. It looked as though it was unscathed. Yes, he rather thought it was, and that was miraculous and only because they'd at least had the sense to send it by courier instead of by parcel post. He felt a presence behind him, a warm presence. Julia, her chin on his shoulder, arms creeping round his waist, unable to restrain her curiosity.

'That's gorgeous. An eagle. What is it?'

Which porcelain factory had manufactured it – that was what she meant. Instinctively he went to lift it up to look for a mark underneath and found that his groping fingers couldn't get a purchase at the bottom edge. It was stuck to the baseboard. Of course it had to be since it hadn't shifted when he had lifted it. Who in their right mind would glue a piece of porcelain of that quality to a chunk of blockboard two feet square. Answer – somebody who was afraid it would topple over. A practical man.

Yes it was an eagle perched on a rock with its wings folded. It had a cream coloured head and neck, imperious eyes, and a hooked beak as black and glossy as bitumen. From the chest down its painted plumage was chocolate brown, the wings being highlighted with bands of a paler shade. Tastefully the baseboard had been painted in one-coat emulsion to match.

'Is that the letter that came with it? Why don't you read it?' Julia demanded. 'That's what it's for.'

He opened it.

Oxgang Farm

Dear Mr Ramsay,

I was over at Bressemer last week for some pheasant chicks and your father mentioned that you were open-ing a new showroom in London which brought it to mind that you were still in the antique trade which made me think all of a sudden that you might be able to help us over our eagle. So here it is.

My grandmother bought it at a sale up at Bishop's Stortford just before the war and I've always wondered if it was worth anything. I wanted to take it to one of those roadshow things but they never come up our way so perhaps you can help. Don't suppose it is worth anything much though.

Your father seemed in good spirits when I called. We're all getting older of course.

Yours truly,
James Rice

'What are you going to do?' Julia asked.

'Find out about it first.' Putting the letter in his pocket he picked up the fierce china bird and took it down to their brand new storeroom in the basement, in their brand new lift.

Conscious of the perils of any partnership it had taken him a long time to make up his mind to go in with Julia but now that they were so close it was more like a husband and wife thing really – as good as. He trusted her and besides her mother had dipped into her capital and come up with a very helpful amount so her side of the family were standing as much of the risk as he was.

He was sure it was the right time. Anyone could see that the recession was coming to an end. With the yen hitting new highs the Japanese would be on the feed again, or soon would be. They had taken a risk with this post-modernist decor but Julia said she was fed up with gloomy pseudo Georgian and anyway half the people with money these days had modern houses – that was the point. What was more they wanted to be able to see what they were buying. He had deferred to her judgement – that was what a partnership was about – seeing the other person's point of view. Therefore stainless-steel fitments instead of brass, plenty of light from above, pale maple floors everywhere, built-in cupboards faced with plate glass round the walls for displaying glass, silver and porcelain – much better than dim cabinets with astragalled doors that always obscured the client's view.

Although it was in a very decent location he had been able to screw a reasonable rent out of the property company which had been eager to do business with so much unlet space on its books. But the fitting out had cost a fortune. Anyway it was all to play for now. He'd better get on. He'd forgotten to tell her to phone the caterers.

His father managed to arrive punctually from Liverpool Street the next day, with the dog flopping suspiciously out of the taxi after him. He couldn't leave Wellington behind he confided afterwards to Julia's mother beside him on the Regency *chaise-longue* with a selection of the hundred or so guests ebbing and flowing around him. Couldn't leave the poor old fellow at Bressemer because there was nobody now he could trust to look after him, not since old Agnes had died. Besides the dog would enjoy this outing – different smells, new people to make much of him. Wellington was stone-blind now but he still took an interest.

'He's not my guide dog, I'm his guide man,' Ernest Ramsay offered, fondling the dog's hot ears and was rewarded with a smile from the woman beside him. They understood one another – both of them wondering how this new venture would work out, standing helpless on the sidelines and hoping for the best while they sipped their champagne.

When the rout had finally ended, the guests gone, the hired waiters departed with their gear, Charles Ramsay took his father downstairs to look at what Jim Rice had sent him, as a diversion.

'Lord, I remember that,' said his father. 'They used to keep it in the dining room at Oxgang next to the fireplace.'

'He wants to know what it's worth.'

'Is he going to be disappointed?'

11

Charles shrugged. 'I hope not. I'm not certain where it comes from yet. I'll get a second opinion as soon as I have time.'

His father looked round the shelves of the storeroom with discernment. 'You've got some nice things here. I like that.' He nodded towards a little Regency chiffonier in faded rosewood with brass fittings. His enthusiasm faded and he looked back at his son with trouble in his eyes. In recent years Charles had grown more adept at reading the signs. Something was worrying the old man and he couldn't formulate it or was reluctant to do so. It would have to be explored.

'Of course I'm taking a bit of a risk but I know what I'm doing. I've been able to pick up some nice things and lock them away in the last twelve months and I can afford to keep them a while longer. Money's cheap and getting cheaper and the market is already picking up.'

His father pretended to examine the eagle's head with sudden attention. That wasn't it then.

Was it the fact that they'd involved Julia's mother in the scheme? 'We laid everything out clearly to her and insisted that she took legal advice. She's not liable for anything the partnership does. Nothing beyond what she's put in, which she can well afford.'

His father shook his head impatiently. That wasn't it either.

'Come along you two, we're ready to go and we're ravenous,' Julia called from the top of the stairs. They were all going out together for a late meal. A family party.

'Something's cropped up,' his father said quickly, 'and I'd welcome your advice. No time to talk about it now. Could you come up to Bressemer next weekend? Any chance of that?' He hurried on without looking at his son, 'I know you're both fearfully busy but I would appreciate it you see.

You could leave Julia in charge. There's no need to drag you both away from London.'

Charles scrutinised his father.

'What's up?' he asked as carelessly as he could, trying to prompt the old man to get it off his chest. But it wasn't the time and place.

'It'll keep,' Ernest Ramsay muttered as he turned towards the stairs. 'Mustn't keep them waiting.'

'Go down to Bressemer next Saturday!' Julia exploded, in the bedroom of the flat four hours later, brushing her hair with fierce indignant strokes. 'You can't be serious.'

'He's bothered. There's something wrong and he needs time to tell me.'

'OK, OK. But not next Saturday. Haven't you any conception of how important the next few weeks are? It's our launch for goodness sake,' she banged the hairbrush down on the dressing table and turned towards him thrusting out her clenched fists in frustration in front of her and bursting out, 'and there's so much to do.'

She'd had a heavy day and a modicum of alcohol at the end of it. She was tired, she was strung up – and she was right. Of course she was right. He'd have to put his visit off for at least a week, probably longer. It wasn't fair to her. They'd managed to stir up a lot of interest in the press here and there and they both had to be around to capitalise on it, to keep things moving. Of course.

Maybe he could get away the weekend after, he told his father when he rang him to make sure he'd got back safely the following morning. The old man didn't make a fuss about it. Just sounded fatalistic as though he'd run out of . . . authority, something like that.

Ramsay was pushed to find time even to ring him. A journalist from one of the glossies had come round to do an

interview at no notice at all and Julia had to cope with her in
the office while he took a Japanese dealer out for lunch at
the Pot au Feu, and afterwards Charles made their first sale
– a small ivory tusk vase carved in low relief with various
skeletons, wrestling, playing *go*, performing on musical
instruments. Hilarious, all those bare bones. Julia had hated
it but Charles knew his market and so did Mr Arai. After no
more than a glance he took it, together with the large ivory
figure of a basket seller.

'Interesting,' said Mr Arai gnomically. 'What else do you
have?'

'It's all in the storeroom. In the basement.'

Mr Arai raised an enquiring eyebrow and smiled. He was
a man who liked to get his own way.

Many of the things down there hadn't been fully assessed
and Charles wasn't keen to let any trade buyers down there
yet. On the other hand the man had just spent several
thousand pounds and he couldn't afford to make him lose
face.

'By all means,' he said, ushering him towards the lift.

He turned on the lights and let the dealer roam along the
long shelves on the one side of the room where the smaller
items were kept. He went from item to item, hands behind
his back as if to make sure that his host understood that he
wasn't going to touch anything, and that he realised that all
these items were still, as it were, in limbo. He spent almost
exactly the same amount of time in front of each one. A
pause . . . footsteps echoing on the new concrete floor . . .
a pause . . . more footsteps. Until he came to the eagle. His
small black eyes betrayed no interest but his hands unlocked
behind his back.

'May I?' he queried and gestured as if to pick it up.

Hastily Charles put in, 'It is stuck to the base I'm afraid.
That is how it was when it came in.' He didn't want Arai

thinking that it was some English practical joke. That would have been most upsetting for him.

'And it is not yet for sale?'

'It belongs to a friend of the family.' That was a fair description of Jim Rice. 'He has asked me to give an opinion on it.'

'And what is that opinion?' The eyes were lively and mocking.

Charles tapped the baseboard. 'I haven't had an opportunity to examine it completely yet.'

The Japanese gave it his attention for a moment. 'We might speak about it when you have,' he said.

Absorbing what he had been told, Ramsay conducted his visitor upstairs and when the Japanese had gone he went back and took another look at the eagle. Whoever had stuck it to the board had done the job some time ago, by no means tidily; and it looked as though he had used animal glue – it would have been out of character for any of the Rice family to have spent money on a fancy adhesive – and if so it shouldn't be a problem to soften it gently with warm water to get the eagle clear. However, to be on the safe side Ramsay rang his favourite porcelain restorer and invited him to deal with it. When they finally removed it from the baseboard they found no factory mark on the underside of the rock on which the bird was perched. Not that Ramsay had been banking on there being one.

Conscious that there were a thousand other things he should be doing he considered the anonymous bird on its anonymous rock. Now then, where did it hail from, this eagle of Jim Rice's? Provenance? A sale in Bishop's Stortford just before the balloon went up in 1939. That didn't get him far.

It was early, no doubt about that.

'Beginning of the seventeenth century,' put in the voice of the restorer behind him.

Yes . . . Ramsay ran his fingers lightly over the surface of the wings. A clear glaze over the brown feathers.

'That's an iron pigment,' prompted the voice. Why didn't it tell him something he didn't know? Then it did. 'I've seen a bird like that before, when I took the kids to visit a country house in Buckinghamshire, but I'm sure that one had a painted decoration over the glaze. They had a white model of it, unpainted, beside it. I remember wondering, if I'd had the whole model to paint, how close I could get it to the original. That would have been a challenge. Worthwhile.'

Ramsay turned to look at the man whose face was rapt, his gaze turned inward.

'That copy, where was it made now? It was German I think.' He shook his head with finality. 'No – can't remember.'

After he had taken his leave it still niggled Ramsay – having to admit that he didn't know for certain what the thing was. Whatever the restorer said it didn't look European. There was something about the modelling of the head . . . and Arai had recognised it and wanted it, Charles thought. For his money that eagle was early Japanese but he hadn't got time to research it. He'd have to take a short cut. Dirk van der Meuwe would know.

Dirk was an old friend of his who went back to the days when they had both been learning the trade as porters at Crowthers, the international auction house. Unlike Charles, he had stayed with them and become manager of their operation in Amsterdam and he was still there, cautious, imperturbable, surviving cutbacks and the recession by running a tight ship and keeping his head.

When Charles rang him he didn't waste time on the

amenities because his time was money too.

'Good morning, Charles. What can I do?'

Ramsay told him. A client was interested in it and he didn't know how long he was going to be in London. There wasn't time to send a photograph.

'The usual story. Describe it please in detail.' Ramsay did so. There was a heavy Dutch silence at the other end of the line. 'Sounds nice. I have business to do in London next Tuesday and I want to see this new showroom of yours anyway. I'll come at about four and you can give me tea and introduce me to your . . . Julia is it?'

'Julia, that's right. Thanks.'

That was all right then – Dirk was strong on oriental porcelain; in Amsterdam you needed to be.

After they closed that evening and they had eaten and gone through their diaries together he brought out a couple of bottles of Macon and they let their hair down.

Julia said she wasn't absolutely certain but she rather thought that eccentric friend of Mummy's, the one in the dramatic hat who was loaded – serious money, was going to buy not only that table but the chairs as well. She would ring in the morning.

'Goodness knows where she's going to put them. Mother says the house – it's a huge house as big as Bressemer nearly – is crammed to the doors. You can scarcely get *in*, Mummy says. Still that's the old girl's problem. Perhaps she's buying somewhere else. Nice old person.'

She folded her legs beneath her on the sofa, took a deep gulp from her glass and set it down on the floor in front of her. He told her how far he'd got with the eagle, that Dirk was coming on Tuesday.

'Sounds good,' she said. 'Good news for Farmer Rice but how much smoke does it put up our chimney?' The light

17

rebuke was not aggressively spoken. 'Do you think he'd want to sell?'

Perhaps. Ramsay was out of touch with the state of farming locally – his father didn't give much away these days. Oxgang was a middling size farm. You never could tell. Sometimes they lived like gypsies and would suddenly appear in a brand new Range Rover. Others' farms were beautifully kept, the latest machinery, everything and then you saw in the *Eastern Courant* that they were being sold up. The feeling in his bones was that Jim Rice would be prepared to part with it if the inducement were significant – not just a few hundred for something which was a small part of the family history, that Granny had bought before the war.

'Why don't you make him an offer, on spec? A couple of thousand or something?' she asked idly, taking a surreptitious look at her diary, preoccupied again with her own problems.

'One couldn't do that.' Charles spoke automatically.

'Why not?'

'He asked me for my opinion. He didn't say he wanted to sell it.' Try to diddle Jim Rice out of his eagle? That wasn't on his agenda.

She glanced across at him with annoyance, a look which said that he was being too honest for his own good. There were other considerations than just the duty of care which he owed to Jim. Like the rates on the business and the interest ticking up at the bank – and the security of the investment which her mother had made in them. She wasn't going to say that he needed a sharper commercial edge but she was allowed to think it.

'It's your *probitas* thing again is it? You've got a touch of the scruples?'

Probitas was the Ramsays' family motto, meaning honesty,

fair dealing. For generations most of his ancestors had lived by it. There had been the odd exception but his father certainly had and he himself tried to although it wasn't always easy to see the wood for the trees. He wasn't being priggish or anything like that. It was just that one had got used to it. It was like wearing a seatbelt in a car . . . You'd been doing it for so long that you felt uncomfortable without it. She knew all about it; they didn't need to go tramping over that ground again did they?

'You'd be taking a risk on it. You don't know what it's worth yet, do you?'

No, but a lot more than a couple of thousand, that was for sure. He said nothing.

'Have it your own way.' She went back to her book, making a neat note in it. She was good value, Julia, but sometimes her logic was a little tortuous.

Dirk's taxi was still there, waiting outside. His meeting had overrun and he would have to hurry or he would miss his flight he said.

'Unquestionably it is an Arita eagle. I thought that was what it might be,' he said, 'which is why I brought you a copy of this.' Clicking open his briefcase he produced a photocopy of an article.

' "Füche japanische Porzellanadler und Ihre verscheiden Nachbildungen".'

Ramsay glanced at it. 'Thanks,' he said. 'Catchy title.'

'You don't read German? Never mind,' Dirk gave Julia a heavy wink, 'it has some pictures.'

His humour hadn't progressed much, thought Charles, since the days when they had lugged furniture around Crowther's basement together, even if his tailoring had. He was wearing the kind of dark blue suit fit for a Eurocrat and he hadn't let the tailor stint on the quality of the cloth. Now, standing confident and foursquare in the centre of their office, he was taking a token gulp of hot tea from the mug in his hand, its handle turned outwards.

'What do you think it's worth? What do I tell my farming friend?'

'He wants to sell? We'd be delighted to . . .'

'That's up to him. He can't decide if he doesn't know . . .'

'Sure, sure. It's not easy. I've looked through the records. The last one we handled made twenty-three thousand pounds in the London rooms but that was five years ago and many things have changed since then.' Recessions, bear markets, revaluations, the rich juggling their wealth between bonds, equities, property, works of art – a lot of things.

Julia was much too well schooled to react visibly to the figure he'd come up with but Charles saw her bend forward a little, tensing a fraction before he cut in, 'Arai looked interested. You can never be quite sure. There was a glint in his eye though.'

'Don't forget the pound sterling is looking very cheap to him at the moment.'

Charles went to his desk and consulted his currency folder. 'The yen's risen by about a third since then so that would be equivalent, other things being equal, to . . .' his hand flickered over the calculator beside him and was still, '. . . about thirty-six thousand pounds today. However other things aren't equal.' The market over there had been down, had been in the doldrums, was on the turn. Perhaps.

'The market is improving,' Dirk announced, setting his mug down, pressed for time. 'I would expect to be able to get you more than a hundred thousand guilders at our big auction in Amsterdam in the autumn. Let me know.'

He turned to Julia. 'Thank you for the nice tea. I must go,' he said and went.

After the taxi had driven off Charles suggested, 'I could go up to talk it over with Jim Rice next weekend and then go on to Bressemer. Kill two birds with one stone.'

'Why don't I come with you?' she said. 'It would be a break.'

'I know, but it would be a lot more comfortable for my father if you didn't. He's never found it easy to communicate and it's not getting any better as he grows older. With you there he might find it just too difficult to unburden . . .' Which would mean a wasted weekend. Time, time, why wasn't there more of it?

'Fine. No problem,' she said, not being the sort who made a fuss. She thought it was a problem though: He could see that.

Tea at Oxgang was a much more leisurely ceremony. In his honour Ethel Rice had laid the table in the chilly dining room and looking round it, at the new carpet heavily patterned so as not to show the crumbs, at the somewhat approximate painting of a couple of Holstein cows, Charles wondered how many times the Rices actually ate a meal in this room. It had an unused feel to it. The eagle would have been safe enough here – out of harm's way in the nook beside the tiled fire surround, 1960s vintage – which was why it still had its beak intact and all its claws.

He judged that they had gone far enough now with small talk – it was time to get to the point of his visit.

'I had to take your eagle off its board so that I could look underneath the base of it. For a mark,' he began.

'That's all right,' said Jim, in his comfortable Suffolk voice, holding out his cup to his wife for a refill, 'that'll be no difficulty. Soon stick it back.'

Out of habit Ethel Rice opened the lid of the silver-plated teapot and gave the contents a good swirl. Then slightly abashed at this lapse she glanced at Charles and said in extenuation, 'He likes it strong.'

Jim went on, 'My grandmother bought that old eagle up Bishop's Stortford way before the Second World War.' He spaced the last three words for emphasis.

'Yes,' agreed Charles. He'd said that already. There was a silence which grew longer as each of the three of them waited for someone else to speak.

It was Ethel who broke the silence, 'Since you're in antiques we were wondering if you might be interested in buying it. Jim didn't want to put that in the letter straight out because he didn't want to be too pushy. But that was the idea, wasn't it, Jim? It was just sitting in here taking up all that space. Great big thing.'

Julia had said, 'Why don't you make him an offer, on spec? A couple of thousand or something?' She was a marvel but what rubbish she talked sometimes.

Ethel's voice went on. 'We thought – might as well get something for it.'

Her husband made a confirmatory noise and boldly stared at Ramsay, watching for his reaction.

The reply came without a fraction of hesitation, 'Look,' said Charles, 'it's worth quite a bit of money.'

'That's nice,' said Ethel, 'we might be able to . . .'

Her husband motioned to her and her voice died away.

'How much is "quite a bit"?' he asked.

'It could be as much forty thousand pounds,' Ramsay said. He didn't want to raise their hopes unduly but it would have been worse to understate the figure and leave a shadow of misunderstanding behind to haunt them later on.

There was another long silence.

'That *is* quite a bit of money,' Jim admitted and his gaze focused in the middle distance on a point somewhere on the floridly patterned wallpaper behind Ramsay's shoulder. Then emotion got the upper hand, 'Gor. That old eagle. D'yew hear that?' he demanded of his wife. 'D'yew hear that?'

Her cheeks had coloured up. Were those tears in her eyes?

Flustered, she looked down at the teatable for some delicacy to offer Charles as a reward for bringing such good news. Her eyes busy, she enquired, 'Another scone, Mr Ramsay? Or a chocolate cupcake?'

Yes, they would like him to handle the sale of the eagle for them, they agreed; his fee would be ten per cent of the amount it realised. He suggested that he should approach Mr Arai first. If that fell through he could send it in for auction by Crowthers, either in London or over to Dirk in Amsterdam. Carefully he explained to them the extra charges they would have to pay if he did that – commission, buyer's premium, a big photograph in the catalogue. Familiar with cattle markets Jim had no trouble with that, although his eyes narrowed as Ramsay detailed the rates of commission they charged.

'They aren't doing badly for themselves then. All that's going to come to quite a slice off the top of the joint, isn't it? Mind you,' he added in case he might be misunderstood, 'your bit – I've no quarrel with that, no objection at all . . .'

'They'll get you the best price,' said Charles.

'The labourer is worthy of his hire,' Ethel said, starting to clear away.

As he was leaving she waddled off to the pantry and brought back a plastic bag full of runner beans and another of carrots, young and fresh with crumbs of earth still clinging to them.

'For your father,' she said. 'I know he likes fresh veg.'

Charles Ramsay felt it had been a good afternoon's work. He wasn't sure how Julia would have seen it and he was glad that she hadn't been there. He felt comfortable though. *Probitas*. The best policy – something he had to live with.

Chapter Two

His father opened one of the white plastic bags and glanced inside.

'For you from Ethel Rice.'

'Runner beans and carrots. Nice of her,' the old man muttered, somehow shrunken and exposed by the great stone doorway of the house surrounding him, the wide steps rising up to it on both sides, lately refurbished, the moss and weeds scraped away and pristine gravel newly spread around at the base. Above them the mansion, Bressemer, made its statement, asserted its presence almost as though it was another member of the family, making its own demands and imposing its own conditions, sometimes infuriating, sometimes consoling. Certainly the only place which either of them recognised as home.

'Come in. Come in.' Seeming even more abstracted than ever the old man ushered Charles into the wide panelled passageway.

'You're in the usual bedroom. Do you want something to eat?'

Already climbing the oak staircase, bag in hand, his son called over his shoulder.

'No hurry. Not after one of Ethel's proper teas. I'll come down for a drink in a minute.'

The usual bedroom looked exactly as it had when he had

left it after his last visit a month or two before – the
Qashquai carpet which filled most of the floor, its big
lozenge-shaped field splashed with afternoon sunlight, the
full tester-bed and the Georgian hanging press against one
wall with its spacious oak drawers lined with ten-year-old
newspapers. Typical of the rest of the house, it was a world
which never changed much. Above him were two other
similar floors of bedrooms and passages, suites for guests
who never came, bedrooms for a family which no longer
existed and for servants who had deserted the house a long
time ago. This room too smelt abandoned, as though it
could do with an airing. He opened both the casement
windows and looked out towards the coast road far off, and
the pewter-coloured sea. It was quiet and it was permanent
– coming from London and the uncertainties of this new
venture of theirs, those were the two things about Bressemer which gave him the greatest solace at that moment. The
leaves of the big lime trees on either side of the avenue were
still an unspoilt green.

During the rest of the afternoon his visit followed the
normal routine – a drink in the kitchen while they decided
what menu for the evening meal would offer the least labour
and most satisfaction. Then they ate it at the kitchen table
just as the Rices would have done because, his father said,
as he always did, that it didn't make sense to open up the
dining room just for the two of them. Over the meal he
made conversation, said how much he had enjoyed the
opening of the showroom, what a splendid woman Julia's
mother was – and that had nothing to do with her birth; his
father was no snob in the normal sense. The exact bed
somebody had been born in wasn't as important as what
they had done since the event. He liked the people he met to
have something about them – to be givers not takers. Not
that he met so very many people these days – didn't get out

26

as much as he used to and one or two of his friends faded away from the local scene every winter, into the churchyard.

He insisted that they should take coffee in the study, in proper cups with a drop of old cognac to keep it company. Laying down the tray on the top of the desk – he had insisted on carrying it in – he opened the cabinet in the corner and extracted a squat bottle and a pair of air-twist cordial glasses which were reserved for this particular use. He was certainly not the sort of man who would use glass balloons; such things belonged in the carveries of metropolitan hotels along with red leather banquettes and expense-account dinners – or so he imagined, having never been anywhere of that kind himself as far as he could remember.

Having opened the door to admit Wellington, he sat himself down in the big wing chair behind the desk. Like Charles's bedroom the study was unchanging. At his father's elbow, the huge battered family tree was still hanging on the wall as it had done for more than a hundred years. No doubt it would be there in a hundred years' time – getting dustier, fading gently more every day. The rows of shields, each delicately painted by some – no doubt underpaid – Victorian artist, still boasted of alliances with other families going back centuries into the past. And surmounting the whole thing the family crest and the single word PROBITAS. A word to live up to. An irritation sometimes.

Someone had once suggested that the artist who had painted the family tree was a miniaturist who had been thrown out of work by the new fashion for *carte de visite* photography in the 1860s. Whose idea had that been? It must have been Jane, the consort of his father's who in his youth had instilled in him a love of objects from the past, had given him an understanding of his inheritance and all at once had departed from the house for reasons which had never been clear to him. It was just the sort of half-romantic thought that she would have had, something which was not a fact – an intriguing idea none the less. Charles wished that she was still around as he watched his father pouring out the coffee. He still hadn't vouchsafed a word about the problem which had persuaded his son that he ought to come up and see him. She would have eased it out of him.

'Well?'

The old man said, 'That inventory you did a year or two back when we revamped the insurance cover – where is it now?' He searched through the pile of papers at his elbow as though he didn't want whole-heartedly to find it. 'Doesn't matter now. At any rate I was going through it the other day and I thought – why don't we get rid of some things?'

Charles sat up. 'What things?'

His father shifted in his seat, awkwardly, not wanting to be pinned down. 'Oh, bits of furniture we don't use – and there's a mass of porcelain in this house that nobody ever looks at. Cupboards full of it. I opened one the other day – I'd broken the bowl I use for my cereal and was looking around for a replacement – and there in that great dresser thing out there,' he nodded vaguely in the direction of the kitchen quarters, 'you know, in the pantry, in the bottom of it I found a dinner service I didn't know we possessed. Didn't recognise it. Derby by the look of it, covered in dust . . .' He sounded resentful as though it had no business to have ambushed him like that.

What was this all about, Charles asked himself. The purpose of it? Not so long ago the cost of work on the house had been a worry indeed. A great deal in the way of repair had been called for; the roof had needed repair on a grand scale but he had seen to all that himself – having it resheathed with lead at great expense and all the outside woodwork repainted from top to bottom. Luckily they had been able to find the money and that with only a temporary recourse to the bank.

As far as he knew his father's income from the estate was enough for his needs which were shrinking as he grew older. So why the talk of selling furniture and porcelain? Ramsay had been a dealer long enough to know the signs when somebody needed to raise the wind – the language that was used, the circumlocutions and excuses. He went straight to the point.

'I didn't know you were strapped for cash,' he said. 'What do you need it for?'

His father pursed his lips and fidgeted with a tense suppressed force, unable to find the words he needed. He rose and began to collect the coffee things. Plainly the frustration he felt was growing inside him and he needed to find a physical release of some kind. Holding out Charles's cup towards him, he said abruptly, 'Have you finished with this?'

The china rattled as he put it roughly on the tray; then he marched out of the room without another word.

Charles didn't follow him. It was better to give him time to get himself together.

When he came back and resumed his chair he sat for a moment, allowing himself a sip of brandy, and seemed to relax.

'It was just a thought. I suppose it came into my head because of this new showroom of yours. If we wanted to sell you would be well placed . . . No need to take the idea any further if you don't like it. Of course not.' He dismissed the idea with a wave of the hand – then caught his son's eye. 'Really and truly, there's no problem.'

Lies, nothing but gallant lies. Charles decided to wait.

The following morning they went for a drive along the coast to find an unfamiliar stretch of beach – as much to give the dog a change as for any other reason. When they left the thin grass verge and plunged into the loose sand of the dunes he wasn't surprised that more than once he had to hold the old man's elbow to steady him – it was treacherous. It was when they reached the beach itself, newly washed by the tide, that it really came home to him how slowly both of the others moved, man and dog.

He thought that a walk in the open air might loosen his father's inhibitions but he offered nothing but more small talk – about the latest political autobiography he was reading, about the ups and downs of local families. There was talk of illnesses. Too much, Charles felt, though that was only to be expected. Looking out to sea he remembered bathing in those cold breakers as a skinny twelve year old; how he had stood up to his thighs in grey water and his father had urged him to dive in, to get the shock over.

'It will be fine once you've got your hair wet. You'll be as warm as toast. You'll see.'

And now the old man himself was holding back, refusing to take the plunge and while he hadn't the heart to bully him Charles felt disappointment – almost a sense of grievance.

They went to a quiet pub for a sandwich and a decorous half of shandy each. It was almost empty – the silence broken only by the occasional burst of conversation from the public bar and muttered exchanges between a couple of tourists in the corner, an almost oppressive silence that seemed to amplify every word that was spoken. When someone coughed it was a noteworthy event. It wasn't the sort of atmosphere which encouraged one to embark on confidences or unveil family privacies. Charles was prepared to allow him that.

When they returned to Bressemer his father had to coax Wellington out of the back of the estate car. While, with head turned away, he was watching the dog negotiate the steps up to the front door he said suddenly, 'It was the bank that put me into it. That fellow Marlowe.'

'Put you into what?'

'Come into the study. I've got something to show you.'

The three of them filed in there, the blind dog bringing up the rear.

Now that he had broached the subject at last Ernest Ramsay loosened up. He seemed to lose twenty years as he reached briskly into the cupboard behind his desk, took out a pile of files, each punctiliously labelled. From one of them, he extracted a sheet of paper and handed it over. His son glanced down at it.

The summary attached to the distribution account which we sent to you at the beginning of June showed that an amount of £174,142.00 was not being called at that time.

The purpose of this letter is to give you early notice that this balance is due to be paid to the syndicate on 25 September. Would you please let us have your cheque made payable to 'The Trustees of SJ Underwriting Limited' in good time to avoid the need for any interest charge?

Syndicate? Charles looked higher up for the subject of the letter: *Non-Marine Syndicate 261232 SMITH, Deferred payment due 25 September* – and it was addressed to Ernest Ramsay Esq. It couldn't be right.

He gave it back with a smile. 'Nothing to worry about.' That figure must have shaken the old man. 'Just a mistake. It must be meant for some other Ernest Ramsay although it beats me how their computer got hold of this address. Something to do with insurance at Lloyd's I guess. But it can't be for you. You aren't a Name are you?' His tone

31

scoffed at the idea . . . that anyone as prudent as his father would have become involved in anything like that. 'Simply send it back with a covering letter putting them right – and forget about it.'

He sat back relieved that the cloud of uncertainty which had been building up for the last couple of days could be blown away so easily. Now that was over he could get back to London – he ought to leave soon. While he didn't want to disappoint the old man he had other responsibilities, particularly to Julia.

The letter had not been laid down on the faded scarlet morocco of the desk top – it was still in his father's hand, a hand which trembled slightly. One noticed it sometimes these days – a tremor which was caused by age rather than anxiety; Charles was sure of that.

'It was the bloody bank that put me into it. The bank.' His father's tone was incredulous. 'Look.' Throwing down the letter he scrabbled angrily among his files, drew out a folder and thrust it towards Charles. 'Look.'

In the oblong window of the neat blue cover it said, LLOYD'S INSURANCE MARKET, AN OPTION FOR LANDOWNERS.

Put him into what? Lloyd's? These days that word was another name for disaster. His father a member of Lloyd's? Not his cautious father – it wasn't possible.

'You can't be. You never said anything.'

As the heir to the place he should have been consulted surely? Seeing his father's miserable face, the sudden flush of guilt and anxiety rising under the skin, he tried to suppress the anger which came storming through him. Fear too, a flood of adrenalin.

What had the old fool done? The fool, the bloody old fool.

Although he tried to control his voice and keep it reasonable, he could hear it through the bones of his head, coming

32

out hard, 'Tell me what happened. *When* did it happen?'

'It wasn't like that, Charles. It wasn't as though I was frogmarched into it. You know as well as I do how difficult it's always been to keep this place going. One has to be fair to the tenants and at the time you weren't in a position to help. The bank said it was the sensible thing to do, to make the estate work for its keep twice over. Everyone round here was on to it in the eighties. It was simple enough. You proved your means, went up to the City and got yourself vetted by the Rota Committee. You were shown round, given a lunch. Then you fixed up the bank guarantee and that was that. You were in – and the profits weren't bad in those days. They made a big difference.'

Charles persisted. 'Why didn't you let me know what you were up to?'

'Can't remember now. It was all of ten years ago. You hadn't really reached the years of discretion then or that was what I thought, and it was my business anyway. Later on . . .'

Later on, when those useful profits had stopped coming in he hadn't felt like mentioning it had he? Had carefully put away in his neatly docketed files those statements of account, underwriting reports and participation statements which chronicled the deterioration in his fortunes as a less than active member at Lloyd's, and had kept his own counsel, hoping that it would come out right in the end, repeating to himself that you had to take the bad years with the good. Trying to keep his guilty secret out of his mind.

Charles threw down the folder.

'God Almighty. Lloyd's. What possessed you . . .'

'It's all very well being wise after the event. It didn't look like that at the time. It had been going as long as the Bank of England, since before Queen Anne. It couldn't go down.'

'But as a Name you have unlimited liability. You were

putting everything you possess on the line. Surely you knew that,' Charles protested, 'didn't they tell you?'

'Of course they did. However they said the chances of the worst happening were infinitesimal – about the same as a meteor hitting St Paul's Cathedral – and those fellows deal in risk. They know about it. It's their business.'

A fine business some of them had made of it.

'May I have another look at that letter?'

He read it again. It told him nothing but the bald fact that the money was due. The printed heading said, 'SJ Underwriting Limited'. Beneath that, on one side an address in Fenchurch Street and on the other what looked like a private address on the Isle of Wight.

'Who are these people?'

'My managing agency.'

'What do they do?'

'They choose the syndicates for me to join each year and they run their own as well. I was in that too. That's the one the letter is about.'

'Non-Marine Syndicate 261232 SMITH you mean?'

'That's it. Smith is the active underwriter. He takes on business for that syndicate and he's in charge of the managing agency side as well.'

Silence. Charles read the brief letter through again and it told him nothing, nothing new. A bluebottle buzzed against the small sunlit panes of the window, fell silent for a moment, then the insistent sound returned, changing in pitch as the insect changed its mind and sailed across the room. Trying to force himself to think he looked up and caught sight of it. It had landed on the upper edge of the family tree on the wall beside his father's head, and was crawling along it. Now it was on the vertical surface, heading head first downwards past the proud motto PROBITAS, down through centuries of Ramsays to the most recently added names, cleaner and brighter than the rest. No doubt it too was giving its brain a rest, fed up with trying to think of a way out of its own predicament. Nevertheless in a minute it would go and try to knock its brains out against the window again.

'There it is,' the old man said and there indeed it seemed to be. It looked as if, one way or another, he would have to pay up. He had taken on the responsibilities of a member of Lloyd's, it had all gone sour and he had to stand the consequences. That was that.

'There is something else . . .' he continued. Expecting another broadside Charles closed his eyes involuntarily.

'. . . It's this . . . I thought that I had given notice that I wanted to resign from all my syndicates some time ago. I couldn't trust my memory you see and I rather hoped, Charles, that you could go through everything for me and see what was what.' He made a helpless gesture towards the tidy heap of files.

Charles took them over, selected the most likely one and began to go through its contents.

What was this?

'*I enclose a revised estimate of your 1988 underwriting year of account result which covers in addition any open years that have passed their normal three-year term . . .*'

Whatever that meant it wasn't what he was looking for. He glanced at more of the pages.

. . . '*The 1988 account has been adversely affected by the run-off of the Aviation and Miscellaneous accounts which have been left open for 1989 . . .*

'. . . *double counting between PSL and Errors and Omissions coverage . . .*

'. . . *are seeking to raise our excess points and intend to buy separate reinsurance cover for each of the other three classes, Bloodstock, Energy and . . .*

'. . . *Profit commission is calculated at 20% of the net*

underwriting result plus gross investment income and capital appreciation less agent's salary, national UK income tax on investment income and capital gains tax . . .'

It amounted to £134.56 he noticed and wondered if their computer had been able to get its sums right. He was aware of his father's eyes watching him. Sooner or later he would have to admit that he too was out of his depth, that the cold grey waves were over his . . . Just a moment. This looked more promising.

'I am sure you are conscious of the approach of 31 August which is the final date for members to give notice of their intention to resign from any of their syndicates by the end of this year and I give my recommendations below . . . I should be grateful for your instructions, to reach me, please, by 25 August at the very latest.'

In the margin, his conscientious father had made a pencilled note, 'Wrote 15/8. Withdrawing all s's.'

But there was no sign of any letter – all his father's letters were handwritten – and he passed the file over to him. 'Didn't you make yourself a copy of your letter?'

Ernest Ramsay frowned, taxing his blank memory. It was almost a year since the note had been made.

'It doesn't look like it, does it? I expect I wanted to get it off straight away so that there wouldn't be a cock-up and I wasn't able to get into town in time.' It had never crossed his mind to buy himself a photocopier. 'But I daresay I thought that wouldn't matter since they would have my letter on their file.'

In his world the word of anyone in the City was still his bond and his managing agent was in much the same category as his stockbroker or solicitor. If you needed a copy of a letter you had written to them you simply asked them for one and they gave it to you.

'Apparently it didn't reach them,' said Charles, then

clutched at the only straw which remained. 'You didn't send it recorded delivery?' There was no reply to his question. 'Did you?' he insisted, and still there was no reply so he left it at that because it wasn't going to help to bully the old man.

There seemed to be tears in his father's eyes. Ramsay looked away. 'I'll take these home with me and go through them. Then, when I've worked out what's what I'll go over to Lloyd's and talk to these SJ Underwriting people. I'll come back to you as soon as I can.'

'It's good of you . . .'

'Don't worry. I'm sure we can sort this out.' What else could he say?

As he drove away down the avenue half an hour later he caught sight of his father for a moment in his driving mirror before the first of the trees obscured his view of him. He had not turned back into the house but was standing beside the stone parapet with its bank of mullioned windows as a backdrop, looking out as though he was determined to enjoy the view.

When he reached the flat Julia wasn't there. The note said,

Ethelred is up here for that collector's jamboree tomorrow. Asked me out to dinner so things must be looking up in Brighton. Didn't want to refuse because he said he had something which we would find intriguing. And profitable. Very mysterious. Back late I expect.

J

It wasn't jealousy he felt. You didn't need to be jealous of Ethelred Lewis – not in that department.

He ought to get on with these files without delay. As soon

as she got back she would want to unload, bring him up to date, consult him on things she wanted to do. There was that big furniture sale in King Street to view, decisions to make.

No, he wouldn't indulge in a whisky and he wouldn't eat now – later when he felt hungry. Having searched round and found himself a writing block and a couple of ballpoints, he placed the files on the sofa in chronological order and sat down beside them. It had to be done.

He picked up the first of them.

Chapter Three

Was it really necessary, Carl asked himself, to use the handpump? He decided to allow himself to be indolent and draw the water which he needed to boil his potatoes from the lake. He could fill the fuel tank on the boat at the same time – an even greater saving of effort. Taking his pale blue plastic bucket he pushed open the door with his shoulder, groped for the fuel can with its metal pourer from beneath the tank of diesel at the side of the house and filled it at the brass cock at the bottom of the tank. Then he made his lopsided way down the path to the jetty, the empty plastic bucket on one side bumping harmlessly against his legs. On his other side the dead weight of the fuel container. Once there he set it down with care on the weathered planks of the jetty before dropping the bucket into the water where it bobbed for a moment sending out agitated circles across the still surface, making the shadows dance along the side of his boat tied up at the end. Afflicted with a sudden spasm of doubt, he glanced at its mooring rope, then squatted down to examine the knot, even to test it, yanking the line once or twice away from the worn iron ring fixed there. In a sense it was his lifeline. Although it might be feasible in theory to make his way back to civilisation through the woods behind him it wasn't a journey he would care to undertake without maps and a compass and then only in an emergency. No, a boat was a necessity or as good as. The only way in and the only way out. It had to be maintained in good order, properly secured, its fuel tank kept topped up so that you didn't end up with a dead motor becalmed on the huge deserted lake.

Having checked the line, inspected the boat and filled the tank he could relax. He turned and pushed the bucket down into the water with the toe of his canvas shoe, letting it almost fill before dragging it up and out by the string attached to the handle. Leaning forward stiffly from the waist he picked it up and went back to the kitchen.

After his meal – grilled fish with the boiled potatoes, salad, and a single can of beer – he washed his crockery in the sink in the kitchen, using the rest of the water, and put the plates in the rack to dry.

He was a methodical man. Only when everything was shipshape did he go to the corner of the living room where he kept his two shelves of books and take down his road atlas. He had left a slip of paper in it to mark the place. Absentmindedly removing it he took the book to the table by the window where the light was better and studied again the route he was going to have to take. It was a hell of a long way to the airport. In his mind he ran over the stages of the journey – by boat to the other end of the lake where he would leave the boat beached. Collect his car from the wooden shed down there which did duty as a garage. Next the twenty-kilometre drive through the forest to the main road which would not be too crowded, not for another fifty kilometres at any rate although it was summer. Even in the middle of the worst recession since the thirties, when many of them were being forced to take their holidays at home, few of his countrymen would come this way. It was too far inland to attract many tourists.

He wasn't as excited by the brief summer they were

granted up here as others were, he reflected, probably because there was too much light for too long and that made him feel exposed. Being a man who, after a long struggle, had learnt to be able to recognise his weaknesses objectively, he was prepared to admit that he had a kind of phobia about it. About light.

He considered the slip of paper in his hand on which he had scribbled down the single word 'Arlanda', and an SAS flight number with the arrival time beside it. There was still plenty of time before he had to make a decision.

Unhitching the binoculars hanging beside the door he went outside and carefully surveyed the edges of the lake. First to his left, slowly all the way round, then the other side. From long practice he had learnt to identify every tree, every knoll and inlet in what to a newcomer would have seemed a fairly uniform landscape. He had chosen his situation well – the forest at his back, a natural forest which had seeded itself for centuries, with no firebreaks or man-made paths across it – and in front the clear sweep of the lake giving no cover to the intruder except along its banks. That was where danger might lie. Not today however. No sign of danger today.

Lowering the glasses he was aware that he had been using this routine reconnaissance of his as an excuse to put off considering the latter part of the excursion to meet the flight – a hundred kilometres along busier roads in broad daylight culminating in the arrivals area at the airport, a public place with foreigners milling about. That was the part which promised to be most disagreeable, when there was the greatest chance that he would be recognised. He felt slightly ashamed of himself but put that feeling out of his mind too. It wasn't important. All that mattered was the simple calculus of gains and losses implied by each fork of the choice which faced him.

41

He listened attentively to the absolute silence and it was good. No, he decided, he would not go to the airport tomorrow. That wasn't the way it would be. His visitor would have to come to him. Let him make the running.

Charles Ramsay looked down from the public gallery at The Room, the marketplace where, according to the ebullient booklet from the middle 1980s he had found among his father's papers, three hundred and eighty-four syndicates transacted business on behalf of nearly thirty thousand Names whose personal fortunes provided the financial backing for the market. In those grandiose days they had seen the need to cater for future expansion as the main problem. Since its beginnings in Edward Lloyd's Coffee House in Lombard Street in the late seventeenth century, the market had outgrown its premises more than once and in the last couple of centuries had been forced to move every fifty years or so. So they had built this place – which was certainly impressive. A cathedral to insurance, full of light and air and complete with escalators, which was capable of expansion to meet their needs for the next century. Unfortunately, he reminded himself, it was a cathedral with a dwindling congregation. Members had been deserting it by the thousand in the last couple of years and there was competition from other newer markets which were not saddled with a deadening burden of old liabilities. Would Lloyd's survive and if it didn't what were they going to do with this building? It would make a rather good antique hypermarket – except that none could afford the rent. He pulled himself up short. At that precise moment a much more pressing question for him than the future of Lloyd's was whether or not Bressemer was going to survive.

How did one make contact with a representative of SJ Underwriting Ltd? He would go downstairs and accost one of those pink-coated waiters they advertised. Considering the gaping hole this organisation was promising to make in his inheritance he had the right to a little attention, he felt.

Although the pink-coated gentleman was a model of courtesy the same could not be said of the employee of SJ Underwriting he was sent to see. No doubt prolonged exposure to angry and bewildered Names had hardened her heart.

He told her his business calmly. Although he was not a Name he explained, his father was, and he had come to make some enquiries on his behalf – about the exact date he had given up his membership of the syndicate. There seemed to be a conflict of evidence on the point – something that needed investigation. He smiled.

Her look said that it wasn't the first time such a story had been offered to her small and interesting ears – each of them adorned, he noted, with a tidy gold stud – and that she didn't at all expect it to be the last.

'Sorry, you have come to the wrong place. All the syndicate's membership records are kept at our offices in Ventnor.'

'Ventnor? On the Isle of Wight?' It seemed a little incongruous to him.

'Yes. Ventnor.' Her reply indicated that anyone who thought that was odd had not yet reached the years of discretion. Ventnor was a very sensible place to have an office it said. Respectable.

Nettled he spoke as one adult to another, 'Do you think you could telephone them for me.' It wasn't a request and she wasn't ready to compromise. He could see that in her eyes.

'I really think it would be easier if you went to see them yourself. We don't have any of the correspondence here – we haven't the space. There are over a thousand members in the syndicate.' In such a large flock for the shearing what was one sheep more or less?

'It's a long way to Ventnor.' She didn't reply – simply watched his face and waited for him to try something else. He drew the crucial letter from his pocket. 'Could I speak to this gentleman – Mr J.L. Smith?'

'He's in The Room I'm afraid.'

'Underwriting?'

For a moment her gaze left his and she showed a sudden unconvincing interest in his tie.

'He *is* the active underwriter to the syndicate.'

'Well. I hope he's making a better fist of it than he did in 1990.'

She turned on her heel and walked away. Evidently the interview was over, such as it was.

'Well,' said Julia, 'what do you think? Do we want to take part in it or not? If we want a good stand we need to let them know by next Thursday. That's what they said. We really ought to have seen to this before you went off for the weekend.' Her voice was neutral because she didn't need to make herself sound reproachful.

The Fine Art and Antiques Fair – Belgravia. Ramsay concentrated on the promotional material she had handed him. First there was the sales pitch which told him that since it began in 1965 the fair had progressed to be the primary trading fair in the United Kingdom and so on and so on, the usual half truths. Could a business like theirs afford not to be represented, it enquired? That wasn't the question he needed to answer. Could it afford to be? That was the point at issue.

He unfolded the big attractive plan and studied it. What about that? Just there. That looked like a good position he thought – on the ground floor, between the entrance and the stairway to the upper gallery. Excellent.

Inspecting the floor plan he remembered how, earlier in the week, he had stood in the public gallery and looked down at the trading floor at Lloyd's. Resolutely he pushed that preoccupation back into whatever compartment of his brain it had wriggled out of.

How much were they asking? He referred to the schedule of rental charges. That much? One had to admire their effrontery.

Something else – he looked about for something else. These charges were twenty per cent up on last year. Was there any point in taking something more modest? Would it project the right image? Perhaps it was just a waste of . . . *Lloyd's. Bressemer. His father. How could the old man have done such a thing?*

They had to be in the top section, that went without saying – early datelines stringently enforced – everything vetted, everything right. The only other option as far as he could see was not to take a stand at all. They could pretend this jamboree really wasn't for them, that they were a cut above even the Belgravia Fair. Why not play it that way? *What about Lloyd's? That was far more . . .*

She broke in on the thought.

'I'm sure we've got to do it.'

All right – go for it, he decided – or rather she had.

'This one, don't you think?' He pointed to the location he had selected first.

'Fine,' she said, marking it, folding the plan briskly.,

They complemented one another. She did the organising and the marketing if that was what it should be called, deftly flattering their male clients, empathising with the women – making herself their ally, understanding their point of view – which left him to get on with buying the stock, making the pricing decisions. Soon he was going to have to broach the

45

subject of the Isle of Wight. Not yet though.

She turned to the next item on the list she had beside her and continued in the voice she always used when she was feeling efficient. 'Jennifer Reed rang. Her client will take the *pietra dura* tables but she is asking for a commission. Ten per cent. What do we do?'

She didn't have to elaborate and it was clear that she had no strong views one way or the other. This decision she really was leaving to him. He had noticed that sometimes he found himself assailed with scruples where she had none. He was never happy with the idea of paying a commission to an interior decorator on something he or she was buying for a client because it was never clear who was doing what for whom and why. Lurking in the background there was a conflict of interests. This time, fortunately, the decision was easy.

'Tell her no. She won't find another pair like that this side of Christmas and I know she's in a hurry.'

Julia nodded. She was no longer the languid girl who had graced Lewis's shop in Brighton – she was becoming really rather formidable these days.

There was something of her mother in her. Her mother, his father. Julia putting her all into the business because of her mother's share in it. His father's problem – he could feel it now, plucking at his elbow. He had to deal with it somehow. The old man couldn't cope.

Julia could cope, however.

It was difficult to reconcile this businesslike person with the woman he knew in bed at night. A woman who was supple, warm and inventive – in a bed where they trusted one another.

He heard himself say, 'By the way, I hear on the grapevine that there's a sale at short notice on the Isle of Wight. Some very good things according to Tony and they didn't have time to put an ad in the *Gazette*. The day after tomorrow. I'll go down. It doesn't need to take long.'

He spoke the white lie casually. He couldn't be expected to live up to his principles all the time.

When the new owner had taken over the hotel on the Isle of Wight a decade earlier he had been determined to restore it to its full mid-nineteenth-century splendour – to give the Albert back the cachet it had possessed when it was newly built, not long after the royal home at Osborne less than twenty miles away had been completed. After an anxious few years he had established it as a place where those who could afford it could enjoy full-blooded luxury. Six-course Victorian meals which wrecked the waistline in a weekend. Discreet private dining rooms. Opulent and shameless breakfasts laid out on the huge dark side-table in the dining room. A billiard room, scented with cigar smoke, where a choice of whisky was left in the tantalus of an evening and guests were trusted to sign their own chits when they had helped themselves. Of course.

One of the features of the place which gave the owner most satisfaction was a vast conservatory of white cast-iron tracery which he had had refurbished, with every pane of glass cleaned and replaced – an operation which had cost him half a year's profits and had been worth every penny whatever his accountant thought. It boasted new tightly joined oak flooring and a jungle of fleshy indoor plants, each carefully groomed.

Quist was in there digesting his old-fashioned breakfast over a copy of *The Times* which he had filched from the library knowing that in a hotel as expensive as this one, nobody was going to take him to task for such a minor sin. When he got up and left someone would merely fold it and return it whence it came. There was an army of such people in the place – most of them invisible – which was one reason why he liked it. Finally, and most important, it was the sort of place which was certain to make the visitor he was expecting resentful and overawed at the same time which was how he needed to have him. Recruitment was a tricky business – not really in his line – and their discussion was not going to be an easy one. Anything which would soften up Begg, make him easier to handle, would be to the good.

He laid the broadsheet aside and opened his briefcase. Instead of busying himself with the notes he had made earlier he couldn't resist taking out a white envelope. From it he withdrew a small catalogue with a matt magenta cover and leafed through it, glancing here and there at the discreet photographs, drawing an inner pleasure from them.

21. *A comprehensive set of Down Brothers instruments, containing assorted instruments for amputation, trepanning, bullet extraction and tracheotomy . . . £1100*
22. *A fine set of surgeon's amputation knives, including six Liston knives . . .*

With impatience he flipped the cover of the booklet closed feeling the edge of his excitement blunted. These were all very well – finely wrought unquestionably, but late. They had been made almost within living memory. His taste ran to earlier, more robust items. Scarcer, of course.

'Mr Quist.' The girl's voice set his brain alive with ideas which had steel about them and would have disturbed her very much had she been able to see into it. She came towards him, her hips swinging decorously, holding herself erect with her tight little bosom forward, while Quist allowed his sweetly cruel thoughts to dance over her approaching shape. Then he pushed the catalogue under the pages of the newspaper. It was not that he was in any way ashamed of his hobby but he was in a foreign country where people's attitudes might not be as emancipated as in his own. One never lost anything by treading carefully.

'Mr Quist isn't it? Room 29? A visitor for you.' She stood aside with her arms pressed back on either side to allow Begg to pass her by, close but not too close, looking after him with eyes which said that she was glad to be able to conceal this particular visitor in a corner of the conservatory which was little frequented at this time of day. A worthy member of society perhaps but one without style or money, who didn't match the type of client the hotel set out to please.

Unconscious of any failure on his part to fit into her scheme of things, Begg sat down in the glossy golden wicker chair and allowed himself to relax along its easy curves. He believed in taking every opportunity to release the tensions in his body. It was something which he was always conscious of, his body – something which he took seriously. He looked after it as carefully as he did his car. It was his major asset and it had to last as long as possible – and like his car it needed more attention every year. It didn't respond to his wishes as readily now as it had when he was twenty. That thought reminded him how long it was since he had quit the army and how urgent it was becoming each day to do something to secure his financial future – something which offered more than his current occupation. He was working in the prison for the time being – a job he had slipped into as a temporary expedient and then found himself trapped into by circumstances – and living near his work in his mother's dark brick terrace house, where she lay disabled upstairs in bed all day, something to see to after every shift but, he suspected, not as helpless as she made out. His time in the army had given him a nose for a malingerer. However, be that as it may, she lay there in that narrow little house which smelt of frugality and pine-scented disinfectant getting more and more greedy for his attention as the days dragged past her. Number 27 Freshwater Walk. Very different from this place. Another world – more promising. He looked round and absorbed the warm ambience of the hotel, sniffed its rich air with appreciation but with no sign that he was intimidated by it. Quist was disappointed.

Begg, his short hair grizzled at the sides, shaven-headed like the guardsman he wanted people to imagine he had been. A mercenary who'd run out of convenient wars to fight. Bosnia wasn't for him – there were manifest draw-backs to signing on for that one – like not being paid, or even fed, someone had told him . . . This venture which Quist was offering – in a civilised unsuspicious country, generously recompensed, quickly done with and out of the way – was a tidy little option. It offered money and that was all he needed to escape from Number 27 – the sound of his mother's stick banging on the floor above him, and her harassing whine: 'Son. Son, I need the toilet.' His dear mother. When this assignment was completed he'd be away and leave her to be cared for by the council's social services department.

He looked at Quist with a superior eye and a touch of distaste. Perhaps the man had heard a shot fired in anger once or twice, he allowed, but only shots that he'd fired himself. Never in the other direction. Still, this interview was too important; he couldn't permit himself the luxury of showing his feelings. All at once he remembered that he hadn't shaken hands with the guy. He leaned forward to offer a neutral hand and felt Quist's firm aggressive fingers close around it. It was a strong grip – something he hadn't expected.

Quist hadn't wanted a partner, had fought against it – a partner quadrupled the risk. However there were three acts

to the drama he had been engaged to play and for the final
one a partner was essential, they insisted. He had to go and
find himself one – somewhere a long way from home. All
reasonable expenses would be paid. They were adamant and
he knew better than to push his luck with them.

He had Begg's awkwardly written letter in his briefcase –
touching, in guarded terms, on his qualifications. Now he
regarded this potential recruit objectively, getting as much
as he could from the details he could see. Cheap off-the-peg
clothes which no doubt were the smartest he possessed –
well pressed. A solid non-commissioned type – not a military genius but that wasn't what he was after. No, what he
needed was someone as professional and uninvolved as he
was himself, someone who'd watch his back, do what he was
told whatever that entailed and keep quiet about it – then
get out of Sweden by the next available flight, back to this
quiet island having expunged from his memory every trace
of what he had seen and done while he was away.

It was decision time for Quist – he had to make up his
mind today, this morning. Whether to take Begg or try and
find someone else in the brief time he had been allowed. It
wasn't easy in this foreign country and he was already
compromised to some extent anyway. When he opened his
briefcase to take out his notes he had all but made up his
mind to take the man on.

That brought him up against the next decision – how
much to tell his prospective recruit about the exact terms of
his contract. Quist's masters had made it very clear to him
that if he failed, or worse, if his connection with them was
revealed whether by accident or design, he would be at
mortal risk and that went for anyone he employed as well.
Two of his assignments had been defined in detail. There
might be others – he was to hold himself ready. If he was
successful well and good. The money was there, a great deal

of it – solid Swedish money waiting for him in a solid Swedish bank. A single decisive signature was all that was needed. He had also been told in very precise terms what would happen if anything went wrong though. Happen to him. Quist knew the market well and he had no illusions about that. There was a lot of competition and people like him came cheap as a general rule. He'd only got this plum job because he knew the country and the language, Like everything else in life it had its downside – he accepted that.

Perhaps he wouldn't bother to give all the detail to the man opposite him. He was short of time anyway because this wasn't his only reason for visiting the Island.

'Mr Begg you are most punctual,' he said. 'That is fine, fine. I like that.' Quist returned his catalogue to his brief-case and withdrew a blue plastic folder. 'Now that we are here, face to face, perhaps you could enlarge on one or two of the statements in your letter.'

Begg tensed and shifted in his seat as he tried to remember what he had said. Being forced to think always put him on edge.

At that moment the girl, anxious to please, came to the door of the conservatory, her small feet silent on the thick carpet. Might she bring them something? A pot of coffee? Tea? – she enquired.

Quist put out a questioning hand towards his guest but didn't give him a chance to express a preference. It was important to establish who was in command from the outset.

'Coffee? Yes? Fine, fine.' He nodded placidly and looked across at her young fleshly presence in the doorway, his thoughts clattering in his head like knives.

'Avalon', Undercliff Road, Ventnor.

The office of SJ Underwriting Limited was what Ramsay had expected from the address – a mid-Victorian villa set

52

back from the road, built in stone under a slated roof whose gable end was decorated with elaborately carved bargeboards. It looked like what it was, a private house trying to double as discreet business premises, not all that far away in style from the bed and breakfast hotels scattered here and there in its vicinity, secure in their cleanliness and white paint and their view over the Channel. Somehow it didn't fit his preconceptions. It wasn't the kind of thing one associated with a Lloyd's syndicate – a million miles from the theatrical opulence of their London building. The woman who came to the door was very much a country cousin too. Grey-haired, much older than her counterpart – the one with the nice ears who had given him such short shrift earlier in the week – and a great deal more polite.

She ushered him into a small vestibule which had been carved out of the sizeable hall of the house when it had been converted, which forced them to stand almost on top of one another although that didn't seem to bother her much, standing erect, a head shorter than he was, allowing him to recite his tale of his father's difficulties without interrupting him. Behind her was a fire door, or what looked like one. The thick glass in its upper half was ribbed, preventing him from seeing clearly whatever lay beyond it. Offices, he supposed, the computers and the personnel of the organisation – its records, its memory.

However instead of leading him in there she took him to a room which lay on her left and seemed to be her office – her desk in the bay window, a word processor with a half-written letter on the screen on a nearby table, the cursor winking.

'I have interrupted you?'

'Don't worry. I was just getting out another letter to our Names. I have plenty of time in hand.'

He half-crouched to glance at the screen and immediately

found his view of it cut off as she moved in front of him to busy herself with saving the letter on disc and shutting off the machine. Obviously she was a very discreet lady. Whatever news of hurricanes, tornadoes and churning reinsurance spirals she had to tell them she was going to make sure that he didn't get it in advance.

It didn't matter. Her name was Barbara Russell wasn't it? He remembered seeing it in bold capitals at the end of many of the letters in his father's files, in the briefcase in his hand. She was the one whose job it was to pass on the bad news, much like a nursing sister – firm but compassionate – taking care to avoid kindling false hopes in her charges, making sure they clearly understood what they were in for as she led them by the hand through the bad news . . .

'We appreciate the anxieties which these worsening estimates are occasioning to so many Names. As usual we are basing our estimates for the syndicate on the most pessimistic forecasts which are coming through to us . . .

'. . . collating underwriting results has become a complex not to say time-consuming exercise . . . nevertheless it is important that you should understand what is being presented. Please refer to the Guidance Notes which should be read alongside the summary of results . . .'

Until finally she brought them face to face with it.

'The figure on Page Two of the Distribution Account, against the heading BALANCE DUE FROM NAME *is your loss . . .'* he felt the words echoing and re-echoing in his head – your loss, your loss, your loss – and wondered if, standing on the sidelines as she did, she had really understood what those two words must have meant to the people she was writing to, whom she had probably never met face to face. How could she understand?

He could imagine his father, knowing all too well where the unwelcome envelope came from, squaring his shoulders to open it and reading line by line through this letter which Barbara Russell had composed so carefully for her Names. His father, referring conscientiously to the Guidance Notes, turning the page and coming to the words BALANCE DUE FROM NAME . . .

It must have been like coming to the end of the world. The last day. Armageddon.

He turned and she gave him a smile. Was it genuine sympathy he saw there or was there a hint of self-satisfaction lurking in her eyes? He could imagine that for all her supportive bedside manner, someone in her position might not be altogether displeased that the Names to whom she, as a mere salaried employee, had ladled out so much seemingly effortless cash in the heady 1980s had come such a cropper, one and all, in the less forgiving 1990s. Did you not recognise, those pale blue eyes seemed to say, the manifest truth of the cliché . . . there is no such thing as a free lunch?

More sharply than was warranted he said, 'For my father this is a matter of some gravity. For both of us.'

The smile was doused instantly.

'Of course. I will go and see if we have a record of any letter from him giving notice of his intention to resign.'

She walked past him out of the room – head up, small and neatly dressed, matronly, someone whom it was difficult to visualise as a teenager. He found himself wondering who there was in her own life. A husband, children? If so how old would they be? One taking A levels and the other a second-year student perhaps. How hard would she be hit if SJ Underwriting was wound up? It wouldn't be the end of the world for her, he decided. She would find employment elsewhere, would cope.

She hadn't come back yet. He looked round for something to read. Although with its functional furniture and plain floor-covering the place had the air of a waiting room of some kind there was nothing, not even the latest accounts for Syndicate 261232 SMITH.

While he was waiting he might as well go through the files he had brought with him once again to fix the details in his mind – on the off-chance that there was something he had missed. Sitting down he opened his briefcase, removed the most recent file and began to go through the loose pages. Some of the letters had got themselves mixed up he noticed and were no longer in the right order. Methodically he began to sort them out. Where did this belong? There wasn't a precise date on it. At the top it merely gave the month and the year. Headed *The Smith Names Association* it was a covering letter forwarding material from the Association to all the Names who had belonged to Syndicate 261232 in the years of account 1989, 1990 and 1991. It was something. At least it told him that there was an Action Group and it meant too that there was cause to set one up. A reason somewhere, a grievance which might be justified and might not but was sufficient to impel a group of members to band together to pursue it.

Closing the file he looked up. Where had she got to?

It was one of those dead moments in mid afternoon. A single car passed by in the street outside and he heard its engine note dying away as it went down the hill towards the town.

He glanced at his watch. It must have been at least a quarter of an hour since she had left the room. These days it didn't take that long to locate a letter surely? Perhaps the registry clerk was new and inexperienced . . . perhaps they had difficulty in recruiting skilled staff locally . . .

He looked at his watch again and all it told him was that fifty seconds had passed since he had last consulted it. It was simple – go and find her. He went into the little lobby, tapped with a tentative knuckle on the upper half of the door and waited, expecting the indistinct shape of someone to loom against the other side of the obscured glass to open it. Nothing happened. He drummed his fingertips more insistently against it – and still no shape appeared.

He tried the handle . . . no, the door wasn't locked . . . He pushed it and went in.

The big room was empty. That was unexpected. There were several work stations, PC terminals, racks of printout, metal cupboards, computers and no people. It wasn't a Bank Holiday and it wasn't lunchtime but the middle of the afternoon in the middle of a normal week. Nobody there in general, and not a sign of Barbara Russell in particular.

Experimentally he called out.

'Hallo. Are you there?' There was no response.

He knew her name but what should he call her? Was she Mrs or Miss? Barbara was much too familiar.

'Ms?' he essayed, 'Ms Russell?' Although to his ears it sounded ludicrous at least she couldn't take exception to it.

There was a door at the other end of the room, painted a restful shade of green and marked STAFF. Was she behind it? He paused and considered what that single word might mean – a rest room of some kind? Could be. For both sorts or just for female employees? He hesitated.

A voice called out, 'I'm in here,' which decided him. It must be where they kept their confidential records. The sign was only there to keep the public out.

Boldly he pushed his way in and found himself in the ladies' lavatory. At least he assumed so since there were no convenient stalls.

He'd never been in one before – of course he hadn't, even by accident – and he felt vulnerable. About to retreat he heard a clink behind one of the partitions.

'I'm here.' Cautiously he looked round it. The door of the cubicle was open and there she was seated, completely decent thank goodness, on the throne, with a half-empty bottle of gin at her feet, pushing the used glass in her hand towards him. 'Come in and make yourself at home,' she invited sombrely. 'May I offer you some of this gin? Neat I'm afraid and you'll have to use my glass because that's the only one I've got. However, you won't catch the plague. I'm not HIV positive or anything – I only wish I were.'

She must have downed two or three glassfuls of neat spirit to have got into that maudlin state in scarcely twenty minutes – as though it was tapwater. She'd been cold sober when he'd last seen her. Why the sudden collapse?

'Ms . . .' he said, 'Ms Russell. Don't you think we would be more at home in your office?'

Rising with care to her proud but modest height she allowed him to assist her, bottle in hand, towards her own room. If he wasn't mistaken she was conducting a one-woman closing down party for SJ Underwriting Limited, presiding over its dissolution. Another syndicate had bitten the dust.

'A cup of tea,' she demanded.

He went to the drinks dispensing machine in the general office, got it for her in its thin plastic cup and set it down on the desk in front of her. It would have to do.

With fierce concentration she managed to get it to her lips and take a couple of sips before announcing, 'Too hot.'

'I should let it cool then.'

Perhaps it was odd to be talking with such familiarity to this woman whom he didn't know at all, taking this trouble, but he couldn't just leave her there. Besides she appeared to be the only one left on the sinking ship who could get him the single piece of evidence he needed. The letter from his father which would tell him whether he had resigned from their syndicate before the 1990 year of account or not. If the piece of paper existed.

What should he do? She was in no state to find the file for him, not for a couple of hours at least.

'Feel sick,' she said. 'Must be this bloody foul tea.'

Patiently he led her back towards the door labelled STAFF.

While she was otherwise occupied he tried one or two of the grey steel filing cabinets in the general office. Every one of them was locked. All the possible cupboards were locked too. Where else was there? Turning, he caught sight of her standing in the doorway watching him.

'I threw up,' she said as though that was an achievement. Then her eyes focused on him more closely. 'What have you been doing? You're one of those men aren't you? You've been at the cupboards.'

'They're locked.'

'You're bloody right they're locked.' Spoken in her crisp business-lady tones the words sounded incongruous, 'and they're fireproof too so don't run away with the idea that you can . . .'

'Do you have the keys?'

'Of course.'

'Where are they?'

'They are about my person,' she replied with dignity, her look challenging him. He didn't rush to snatch up the gauntlet. Searching middle-aged ladies who were the worse for drink wasn't much in his line.

Close at hand there was a swivel chair, a plain one without arms. She subsided onto it with a grunt of satisfaction. Next she began to swing from side to side, fidgeting as a child might do, and then suddenly with a kind of anarchic gaiety she was pushing down and away with one trim shoe in order to propel herself, lifting her feet clear of the floor to whirl round twice with her knees raised.

'Whee . . .ee,' she cried out and the sound had a touch of desolation in it.

'I felt like giving it a whirl,' she explained and giggled shyly at her little joke.

It looked like being a long wait.

Now, having exhausted the possibilities of the chair she clearly felt that it was time to put him at his ease.

'You speak very good English,' she tendered.

He did indeed but it wasn't something people usually . . .

'A lot of you Scandinavians do. You're from the other lot aren't you? The action group they've set up over there. On the prowl for information you can use, aren't you?'

'My name is Charles Ramsay and I'm here in good faith.'

'Oh yes?' Her tone invited him to tell that to the Marines.

'Yes,' he insisted. 'I told you. I have come here on behalf of my father who is a member of the syndicate . . . or rather *was*,' he amended quickly. Looking for proof in his briefcase he found one of her own letters and offered it to her, stabbing his finger at the name at the top of it. 'Ernest Ramsay. And see, here's yours at the bottom of the second page.'

'I saw your car. That big blue one. Swedish, isn't it?' She made a knowing face. The gin had got to her brain. There were hundreds of estate cars like that in the UK. Thousands.

'Look I promise you . . .'

'All right, all right, all right,' she reiterated, coming down the scale with a final emphatic, '*all . . . right*' – to make it sound as though she believed him. It was obvious, though, that she wasn't going to surrender the keys or help him to plunder her sacred files for his father's letter. Not for a long time yet, at any rate. How could he persuade her?

She stood up, drowsily.

'Tired. Time to go home. Back to my dear little cosy little village. Finish it off tomorrow.'

Presumably she meant the letter to her Names which she

had been working on earlier – the farewell missive from her to them.

Village? How was she going to get there? He had too much respect for the townspeople of Ventnor to allow her out on the road behind the wheel of a car in her state. And if he lost touch with her now he might have missed his only chance of lifting the cloud which now lay over Bressemer and over his father – that was the other thing.

'I'll drive you there,' he said.

In the car she lapsed into a morose silence for most of the time as she sobered up and the inhibitions which the gin had loosened closed in on her again. She spoke only when he had to be given directions, driving along narrow roads which, because they were moving inland away from the holidaymaking coast, were almost deserted. As they came down a hill past a grey stone barn, the shallow arch in its façade dated 1832, and an empty farmyard, she burst out impatiently, 'Left here. Left.'

Obediently he spun the wheel turning the heavy car along a side road, taking them beyond an unassuming medieval church.

'. . . and it's on the right.'

The house was hidden from the road behind a dark overgrown hedge. The drive led down beside it to hard standing at the back with a view over deserted fields to a low range of hills to the north.

'This is goodbye,' she said.

Getting out of the car she rifled her handbag for her key. Not there, nor in there. She became more and more impatient as she felt him approach as though that implied that she wasn't even capable of getting into her own house. Burrowing further she was driven to the indignity of handing him a purse, some loose coins, a diary. All of a sudden her agitation came to the boil and anarchy took over again. Desperately she upended the bag and emptied the rest of its contents on to the doorstep. Credit cards, diary, scraps of paper were vomited on to the ground.

Ramsay picked up the key and handed it to her – then took the bag from her and patiently refilled it while she waited with one impatient foot on the step, looking down at him.

'Thank you. Really that'll do. I'll see to it.'

As she spoke, the last of her carefully husbanded control left her, her legs buckled and, like a collapsing puppet, she fell on top of him – bouncing off on to the ground.

She lay crumpled in front of him with her skirt above her knees, underwear visible, her hand flapping about trying to shield herself.

When he bent down to pick her up, she wriggled quickly away, 'Hands off.'

Rolling over on all fours she managed to struggle clumsily to her feet, tears of humiliation glistening in her eyes. Clearly she couldn't be left in such a state – one of her knees was grazed, her sensible skirt muddied.

Hobbling in front of him she made no attempt to prevent him from following her inside.

At length, once she had changed out of her working clothes and dealt with her knee, she seemed to be glad of his company. In the sitting room she found a drink for him, taking nothing stronger for herself than tonic on its own with a slice of lemon. She hadn't got her spirits back but was making an effort to recover her poise just as, he imagined, she had been brought up to do. No doubt it helped to be back on her own territory, among the evidence of her private life – an embroidered cushion, a plain carpet in a practical colour, a pair of good Rockingham vases, inherited from an aunt she said. Wanting to cheer her up and because he felt she ought to know, he told her what they were worth. She didn't show much pleasure at the news, perhaps because she thought it an intrusion. However when he steered her on to the subject of SJ Underwriting Limited she became more forthcoming. She had been with the agency for years, had grown up with it, and when Smith had arrived on the scene he had found her indispensable – his liaison officer.

'Why did you think I hailed from Sweden?'

'Ericsson, Lundström, Andersen, Gustafsson, Winblad . . .' she recited in a gloomy monotone. She had some trouble getting her tongue round Gustafsson – a bit of a mouthful.

Who were they?

'Our Scandinavian Names,' she informed him with a touch of self-importance, as though she was back in the prosperous eighties.

'Members of your syndicate?'

'Yes. We had three hundred and twenty of them all told.'

That struck him as strange.

'There's nothing in the rules against people like that . . . foreigners,' she countered.

'Right. But so many from Scandinavia in one syndicate? How come?'

'The first of them was a close friend of Smith. He brought the others in. It had a certain cachet and at that time they had plenty of money looking for a home – some of them had bought property in London. By pledging it at Lloyd's they could make it earn its keep twice over. The usual sales pitch. A clever thing to do.' She glanced at Ramsay with something like bitterness in her eyes. 'And then it turned out to be not so clever. So now they have an action group and they are after somebody's blood.' Smith's evidently. And they weren't alone.

'When I tried to get to see him a couple of days ago I was

given to understand that he was in The Room. Still operating on behalf of the syndicate. Is he in London?'

She didn't respond.

'Is he? What's going on? Where is he?'

'I don't know.' She rose and went to pour herself something stronger than tonic on its own. With her back towards him she said, 'He hasn't been in touch for a week. You've seen how things are down here.' He had. Crumbling.

Certain that she was covering something up he was aware as well that he was there on sufferance, always on the edge of antagonising her – and she was starting to drink again. Better to leave it alone. He ought to leave before she grew quarrelsome again. He could only hope that he would be able to make contact with her at the office in Ventnor tomorrow and prevail upon her to try to find the letter. There was no guarantee that she would be there. Looking for words that would somehow improve the odds, he got up to go and the words wouldn't come.

She sat, saying nothing, then defiantly drank the contents of her glass – it looked like whisky now – straight down in a single gulp. So she was out to get paralytic again. What good would that do?

'It's no business of mine . . .'

'That's it, young man, you've said it. No business of yours. No business of anybody's except me. It's my business. The buck stops here.' She banged her free hand fiercely against her chest to demonstrate where it stopped before jumping to her feet and pushing past him, back to the drinks cabinet again, a walnut-veneered 1950s affair with mirrors and a light that went on automatically or had done so once. The bottle chinked against the glass.

'Come on, have another. Loosen up.'

'Not for me.'

'Come on.' She pushed a second glass into his hand.

Wanting to put it down he held on to it to humour her, awkwardly.

'Nobody can blame you. It's not your fault that the agency has—' Gone into liquidation? Been suspended? Not knowing exactly what fate had overtaken it he left it open. 'That's the management's responsibility surely?'

'Exactly,' she agreed, which threw him but he ploughed on.

'What's the worst that can happen?' he demanded, banging in the answer before she could reply. 'You may have lost your job. So? You're a competent woman – you'll be able to find something else. Think of your Names, up against huge calls they can't meet, facing years when the accounts cannot be closed, knowing the verdict but not the sentence. You could be a great deal worse off.' Yes, he was playing Job's comforter, he admitted, but it was true enough wasn't it?

'How do you know I'm not a Name?' she demanded.

That caught him off balance. Involuntarily he glanced round him for evidence of wealth and saw none. The house was pleasant enough, modest though, and this room was unremarkable, apart from the Rockingham vases. Perhaps she had inherited, along with them, a fat portfolio of stocks and shares. For the first time in their short acquaintance she smiled.

'That took you by surprise didn't it? Sit down and I'll tell you about it.' He obeyed. The story didn't take long. When Smith had taken over the agency she had already been working there for over twenty-five years and the retiring directors had wanted to give her some tangible recognition of her faithful service. What better way to reward her, they had thought, than to make her a Name herself? At that time the profits from Lloyd's had seemed ample and effortless; it was only right and proper that she, who had doled out the rich harvest to their Names for so long, should be put on an equal footing and be given a share in it herself. The bank guarantee had been fixed up, the interview arranged and she had signed on the dotted line. There had been a long and rich lunch in her honour with short and witty speeches. And now it was the morning after.

'I shall be allowed to stay here,' she said, looking round her living room dispassionately, 'I think I shall, although I haven't been told yet. They try to be merciful but it will be a strange feeling knowing that everything I touch, the glass in my hand, the chair I am sitting in, the carpet under my feet, the oven and the dishwasher in the kitchen – knowing that they will all belong to somebody else and there is no way that I will ever be able to possess them again.'

If they couldn't make their case and the worst happened he wondered, would his father be allowed to stay on at Bressemer? As a tenant? Would it be like that? It was an idea that would take some getting used to. If the worst happened.

In that case everything would go under the hammer sooner or later.

That thought reminded him that he was supposed to be on the Island to attend a sale – that was the excuse he had given Julia.

He explained his predicament to Barbara Russell.

'Help yourself.'

She watched him ironically as he told his tale on the borrowed telephone. The sale? . . . No it wasn't what he had been led to expect. No nothing of any real quality. It was getting on now. Better to stay overnight and come back to London in the morning.

'Miss you,' he said, honestly enough.

'Be good,' said Julia.

He could have been an erring husband he reflected as he put down the receiver, wondering whether the story he had told had really hit the button. Turning to the woman with the grievance on the other side of the room he saw that the same idea had occurred to her although she kept it to herself.

'I'd better find you something to eat,' she said, suddenly throwing off her lethargy and turning capable. Because he wanted her on his side and the alternative was a solitary meal in a hotel, he didn't refuse. She made no apology for what was on offer – half a cook-from-frozen pizza and some re-heated vegetables. She allowed him to help her stack the dishwasher and make the kitchen shipshape.

Afterwards she seemed to be in no hurry to see the back of him – rather the reverse. It was almost as though, well aware of his need for her co-operation, she was exacting a price – a few hours of companionship, the right to tell her story to him, because there was nobody else available.

She showed him over the house – her realm which was soon to be usurped. Unpretentious, it had potential and somebody like Julia could have made much of it. It was a low building sprawled behind the lawn which sloped down towards it from the road. It had started life as a large cottage, she told him, and had been added to in the mid nineteenth century to provide extra space for a Victorian farmer's family. She had been lucky enough to find the plans in the local library's archive – she had the photocopies somewhere but she didn't think she could lay her hands on them just at the moment she said, throwing the words over her shoulder as they went upstairs. There were unexpected steps – to the bathroom, to one of the bedrooms – showing how the builder had been forced to improvise when the house had been extended.

She made the small talk which went with the house and its neighbourhood. There had been smuggling, of course – the crypt of the church had been a storehouse for brandy – and wrecks on the coast. She told him the story of the chantry built on the hillside behind St Catherine's Point as a penance for the plundering of a ship carrying wine from France in the Middle Ages – wine which belonged to the Church. A mistake.

She took him out on to the lawn to show him the front of the house before the last of the sunlight from the west disappeared. It was a quiet and private place. He could hear no traffic on the other side of the hedge, no sound from the terrace of cottages further down the road. The whole village seemed to have gone to sleep.

Although it was too cold to sit outside for coffee she insisted on opening the French windows in the sitting room to give them both the benefit of the evening. Gradually she ran out of conversation, passed the onus on to him, putting in the odd word now and then but becoming less responsive, falling back further and further into the comfortless world from which he had rescued her for half an hour. Eventually he saw that she wasn't even listening to him. He fell silent.

The telephone rang, making a discreet buzz. Again – and again. At length she had to pick it up. 'Barbara Russell here.'

To give her privacy he went into the panelled hall with its polished quarry-tiled floor to find his briefcase. When he returned he found her sitting crouched over the receiver, trying to break in, to get whoever was haranguing her on the other end of the line to listen to her.

'I have told you, I have nothing to do with that side . . . Mr Smith who is our leading underwriter . . . I don't . . . he hasn't been . . . Listen, will you please listen . . . You must understand, it is not my responsibility.' She closed her eyes as though to shut out what was being said to her. 'No.' The word exploded in the room. 'No, I am not to blame. Believe me.' Now there was fear in her voice. 'I don't know where he is.' A tic started in her eye as she listened for a few moments longer then she pressed down with her forefinger to cut off the call.

'What was that about?'

'I'm ex-directory,' she said, 'I don't know how he got hold of my number.' She laid her head back against the cushion of the chair and tried to gather strength.

'Who?'

'He didn't say but he said he represented one of our Names – that was what he said.'

'Where was he speaking from?'

'I don't know. He said he was on the Island, only that.'

'Did he threaten you?' She nodded.

'What with?'

'Disembowelment.' Although she spoke the shocking and extraordinary word in a detached way, allowing each syllable its due weight, it still almost made him laugh – surely such an idea belonged only in late-night horror movies. Didn't it?

The look she returned allowed him no room for doubt that it was a reality to her, and to the man at the other end of the line. She was sober now, completely. 'He was going into detail when I closed the conversation,' she said primly.

What sort of a man would do that or cause it to be done? Somebody, he imagined, whose life had always run on easy rails and who now found himself facing a concrete reality which he couldn't come to terms with – so he was casting round for a victim. There were over a thousand members in the Smith syndicate and plenty more for whom the agency acted. Statistically there had to be a small percentage of actual and potential psychopaths in there.

'Have you had to put up with much of this?'

'Some.'

'Can't the police—?' Halfway through the question he

abandoned it, left it to answer itself.

Of course she had sought their help. A frightened grey-haired woman living on her own – with nothing much to offer these days and all too aware of it – who had done what she thought was best and was now under fire.

'I think you should leave,' he said. 'Go and find a room for the night somewhere. Sandown. Shanklin. I can drive you over now if you like.' At least he'd paid her the compliment of taking her seriously.

'Not now. I can't trust myself to make decisions now,' she replied. 'Give me until morning.' She paused, to prepare herself for the request she had to make. 'I'd feel much safer if you could stay the night. Would that be possible?' He couldn't refuse.

Unused to visitors she forced herself to concentrate on what he would need – found sheets and pillowslips for him, towels and a bar of scented soap, a new toothbrush still in its oblong cardboard and cellophane pack. She tried to help him to make the bed and when he brushed her aside, stood watching him absentmindedly with empty hands, seeming, he thought, to have retreated further and further into herself, almost beyond reach of his attempts to reassure her. Putting it down simply to nervous exhaustion, he ordered her briskly off to bed.

Before venturing there himself he listened for the noises of her in the bathroom, a tap running then shut off, the sound of water moving through the old plumbing of the house. With his bedroom door ajar and one ear cocked he waited for her bedroom door to close. She was safe.

He slept like the dead, with no memory of any dreams when he awoke. Opening his eyes he saw the sun streaming hot already through the gap in the flowered curtains – curtains which he for a moment didn't recognise; and that white laminated wardrobe was new to him, not his style at all. Why was he naked in this bed? Why no pyjamas? Why no Julia? It wasn't until he caught sight of his briefcase beside him on the floor that he remembered where he was.

He rubbed his jaw and the stubble bothered him. He'd have to put up with it. No razor with him, of course, and there wouldn't be one in the house.

He dressed himself – irritably because he wanted a shower and he would be forced to undress again in the bathroom; having no dressing gown there was no alternative. He made his way down the dark passageway, wondering if Barbara Russell had got up yet – he could hear no signs of life downstairs.

When he descended a few minutes later she wasn't in the kitchen. In the sitting room the unwashed glasses were still there and the window had been left open which gave him a twinge of guilt. He should have seen to it. Instinctively he closed it, and took the glasses to the dishwasher in the kitchen.

At least the back door was locked, that was something. Turning the key he pushed it open and went outside into the sunshine. There were still signs of dew on the windscreen of his car. Only half concentrating, he checked it over. Everything was in order – tyres, bodywork, aerial – not that he had expected it to be otherwise out there in the country.

He looked up, at the landscape to the north; apart from a distant farmhouse it was open farmland – grazing for a herd of lethargic cows this morning. To his left beyond the garage was a hedge with an opening in it. The gate dragged on the ground – its corner had worn a quadrant in the dry earth. Ducking his head beneath an unpruned mass of roses supported by a rusty arch of wrought iron he went through into what had once been an orchard. There was nobody there either. Was she playing some kind of game again? – a flirtatious game perhaps?

He looked back at the house and tried to work out which was the window of her bedroom. That one over the kitchen, he decided, and walked quickly back in that direction.

'Hallo.' His intrusive voice disturbed a blackbird which had been busy tormenting some earthworm under the hedge; it fluttered past him and there was silence again with no response from the curtained window above him. 'Good morning,' he called out again cheerfully. This time the blackbird ignored him and again so did she – if she was there.

He went back into the house and searched quickly through the ground floor, opening doors to rooms which he had not visited before. A small workroom, another living room on the sunless side of the house which looked as though it was never used. She was nowhere to be found. Since they had left her car behind in Ventnor she had to be within walking distance, wherever she had gone. Unless she was still up in her room and simply hadn't heard him. Perhaps overcome with her troubles she had come down-stairs in the middle of the night for another drink, more than one, and was now sleeping it off. He climbed the stairs and approached her bedroom door.

'Are you there?' he called.

No reply.

He knocked. Nothing.

'Time to get up I think,' he insisted.

He turned the door-handle and looked round the door into the scented half light of her room, taking in first the dressing table beside the window – a cut-glass pin tray, emery boards, an opaque jar with a pink lid. Beside it was a low padded chair upholstered in an Art Nouveau fabric and, sitting on it, a doll, dressed fashionably as a child of the 1860s. A valuable and rather flamboyant thing to find there. He could well imagine that it had a special meaning for her – a

72

well-loved companion – somebody to talk to. His gaze moved to the bed and the shape beneath the counterpane which had come adrift in the night and was sagging to the floor.

'Are you awake?'

It was then that he suddenly felt the need to focus on the figure, to watch it with especial care. Of course she was breathing. You couldn't tell straight away, you had to keep your eyes fixed . . . He went to the window and pulled the curtains open. She was lying with her knees drawn up to her chin. The head turned away from him with one or two hairpins in evidence above her right ear.

He shook her shoulder. 'Wake up.' She wasn't awake. She certainly wasn't awake.

Feeling himself an intruder, he pressed his hand down where he imagined her heart would be, under her left breast. There was no protest from her, no movement at all, and as he pulled her over on her back she was a dead weight.

At that moment the word *disembowelment* jumped into his mind. He looked down. There was no blood was there? No, the sheets were white – no ultimate horror at least.

Although he had never bothered to learn anything about resuscitation techniques there was something he dimly remembered, something he had seen once on television. He opened her mouth and putting his against it, lips closed against hers, he blew into her lungs while he held her nose closed – again and again and again. The scent of the astringent lotion she had used the previous night still lay on her skin like a broken promise. She was inert.

Setting the heel of his hand over her heart he pressed down fiercely with his other on top of it and pumped away in a desperate crescendo of effort, feeling the sweat springing on his scalp, trickling down the side of his face. Again he tried his version of the kiss of life.

At length he had to give up. The work had become

73

meaningless, almost obscene – the pounding of something lifeless. Feeling sick, knowing it would be too late, he went downstairs and telephoned the emergency services.

He had no idea how long it would take them to arrive but before they did so there was something he had to do. Although he hadn't the least wish to go back into her bedroom he forced himself to remount the stairs.

Into her room again. It might be his only chance to find the key to the office in Ventnor.

Even in high summer, sunlight would never reach inside that room – it was on the wrong side of the house. None the less there was still too much light in it for him. Nothing had changed – the curtains, the glass tray, the doll seated in its chair watching him. The woman on the bed was still lying where he had left her, flat on her back with her eyes staring upwards. He made himself close them before he began his search.

Her handbag first. Would the police be involved? He had no idea of the cause of death and he would have to be careful. Instead of emptying the bag out on to the floor he removed the items one at a time and laid them on the edge of the dressing table – the purse, the folder of credit cards, the diary – and then rummaged among the coins and bits and pieces for her keys. There was no sign of them at all.

The only one he had seen the previous evening was now in the back door. He had turned it in the lock himself when he had gone out into the garden less than half an hour earlier.

She ought to have brought the others with her but had she actually done so? Had she been sober enough, sufficiently in charge of herself, to remember them? Was it possible for her to have left the key to SJ Underwriting's offices behind?

He tried to think it through, taking himself step by step through yesterday's journey. First of all, had she closed the front door to 'Avalon' behind them or had he? Shutting his

eyes he tried to conjure up the detail . . . Going through
the door she would have been in front of him, he was sure
of that because he had been conditioned since his school-
days to let ladies go first – it was automatic. Had she gone
back past him to close the door? Was it he who had
slammed it? Angry with himself he shook his head. He
couldn't remember.

However she had said something about the other keys –
to the filing cupboards. They were 'about her person' –
that was what she had said. Had she been telling the
truth? Feeling as though he owed her an apology he began
to look for the clothes she had been wearing at the time.
The jacket? In the wardrobe – nothing in the pockets. The
skirt was hanging on a plastic-coated clothes drier. As he
ran his hands over it he realised with a kind of pang that it
was still slightly damp – she had found time somehow to
sponge that muddy mark off it before going to bed. No
keys there.

Reluctant to invade the privacy of the dead woman on
the bed he patted the rest of her clothes, lying folded on a
chair, with the flat palms of his hands – tentatively as
though he was afraid to wake her up – the slacks and shirt
she had changed into after returning to the house, her
underwear on top of them. There was nothing there
either.

What about the drawer of the bedside table? No, that was
empty except for a paperback novel and half a tube of
yellow cough sweets.

Obstinately he returned to her handbag to check it again
with the same result. He was downstairs searching her little
bureau in the sitting room, still searching, when he heard
the ambulance drawing up on the drive beside the house; he
had the door open before the driver reached it, a tall fellow,
with blond hair, short back and sides, who gave Charles a

look of jaded resignation, the sort of look one gives to a colleague who has also suffered.

'What's she been up to now?' he sighed.

Ramsay wasn't sure whether he had been altogether well advised to go to the police and volunteer a statement. However, the thing was done now. The real reason, he admitted to himself, was that while he wanted to divest himself of any responsibility for Barbara Russell as quickly as he could, he also felt obliged to see she wasn't left in limbo, a victim without a home. That idea troubled him. The police would have a procedure for coping with the fallout from the death of a solitary woman – would be able to trace her solicitor and contact her next of kin – would make sure that everything needful was decently done.

His statement, which was comprehensive, was taken by a constable in a non-committal way. They would let him know if they needed him, he was told as he was invited to sign it before he was sent politely on his way. He made no enquiries about the possible cause of her death nor when it would be established for certain. Blameless as he was, there was no point in giving hostages to fortune – the less interest he showed in the matter the better. He sensed that the event had left him with a liability which it was still not possible to estimate. He was like the member of a syndicate at Lloyd's which could not close one of its years of account – left with an uncertainty at the back of the mind which he knew would come back to plague him from time to time. He had been, he told himself again, no more than . . . a passer-by, somebody who happened to be there.

Now he happened to be here, sitting in his car on the opposite side of the road from 'Avalon', a little way down towards the sea, trying not to look conspicuous which wasn't easy because the place was deserted again. Except that today the proprietor of one of the guesthouses was taking advantage of the mid-morning lull to mow the grass in front of his establishment.

Sitting in the driver's seat with the file on his knee Charles could have been a sales rep going through his paperwork before his next call. What was his next move?

Somewhere in that file there was a letter headed *The Smith Names Association* with enclosures. He turned the pages to find the name of the man who ran it.

Please consider carefully what the Association can offer you. Only by standing together can we find a solution to the problems which are facing us today.

Yours sincerely,
John Clarke
Chairman

While he was ready to stand together with other members Mr Clarke obviously didn't believe in letting them get too close. He hadn't put his home address at the head of his call to the troops but only a box number in Berkshire. That problem would have to be overcome since Mr Clarke was now his best if not his only hope. Clarke would have to be found.

In the few minutes Charles Ramsay had been waiting by the kerb, nobody had gone into 'Avalon' or had come out. Suppose Barbara Russell had not locked that door. Getting out of the car he sauntered over to it and tried the handle. No, it travelled a quarter of an inch and that was all. It wouldn't budge a fraction further and the door was as firm as a rock. He didn't consider any other way in – there was a red box marked helpfully with the words SECURITY ALARM screwed to the wall above him.

He strolled back to his car past the gardener who had

finished his little bit of mowing now and was pulling in his orange flex, hand over hand.

'Seems deserted,' Charles observed.

'I saw somebody there yesterday. The boss lady. But there hasn't been anybody else lately.' The man looked him up and down with a grin, taking him perhaps for a debt collector who had missed his quarry or something equally unpopular.

'Thanks.'

Ramsay got into the car and left, the frustration growing inside him as he drew away. Changing up sharply at the end of the road he asked himself what else he could do. Nothing.

Chapter Four

Begg laid the tray on the bedside table. He had taken particular care over it – the cup of tea, the toast and marmalade cut into neat triangles, the plate of cornflakes. He wanted it to be right today.

His mother lay with her face to the wall pretending to be still asleep. It was all part of an endless game she played to keep him guessing. Her bedroom offered little in the way of diversion and she needed some amusement – making him suffer a little was as good a way of passing the time as any other.

When he had first come to live with her he could have killed her for all the trouble she caused him – adding avoidable strains to all the unavoidable chores her disabilities created for him. Gradually his slow mind had worked round to the conclusion that to murder her was quite unnecessary. Not least because it would be unprofitable. Any killing which he did, any risks which he took, had to be rewarded. That was a central rule of his and one which helped him resist the temptation, when she was more than usually irksome, to suffocate her with one of those dingy pillows lying underneath the straggled hair which was all that he could see at the moment, poking above the bedclothes.

'Wakey wakey,' he said, his voice jovial for once. She

rolled over and made an elaborate show of waking up, taking as long as she could.

'Your breakfast,' he said betraying none of the impatience she had come to expect. Today he was relaxed and benign – because it was for the last time. His small eyes watched her yawn. It was the last time that spectacle would be inflicted on him too.

He was afraid that his excitement might show through and set off a long querulous crescendo of suspicion and self-pity but she noticed nothing.

'The tea's hot,' she announced judiciously after just sipping it, that was all. Then for a minute or two they swapped banalities. Those were the last words they would ever speak to each other and the knowledge made him tolerant, up to a point.

He glanced at his watch.

'Got to go now,' he said, 'or I'll miss me shift.' Those were his final words, he was convinced of that. He moved to the door and called out over his shoulder without looking back, 'Cheers then.'

Her mouth was full of cornflakes. She made an indeterminate noise and nodded in his direction trying to clear her mouth to speak to him but by the time she got there he had gone – was halfway downstairs, picking up his flight bag, swinging it over his shoulder. Front door open, front door shut. Crossing the road outside he glanced up at the window of her bedroom. He had been merciful he told himself. When all was said and done she was his mother.

He marched up to the reception desk. It was the same girl as the day before. He liked the look of her but knew she wasn't for him.

'Mr Quist. Room 29. He is expecting me.'

She dialled the room and waited, giving Begg an automatic

80

smile, then waiting again. Replacing the handset she looked up at Begg. 'There's no reply from his room.'

'You sure?'

'He's not answering. Perhaps you'd like to try later. Phone him direct.'

He felt as though somewhere in the structure he had created in his mind something small had slipped out of place. No, nothing was wrong. He checked the cheap black watch on his wrist. He had been told to arrive at eleven in the morning and it was only six minutes past. Quist might be taking a bath, might have gone out in the grounds to take the air for a moment. The Swede hadn't struck him as the unpunctual type – very much the reverse – and you couldn't call this unpunctuality yet. Not six minutes.

'I'll wait,' he asserted, facing her down, knowing she wasn't enthusiastic. That was her problem – she would have to put up with it. He wasn't leaving.

'You could sit over there if you like,' she conceded, making the best of a bad job. She didn't want him wandering around the hotel unaccompanied. He could sit down under her eye in the spacious reception hall of the hotel. He took a deep chair as far from her as possible.

She answered the telephone, took a booking, sat at her word processor and typed out the confirmation letter there and then. A chambermaid came and handed in a key she had found in one of the rooms.

Begg looked at his watch. It was eleven fifteen. He collected a thick country magazine from a table and returned to his seat. He studied the advertisements for a minute or two. Where was Quist? Where was he hiding? He persevered with his reading trying to take in an article on thatching. After a while he put the journal away and checked through the contents of his flight bag.

The girl at reception looked up and he caught her glance.

He had been there more than half an hour and he knew what her look meant. That he was unimportant enough to be kept waiting.

He got up and went to the toilet, the bag slung over his shoulder. He wasn't going to let go of it. Ignoring the girl as he passed the desk he returned to his seat, slumping into it with resignation. Since he was neither quick witted nor imaginative it always took time for messages to get through to him but now a doubt sidled into his mind. It hadn't all been a hoax had it, this story of Quist's? The man hadn't decided overnight that he didn't need him after all and ditched him – just as he himself had deserted his mother earlier that morning. If he had done, nothing would have been lost, Begg considered – nothing except his pride and another of his hopes. He would have to slink back to 27 Freshwater Walk but she would be none the wiser. He congratulated himself on the manner of his leaving that morning.

It was three minutes to twelve.

Another possibility hit him. That in some way Quist was an informer for the police who had been sent to entrap him. Slowly his mind turned over the possibility as well as it could, tried to recall the interview, to remember which parts of it might have been incriminating. The whole thing demanded too much effort and gradually the thought receded until nothing of it was left but a feeling of mental discomfort.

When he looked up and saw Quist coming briskly in through the Gothic, golden oak front door of the hotel he gave a triumphant glance in the direction of the girl as if he had been vindicated. He rose to his feet.

Quist offered no apology but said merely, 'You have arrived then?' as though it was his recruit who was at fault, who had caused the delay. 'I had other things to do.'

That was clearly all the explanation Begg was going to get and he wasn't in any mood to press it. He was too relieved to see the other man who went on crisply, 'I have my luggage to collect and my bill to pay. Wait here.'

The sharp note in his voice caught the girl's attention as Begg subsided again into his seat. Her assessment of him had been correct. He was a subordinate, that look said. You should see me in action he thought, remembering Angola, the Middle East. There were photographs he could show her – he had them in his flight bag – he had left everything else behind but not those. All at once he was seized with a desire to lay them out like a winning poker hand on that polished oak table over there and make her look at them – at what happened in the world of men – his own world.

Eventually Quist came back, a heavy bag in either hand. Catching the red look in Begg's eye he didn't ask him to carry one of them for him.

Outside they crunched together down the gravel drive – the rhododendrons still flaming lavishly on either side.

'We fly to Stockholm this afternoon – from Heathrow. I will brief you fully before we leave. When we arrive we will separate and I will go my own way for a few days.'

'Money? Where do I stay?'

'All arranged.'

Quist didn't give much away. Begg wondered once again what had delayed him that morning but was quite content not to ask.

The lake was dark, deep and glassy, under the pearl grey clouds that had replaced the threatening sky of earlier in the day, asleep now in the afternoon. Carl had always found it uncomfortable to hold binoculars to his eyes for long so he lowered them, something to do with his shortened tendons he supposed.

Hearing a splash he looked down over the water and saw ripples spreading across its surface. Their cause he couldn't see however – a beaver perhaps, turning in the water over there where the birches lined the edge. After three days his visitor still hadn't arrived. He was used to waiting though – it was part of the hand he'd been dealt in life. Something to be accepted.

There was a different sound, a purposeful thrumming beyond the end of the lake. He put the glasses to his eyes again and studied that sector of the sky, then turned and began to run with heavy strides towards his small wooden house, the binoculars' case bumping against his back as he ran. He reached the porch, pushed hastily through the door and once he had reached the sanctuary of the living room continued to watch the red helicopter, about three hundred metres up, flying steadily towards him like a large and complicated insect. As it approached he heard the quick slap-slap-slap of its rotors above the noise of its engine which reached a crescendo as it passed over the roof. He stayed indoors long after the sound had died away completely and it was a couple of hours before he emerged from the house. This time he was wearing a dark blue hooded anorak although there was no expectation of rain in the air. Going down to the jetty he stepped into the boat, untied the painter and moved to the stern, crouching to keep his balance as it bounced and swayed underneath him. The sudden roar of the engine as he started it up sent a family of inquisitive ducks scurrying away for cover.

At the other end of the lake there was a small group of houses, all built of wood, painted uniformly a dull red colour. A farmhouse, with white windows, storehouses, a huge barn where Hansson wintered his beasts and the shed where he allowed Carl to keep his car.

The farmer himself was nowhere to be seen but the shriek

of a circular saw in the workshop on the other side of the yard gave a clue to his whereabouts. Carl did not seek him out but instead made straight for the shed, got out his grey car, a seven-year-old Swedish-made saloon, and drove off down the unmade track leading to the road which snaked through the forest.

When he reached the neighbouring town the tidy streets were empty – he had chosen his time well. Nevertheless, before quitting the car, which he parked as close as possible to the post office, he raised the hood of his anorak and zipped it up to the neck. Inside he walked straight past the idle assistants at the counter, going instead directly to the vacant glass-lined payphone at the end of it without looking to left or right. He made four calls altogether, with his back turned towards the room, shutting out the gaze of intrusive eyes, keeping himself to himself. Since there was no one else waiting to use the phone he was able to take his time, stopping methodically after each call to consult his diary to check the number for the next one. After the last of them he put down the receiver and swore to himself in an explosive whisper which was quite inaudible outside the glass box in which he was confined. Turning impatiently to push against the door he trudged outside, head averted.

When two hours later he got back to his refuge it was still broad daylight of course and it would be for hours yet. How he execrated these interminable days of summer with their pitiless light. It was only in his small starkly furnished bedroom that he could escape from it. In there he had pinned brown paper over the window to the side of the room. There had been enough to cover it but not the other window at the front, so he had taken up from the floor the heavy rag mat which Hansson's wife Ulla had given him – to cheer the place up, she said – and had nailed it sacrilegiously over that one. It was a dense affair which she had woven on her own loom out of lengths of scrap material, strips of old skirts and dresses for which even she could find no other use. There might even be a pair of Hansson's pyjama trousers in there somewhere. This multicoloured weft had been forced down hard against the strings of the warp making a thick mat which was ideal as an excluder of light – not a speck could get through. It provided him with necessary darkness in there – the darkness which he had to have before he could sleep.

Chapter Five

'My dear,' exclaimed Ethelred, 'you have moved up in the world.'

He had just walked in through the door – suddenly appeared – a rather dumpy apparition. He really needed to get some weight off, Julia thought, although she wouldn't have dreamt of saying it because it *was* a pleasure to see him. She regarded him with an indulgent eye – Ethelred Lewis, her former boss.

His envious gaze darted here and there, sizing things up. All this light and space, these floors . . . not very cosy was it? That was what he was thinking, she guessed, and it was only natural. His shop in Brighton where she had worked was fine in its way but not in the same league. Even when Ethelred had operated in The Arcade off Piccadilly, it had been on nothing like this scale.

'I wasn't invited to the opening,' he said reproachfully, which was childish of him, since he knew very well that Charles couldn't stand him. One good thing about his being away, the only good thing as far as she could see, was that she could settle down to a heart to heart with Ethelred. She had a need to unburden to someone and with him you knew he wasn't on the make, in that sense at least.

'That's nice,' he said, laying a judicious forefinger on a pie-crust table. 'What are you asking for that?'

When she told him the figure he drew in a sibilant breath as though a sharp little pain had been inflicted upon him – as though she had dabbed disinfectant on a wound a touch too stringently.

'I couldn't do anything with that, not even with the usual percentage off for trade.' The word jarred harshly in the surroundings which she had created with so much care. She hadn't posed the table there on that Senneh rug to be tradeable and he wouldn't be in the running for it anyway. She let the remark pass her by, as a sop to his pride.

'Charles is away is he?'

At a sale in the Isle of Wight, she told him – some country house thing organised at short notice.

He looked theatrically blank. 'Where?'

'Somewhere near Ventnor I think.'

Ethelred already felt put down by the austere luxury of this new place of theirs, its desirable position, the quality of their stock, the prices they might even get away with. He caught sight of a gilded George II mirror on the wall behind her, went over to peer at it hopefully . . . and pulled a face. It was right, depressingly enough.

A sale near Ventnor? He felt offended by Charles Ramsay's presumption, discovering a sale which he hadn't heard of on his own stamping ground, the South Coast. He wasn't going to let that go by without a challenge.

'Have you got a copy of the *Antiques News?*' – the weekly that listed most of the antique auctions in the country. To humour him she went into the office and found their copy for him to riffle through so that he could prove his point.

'Nothing in there. I thought there wouldn't be,' he said with satisfaction in his voice, putting the tabloid pages back together carefully and handing the paper back to her with a malicious little nod of the head.

Taking it she answered casually, 'He did say it was at

short notice.' Charles wasn't the sort of person who made things up.

'There's more to this than meets the eye,' he insinuated.

'Don't be silly Ethelred.'

'I bet you fifty pounds. There.'

'Fifty pounds that what?'

'That your Charles Ramsay wasn't at that sale.'

'Why?'

'Simply because the sale wasn't there for him to be at, that's why, lovey.'

She would have liked to take him on and teach him a lesson but she knew from experience that for Ethelred betting was a one-way affair – his way. He was always ready to forget a debt of honour.

There was something else besides. She was feeling resentful – she didn't see why she should put fifty pounds of her own money on the line to back up Charles's reputation for telling the truth. On top of that the fact that this sale of his wasn't featured in the *Antique News* made her pause. If for some reason he was telling a fib it would be more than galling to have to admit it to Ethelred.

'Well?' he demanded.

'I never bet on certainties.'

Intrigued at the evasion he pressed home his advantage. 'When are you expecting him back?'

She glanced at her watch. Was it already three o'clock? Where the hell had Charles got to?

'Not for an hour or two yet,' she lied. Bypassing a Regency sofa which was elegant but insufficiently upholstered he made for the plump seating in their reception area and subsided into it with a gesture that invited confidences.

'Then you can take a break, sit down and tell me everything that's happened since we last met. I'm not going to budge until you do.'

She brought him Lapsang Souchong tea, his favourite, and thin crisp biscuits to nibble. At first she was robustly upbeat – the opening had been fabulous – marvellous write-ups in the press and everything. He seemed truly to be pleased for them, for her anyway, which was something she hadn't really expected. There were no small flashes of bitchery.

Encouraged she showed him the side galleries, the big storeroom downstairs, explained the whole set-up, while he made all the right noises. In no hurry to leave he was still there after a couple of hours – keeping out of the way when she was busy, nosing about – and Charles hadn't put in an appearance yet. Where had he got to? She was damned if she was going to wait for him. She would take Ethelred out to La Roma down the road and buy him dinner. He was no girl's idea of the perfect escort but at least he was there.

By the time they were into the second bottle of Barolo she was ready to unbutton to him and come across with some of her anxieties – without being at all disloyal to Charles, of course.

Instead of inducing mischief in Ethelred the wine had made him more genuine, readier to listen with attention to what she said and also what she didn't say. No one knew more about survival in the business than he did. He had a battered wisdom about him which gave him a kind of dignity, she felt.

While he would never have admitted it to his face he was willing to concede that Ramsay wasn't the sort who would cheat her. On the other hand she was right to be concerned. They had put a lot of money at risk – he hadn't realised how much – and of course her mother's interests had to be protected. The venture was at a critical stage and it needed the full-time commitment of both of them. It would be crazy to rock the boat now. However if it turned out that she and

Charles didn't hit it off and she felt she needed a different partner in the business, he had no doubt that he could find one for her. He did have contacts, he asserted proudly. Did she want him to make one or two enquiries – ask around?

Certainly not, she said. His hands on the tablecloth were animated by a gesture which said, 'As you wish,' and which caused the ring on his little finger to flash a tiny message of discontent in her direction although his face remained judicious. She was sure that for once he was sincere in what he said, not motivated by malice or the wish to settle some old score with Charles. That thought made her reconsider her refusal as she took refuge in a sip of wine. Loyalties were such slippery things to deal with. Placing her glass with care on the tablecloth in front of her she turned to him.

'What do *you* think I should do?' she asked.

Chapter Six

John Clarke's soldier father had always taught him that difficulties were there to bring out the best in you, and that meant that when you were up against it you had to make a special effort to keep fit and maintain self-discipline. Never permit your standards to drop, he had been told and he hadn't. Which was why he was determined to run a third time round Long Field. He had a good sweat going now and his breathing was deep and satisfying as though he had unlocked his lungs at last. The last circuit completed he let himself out through the gate making sure that it was securely closed before taking to the road, a small wiry man with a receding chin in a blue and white tracksuit – his glasses misted over. He pressed forward, refusing to allow his legs to flag, just as he had at school in the last muscle-burning mile of the Whitsun cross-country run. Willpower, that was the only way to do it . . . it was all a matter of control – which was what Carol had signally lacked and why she had fallen by the wayside. She was better out of the way, he thought, as he came pounding towards the drive of the home which she had deserted in such a flurry not so very long ago. He wasn't sure that he, not even he, could have coped if she had stayed.

Hanging on to a routine, that was the secret which had enabled him to hold anxiety at arms length and keep his mind clear to face up to the disaster which had so panicked her. Routine. In the programme in his mind he ticked off, *4 p.m. Run*, and considered the next one with a rare touch of pleasure, *4.25 p.m. Shower and change*.

He always liked to sprint the last fifty yards or so – to him it was an affirmation. Turning into his gravelled drive between the white painted gateposts he put his head down and let rip, legs driving like pistons, his tracksuit trousers flapping in a frenzy. Coming to a halt beside the big pseudo-classical front door he allowed himself the luxury of flopping over to release the tension and let the pain gradually ebb away from his muscles.

Beside him, a voice said, 'Congratulations, Mr Clarke.'

He could make nothing of the shape he could just discern through the blurred lenses of his spectacles. Hastily wiping them he looked again.

A dark young man – younger than himself – leaning against an estate car parked in his drive. In front of his garage, beside his house – all this belonged to him and no one was going to take away or diminish his right to it. That was a vow he had made to Carol before she had left.

'Would you move it, please? Your car. This drive is private.' Private. *Private*. Didn't he understand the word? Why wasn't he moving? Must be another pernicious journalist. 'I am not giving interviews at the moment. I am far too pressed for time.'

Standing there still panting and perspiring in his tracksuit he felt that he was being placed deliberately at a disadvantage. He couldn't afford to have his routine broken – it was much too important.

Now the young man was offering him his hand. 'How do you do? Actually I'm not a journalist . . .'

'Your car. Please be good enough to move it.'

Without looking back to check whether his order had

been obeyed, Clarke let himself into the house, shutting the door behind him as if it could close his mind to the trespass, and went and took his shower in the downstairs bathroom as he always did.

4.30 p.m. Change into clean clothes.

Descending the stairs he felt fighting fit – ready to begin the battery of telephone calls he had to make before five. Since he hadn't spoken to Carol for five days he would ring her as well.

As he was about to enter his workroom there was a solid knock at the door. He opened it. Yes? The young man again.

'Mr Clarke, my name is Charles Ramsay. I am nothing to do with the press and I need to consult you as Chairman of the SJ Names Association.'

'Where is your car this time?'

'I have parked it in the road.'

He threw the door open to give himself a clear view and saw that it was no longer in the drive. Right, he could come in.

'You'll have to wait. I have telephone calls to make . . .'

They were standing in the workroom which was orderly to a fault – a plain table empty of papers, a state-of-the-art word processor in lonely splendour on its stand with a mobile filing rack on castors beside it. It was as functional as the bridge of a warship or an airport control room. Nowhere was there any clue to Clarke, the person – no scribbled notes, no jokey postcards. The only thing thumbtacked to the pinboard was an outline-planning schedule for the year and it didn't look as though many laughs could be squeezed out of that. He glanced up from the luminous screen.

'I can't find your father on our list of members.'

'He probably overlooked it. He has become forgetful lately.'

'Equally well, he may have forgotten to resign from the syndicate . . .'

'That is exactly what I am trying to . . .'

Clarke overrode the interruption, '. . . and if so I'm afraid I have bad news for him.'

He wasn't taking any pleasure in what he was about to say, simply stating the fact, like a lawyer wanting to get the ground cleared. '. . . the substantial call he has received is not the end of the story for that year of account. Part of it has been left open, due to material uncertainties concerning the syndicate's exposure to Personal Stop-Loss risks.' The last words were spoken sarcastically, as though he was quoting from one of Barbara Russell's tactful circular letters to her members.

Ramsay subdued his irritation. 'What does that mean?'

'They don't know what their liabilities will be and they haven't yet found anybody who is prepared to reinsure them,' Clarke translated.

'To cover them?'

'If you like.'

'So this one hundred and seventy-four thousand is not the last of it.'

'Not if your father failed to send in his papers early enough.' Having been brought up in a military family the out-of-date phrase came easily to Clarke.

'Leave the syndicate you mean?'

'Yes.'

'Then why not say so?' Provoked by this new reverse Charles Ramsay spoke the words too sharply and regretted it.

The other man shot back, 'You *are* seeking my help I take it?'

'I apologise. I'm in your hands. There is nobody else to go to.'

Mollified, Clarke squared his shoulders. The SJ Names Association was his lifeline – it was all that kept him from the chaos of despair. It meant as much to him as the regiment and the men who served in it had meant to his father, and it was clear that Ernest Ramsay was properly one of their company, while not officially on the strength. That could soon be put right. He went to a drawer, found a membership form and gave it to Charles.

'Please ask your father to complete this and return it to me with a cheque for the annual subscription – £90. There is a newsletter, a helpline, and we hold quarterly meetings to bring members up to date with developments.'

That essential formality completed he eased up. 'So you have already approached the syndicate . . . in the Isle of Wight?'

'Yes – Barbara Russell. She was unable to find the letter from my father,' Ramsay said, confining himself to the literal truth.

Clarke grimaced. 'That woman is no favourite of mine.'

'I asked her where Smith had got to.'

'What did she say?'

'That she didn't know,' Charles replied.

'That's not the story she told me.' Clarke looked adamant, his mouth a thin line above his unimpressive chin.

'Oh? What did she tell you?'

For some reason of his own Clarke wasn't going to say. 'I suggest that you get back to her straight away and ask her again. Do it now.' He gestured towards his telephone.

'She's not available.'

'Not available?' Clarke huffed indignantly. 'Don't you let her get away with that.'

'I haven't much choice. She died this morning.'

'Died?' All at once the curt voice was diminished. 'How?'

Ramsay told him, keeping nothing back. How he had met her, how she had been a Name herself – in the same predicament as the rest of them. There was no point in being other than candid if he wanted to keep Clarke on his side. He watched his ordinary face – the small beak of a nose, the eyes masked by the light reflected on the lenses of his spectacles – and was quite unable to guess his reaction to what he was being told.

When the recital was over Clarke said nothing for a moment. Nervously he pushed his glasses up on his forehead and rubbed his eyes. The gesture suggested that he was dropping his guard, but still he didn't speak.

'What did Barbara Russell tell you?' prompted Ramsay.

'She said that Smith had gone to Sweden to consult his partner . . . the Coathanger.' Clarke's voice was tinged with contempt.

'The Coathanger? What do you mean?'

The question was ignored, as if the other man was embarrassed in some way at having spoken the nickname and wanted now to pretend that he hadn't.

'I thought she was stalling me. I had her down as just another loyal cog in the machine, the subordinate protecting her boss right or wrong to the bitter end – perhaps I was wrong.' The admission didn't come easily from him.

Ramsay wondered just how far that image of the dead woman had become accepted as part of the mythology of the SJ Names Association. The picture of her as a hypocrite, a double dealer, sending out demands for money on behalf of a management which, if not corrupt, had operated the system in its own interest, taken advantage of its knowledge of the law of its own particular jungle. It was easy to imagine one of the members flipping his lid and deciding to kill the messenger even if he couldn't reach the people behind her.

Where did that leave Ramsay? Feeling less than comfortable until the cause of her death had been established. Suppose the post-mortem said that she had not died naturally? Motive and opportunity was what the police would be looking for and he stood out starkly from the background on both counts. Of course he could establish his innocence. Of course he could – if he said it often enough he might convince himself that it was true – but how long would it take to do it? He might be remanded in custody; even if he were bailed there would be conditions attached. His passport would be taken away. By the time he was free to follow him Smith could be anywhere.

The other man's voice had broken into his thoughts but he hadn't heard what he'd said.

'What was that? Say again.'

Impatiently Clarke repeated, 'I said, we had quite a long conversation on the telephone, she and I. She couldn't or wouldn't produce some of the facts I needed – for members who were disputing calls. When I pressed her she said the syndicate records were incomplete.'

'Incomplete?'

'I said I didn't believe it, that I was coming down to the Isle of Wight to see her.'

'Did you go?'

'I didn't.'

'Why not?'

'She told me it would be pointless because the key records and accounts weren't there – that I ought to get in touch with Smith himself – discuss it with him. In the end she admitted that he had taken them with him.'

'To Sweden?'

'Yes.'

'He can't have done, the syndicate had more than a thousand members. He would have had to take a truck.'

'How do you know he didn't? Anyway most of it would have been on magnetic disc.' Clarke glanced at his watch as if to underline that this unexpected interview had disrupted his routine and it was time to bring it to a close – he had been robbed of his privacy for the best part of half an hour.

'I think we should call a halt there. My time is not altogether my own – I mustn't forget that all the other members of the association have their right to a crack of the whip as well.'

He put out a hand to guide his visitor to the door but found that Ramsay wasn't leaving yet.

'I shall go over there and find him. It's the only option,' Ramsay said, half to himself. But if he went he would need an ally there, somebody who knew his way round the country and had an equal interest in Smith's whereabouts. She had intoned a litany of names, he remembered.

'*Ericsson, Lundström, Andersen, Gustafsson . . .*'

That was the one that had given her trouble . . . Gustafsson. They were all aggrieved clients of SJ Underwriting. 'You must know people there, members of your association,' he insisted.

For a moment they stood in silent opposition to one another, in balance, head to head. It was Clarke who gave ground, seeing it perhaps as the quickest way to get rid of his visitor and have the house to himself again.

'An action group has been set up in Stockholm for Scandinavian Names,' he admitted finally.

'There must be somebody running it. Someone like yourself, and he's the most likely one to know where Smith has got to, isn't he?'

Reluctantly Clarke nodded. 'I'll give you his name and address.' His tone said that was the exact limit of his co-operation. Consulting an address list he wrote down the details on a slip of paper in an urgent, tightly controlled script. 'Here.'

Ramsay looked at it. Bengt Winblad . . . an address – Biskopstorget 42 . . . other numbers – that was some kind of postcode presumably and that the telephone number. He turned back to the man who had given him the information as though there was something more he had to ask – thought better of it and moved at last towards the door.

When he had gone Clarke went back into his workroom and sat down. The feeling of well-being which had built up inside him after his afternoon run had all been dissipated. Helpless for a moment he felt a grey sea of anxiety wash over him, sweeping away his command of himself. He had to re-establish it, to climb back on his rock.

Then the murmuring of guilt began again, far away at the back of his mind, rising in intensity until the reproaches were swarming around in his head like bats in a cave. He had only himself to blame for what had occurred, only himself. Gradually he beat them down – restored order in the darkness, calmed himself, with a ghost of panic still in the pit of his stomach.

Ought he to contact Winblad? He was about to consult the address book which still lay on the desk in front of him when he thought better of it. The period he set aside for making calls each afternoon had all been used up; Winblad always talked too much and would persist with time-consuming questions. The only way to get through this marathon was to stick to his programme. He would do it tomorrow, at the allotted time.

Chapter Seven

'I don't need a bloody apology – what's the use of that? I want somebody to explain to me what is going on here. A simple explanation, that's all.'

Julia's voice resounded against the concrete walls of the basement storeroom where he had found her. He had known that she would still be on the premises, working late, and that hadn't made his conscience any easier.

She found it impossible to look at him; her gaze was fixed on a point somewhere alongside him. That was the nearest she could get. Her arms were clasped across her chest as though it were cold down there and it wasn't in the least. Stepping forward to try and make contact with her he stumbled clumsily against the tapered leg of a *demi-lune* card table, a delicate thing which he remembered she had particularly liked when it had come in. She shied away, backing herself up against a linen press, trapped in a gulf of antique furniture – too much of it mahogany, it occurred to him. He could have tried to make a minor joke out of that but knew it would have died, plumping down like a stricken bird at his feet. She was in no laughing mood. Jokes were out.

Charles examined the slender leg of the table for damage. Smashing up the stock wasn't going to improve his rating.

'No harm done,' he reported automatically.

A simple explanation? He had provided that twice already . . . this was the third time of asking. Perhaps, without being niggardly with the truth, he had left out the odd detail here and there – the death of Barbara Russell, for example; he hadn't got to that yet.

'I don't care what you have been up to in the Isle of Wight or why you saw fit to mislead me about it. That isn't so desperately important' – which meant that it was. 'What really gets to me is that ever since the opening you seem to have lost interest in the business – completely lost interest.'

Now she was advancing on him, reducing the gap between them to no more than a couple of feet. Any attempt at this stage to cross it would be a disaster. 'My mother and I trusted you, you know, and you're letting us down. It was your skill that was going to make or break it, I knew that, but I thought that I could bring something of my own to it as well . . . I had a contribution . . .'

The problem wasn't that women had bigger guns than you had, he reflected, it was that they possessed a much greater *variety* of weapons.

'Come upstairs,' he said, 'and I'll tell you all about it.'

No, she said, hugging herself again, almost shivering, not until she'd had a coffee and something to eat.

When that was out of the way he made her sit down in the office and listen. He unloaded the whole thing, exactly as it had happened – from the moment his father had told him about the call on the syndicate right through to his encounter with John Clarke earlier that day.

When she realised that now he was serious she did begin to concentrate on what he was saying, interrupting him only to get this point or that clear in her head. However, when he came to the episode at Barbara Russell's home her questions became perceptibly sharper and more engaged, and by the time he had finished she seemed almost detached.

'What do you propose to do now?'

Her tone made it sound almost as though she was trying to distance herself from him, and unsure how much credit he still had with her he patiently went through his justification. Yes of course, with hindsight, his father should never have got involved with Lloyd's in the first place but the fact was that he had and the only hope of saving Bressemer from the results of his folly was to find Smith quickly; the underwriter was the only lead he had. Surely she could look after the business for another week or two? If she had to cope on her own it wasn't so much of a big deal, was it? For only a couple of weeks?

The facts he had given her were open to more than one interpretation – neither of them needed to say that out loud – but they had been together long enough, he thought, for him to be able to claim her support.

There was no response. He broke the silence. 'I feel like a life-insurance salesman who has just lost a prospect.'

'Do you?'

Her falling inflection told him that it was exactly what he had done. Simple, wasn't it? A single false step. He shouldn't have told her the white lie about the sale. In her mind that pretence had tainted with doubt everything he had just told her. It was a story that you had to take on trust.

Her unspoken question was – why was he so anxious to rush off to Stockholm? Commonsense said that since he was innocent he should wait for the outcome of the post-mortem – it couldn't be long. The police would know.

'I'll contact them in the morning.' Would that do?

At the flat, in the desultory two hours before they went to bed, there were silences which neither of them found the energy to bridge. Once she reminded him of an appointment the following week, halted herself in mid-sentence and had to backtrack . . . if he was taking this trip to Sweden he would have to cancel it. Don't forget that.

Another time, she said briskly, 'It's a question of your priorities really, isn't it?' and left the sentence hanging reproachfully between them. When he tried to follow that up she announced that she wasn't going to be drawn further into an argument and he left it. He was exhausted too.

In the bedroom they undressed in opposite corners, in the privacy of their own thoughts. For him it was a troubled night while she slept the sleep of one who is in the right.

He was up early, too early to telephone the Isle of Wight. Impatient, he shaved and breakfasted in a hurry only to find he still had to kill time before he could make the call.

When the time arrived he made all the needful explanations with precision. Could he be put through to the officer in charge of the case?

'One moment please.' A click, and a feeling of being left in the air, uncertain whether the electronics are working or not.

Standing beside the door with one urgent hand on the handle, Julia was ready to leave for work in her smart clothes – alert, waiting for the verdict . . .

'It is about Miss Russell who was found dead yesterday morning. You may remember me . . . my name is Ramsay.'

The voice at the other end of the line assured him politely that he had not been forgotten. Yes, the cause of death had been established. No, it could not be revealed to him at this stage but he, the voice, could tell him that an inquest would be held in ten days' time and all the circumstances would be thoroughly gone into then. Just like any other member of the public he was entitled to attend.

Now he had reached the point of decision. As he put down the phone he could feel Julia's gaze on him.

'Well? What did they say?'

He told her.

'And what will you do?'

He told her that as well.

'So you are going to cut and run.'

She was deliberately ignoring the size and complexity of the crisis which he had on his hands. How often in her well-protected life had she come up against anything remotely as challenging as this? Never. In his place she would have retired hurt in ten minutes. All she wanted to do was to provoke another clash and he wasn't going to waste energy on that.

Despite her good night's sleep she sounded as though she was at the end of her tether. He thought of his father walking through the rooms at Bressemer. Obligations, duty. He had made his choice.

'Be warned. I may not be here when you get back,' she said.

Clothed in self-righteousness she left the room, shutting the door with deliberation. There was a pause. He imagined her collecting her briefcase, checking that she had her car keys, credit cards and the rest. He knew that if he went over to the window and looked down he would see after a minute or two the top of her blonde head as she emerged from the entrance of the block to cross over the road, elegant, ready for the morning.

He didn't go over to the window. Instead he went into the bedroom to pack.

Chapter Eight

It was a fine afternoon for a flight. The weather had been kind to Erik's new venture so far this summer and business had been good – he would have to remind Karin to get more champagne from the Systembolag. His wife had got into the habit of counting the empty bottles after the day's business was over as a quick check on her takings but for once she had forgotten to count the full bottles left in their cellar and he had noticed last night that there were fewer than there should be – no more than a couple of dozen left. The champagne – the decapitation of the bottle with the sword – it left his passengers in an upbeat mood when they quit the park at the end of the flight with fifteen hundred crowns less in their wallets, minds full of a new experience and the knowledge that today they had been a little more reckless than yesterday. Deep down they too would be savouring a feeling of relief, which he always shared with them in secret – the knowledge that nothing had gone wrong.

Novelty, self-esteem and then safety. It was a heady cocktail of sensations but it wouldn't be the same without the champagne. Besides they'd paid for it and he couldn't offend them. These days tourists were important to the Swedish economy, to its balance of trade – the papers said so – and tourists were no less vital to Erik.

Dear *Isolde*. She was lying on her side on the ground,

heaving and swaying, on the edge of the struggle to escape from the flames roaring at her bottom end. *Isolde* was big and beautiful and blue – his own hot-air balloon.

He walked over to the caravan which they used as a booking office to remind Karin about the champagne order before he forgot. There would be a Japanese in the basket this time, he saw – they were never any trouble, they had too much face to lose – but who was this guy counting out the ticket price in used ten-dollar notes while Karin dabbed out the exchange on her calculator? A used-up looking type in a cheap red sweater and worn jeans who looked up from his task and spoke in English, his tone loud, unmodulated. 'When? Balloon. When?'

Erik threw two bunches of fingers at him. 'Ten minutes' – he threw an extra bunch – 'fifteen maybe. Maybe fifteen. Understand? You have the park, sun, sky.'

He made an encompassing gesture at the amenities that were available to patrons while they waited for Isolde to take her fill of hot air.

Lips muttering the shabby man went back to his task and at length gave up his little wad of money in exchange for his ticket, his change in Swedish crowns, and his receipt. Karin explained it to him, the numbers, the current rate of exchange, and gave him a bright smile. Doubtfully he took the slip of paper and scrutinised it.

Dollars. They were probably like golddust where he came from and for a moment Erik's sense of what was proper overcame his instincts as a businessman. What did this fellow think he was doing, spending his dollars this way? One would have thought he had better things to do with them. Clothes for a start. When all was said and done a balloon flight was a frivolity. A charming one however.

He glanced at *Isolde* with affection – she was filling out nicely.

★ ★ ★

In due course, she was carrying them far above Stockholm in majestic silence.

Far below them and to their left was the familiar overview – the brick-built City Hall looking like a tiny model of itself, its massive blind tower topped with a golden cupola, the royal palace, Riksdaghuset, the black skeletal spire of the Riddarholms Church. It was a panorama which, although he saw it every day in summer, never failed to satisfy him. They were passing Gamla Stan, the kernel of the city and where it had begun, where the Hansa merchants had traded in the Middle Ages leaving behind the German Church as a memento. But it was not so much the buildings as the huge expanses of water surrounding them that gave the capital its special personality. And everywhere there were ships, sailing boats, along the quays nearest to them the heavy black and orange icebreakers which would return to the north before winter, huge cruise ships with layer upon layer of glass-enclosed decks which plied between Stockholm and Helsingfors, and over the glittering surface of Saltsjön a scattering of motor boats, yachts, old-fashioned ferries with black funnels, long excursion boats doing round-the-city trips.

Erik didn't have a set spiel because he had found that the sort of client who could afford fifteen hundred crowns preferred the more personal touch. He spoke to the Japanese standing beside him, pointing, 'Over there is the Deer Garden where one can find the diplomatic quarter and where many important people live. It is also the home of Skansen, our open-air museum.'

The Japanese nodded, half-comprehending, and leaning against the edge of the basket loosed off another quick burst of shots with his camera. Click, whirr, click, whirr, click . . . he had run out of film. Handing the camera to Eric with a single, sibilant, 'Please', he searched in the black pouch in front of him for a new canister, rearming his camera with efficient fingers, bringing it back to his eye to make a stable triangle with his elbows firmly placed on the wicker parapet.

Isolde needed a boost, some new fire in her belly. Pulling on the toggle which controlled her flame Erik let it roar for a few seconds. The Japanese turned his head and nodded his approval with animation.

'Yes, higher. Good,' he urged with a smile.

'Yah. Higher up,' chimed in the deeper voice of the man standing at Erik's shoulder, outside his field of vision. For a moment he had forgotten he was there. Where did he come from? Poland? Estonia? – somewhere to the East – a Russian even.

Well, if they wanted to climb another thousand feet there was no reason why not. Again the flames roared above them and *Isolde* sailed effortlessly up towards the sun.

He turned to look at his other passenger and was surprised to find that he wasn't facing towards the city where all the interest was but the other way, to the east towards the skerries, the thousands of islands in the archipelago. In front of him he had a map, but it wasn't a gaily coloured tourist map or the sort you get in a motoring atlas, basically yellow with roads marked in cherry red and blue. Nor was it a plan of the city. It was sparse and monochrome, more like a mariner's chart, folded clumsily. He made no attempt to hide it.

Various intriguing possibilities flickered through Erik's mind. Years ago, before the USSR had fallen to pieces, the Soviets had shown a persistent interest in the naval installations on the islands. One of their submarines on a spying mission had even been apprehended at Muskö some way to the south east. Ten years earlier he might have considered contacting the authorities but today espionage didn't seem likely. The Russians had problems of their own. While he didn't wish them ill, it did mean that the threat from the east had gone on to the back burner, as it were, for a while, and anyway if the KGB were still monitoring the area they would scarcely need *Isolde*'s assistance, even as things were in Russia these days. Reluctantly he surrendered the idea. It would have been great publicity.

Otherwise, he speculated, the guy might be a treasure hunter engaged on some research to do with a wreck. There were still sunken ships like the *Vasa* around – well preserved because the waters of the Baltic were not salty enough to support *Teredo navalis*, the ships' worm. From his visits to the *Vasa* museum he knew the names of a few of them – the *Roving Man*, the *Green Huntsman* . . . Hansa ships like the *Swan of Lubeck* . . . and warships – the *Mars*, the *Orb of the Realm*. Many of them had been located in the channels between the islands but there were others still to be discovered. Hand on the toggle he lifted his eyes to the horizon like a seafarer and gave *Isolde* another burst of fire to send her soaring.

When they landed the burner gave no more than a sigh as *Isolde* set them down with her customary care – scarcely a bump. Karin was standing beside the champagne table with a big smile and the cavalry sabre at the ready for the ceremony. While she stood by expectantly, he slowly abraded the wire at the neck of the bottle; then using just enough force he chopped with the sword and had it off neatly, the foaming wine sparkling on the grass like diamonds. The Japanese was pleased and took the glass which was due to him from her hand with a polite grin, but the other one, the man from the opposite side of the Baltic, was churlish and wouldn't enter into the spirit of the thing at all. One would have thought, considering what sacrifices the trip must have cost him, that he would have accepted this touch of high living with a better grace somehow.

Ramsay hadn't expected the rain and it didn't make him feel at home. Coming after thunder it was fierce and sudden, hammering down on the window-shoppers surrounding him, swirling along the stone runnel in the centre of the cobbled street. To either side of him there were shops selling souvenirs – wooden horses, painted scarlet and in an improbable range of sizes, postcards . . . or export goods – expensive leather, handmade glass. He glanced at the sodden piece of paper in his hand, then at his equally damp tourist's street plan of Gamla Stan – the earliest part of the city, one of the tidy paragraphs around the edge of it told him – the Old Town. Biskopstorget? He would have to ask. Going into a shop crowded with gently steaming tourists he made his way slowly towards the rear. The small Hindu who stood beside a rack of T-shirts gave him a friendly smile.

'Can you help me please? I'm looking for . . .'

The man shook his head regretfully.

'Kan inte tala engelska,' he said.

That wasn't right, thought Ramsay, the chap must do – he was from India where everybody spoke it . . . the English language had been the Empire's lingua franca . . . one of the benefits bestowed on his country by the Raj . . . for an Indian to speak Swedish as his adopted tongue smacked somehow of ingratitude.

At the end of a narrow street, scarcely more than an alley, he discovered Biskopstorget eventually: a small tree-shaded triangle of space surrounded by tall stucco houses whose fronts were washed in pale colours – dull yellow, brown, blue. He had no idea how old they were and he found that slightly disconcerting.

It was equally difficult to guess the age of the girl who

came to the door. Small, elfin, she looked about fifteen.

'Come in out of the rain,' she said. She spoke in English with an easy familiarity and no trace of a sing-song accent. Between lean fingers she took the trade card which, to save time, he offered her, and before he could get out the explanation he had prepared she exclaimed, 'You saw my advertisement then in the *Antiques News*? Or was it the *Daily Telegraph*? Come in please and I shall show you. Why didn't you tell me you were coming? I would have prepared a welcome.'

It was a large low room which ran the length of the house, the walls panelled in grey, with a *trompe-l'oeil* decoration of cupids and swags in faded green and gold painted above the door. At the far end a pair of plain square casement windows gave on to a small courtyard decorated with plants in pots. A crimson clematis clambered up a whitewashed wall.

'There you are,' she gestured with hands outstretched on either side of her, 'Grandmother's furniture. As you see it is all of first quality and all of it classically English.'

His first glance told him that what she said was true: it was indeed English and most of it early. She had put him back into his familiar territory. When he looked round again, his eyes took their time. A pair of splendid wing chairs, that long-case clock – Chinese Chippendale, a walnut bureau, the colour of dark honey, from the reign of William and Mary. However . . .

'I'm afraid we are at cross purposes. It is Mr Winblad I was hoping to see.' Her father presumably, though she couldn't be as young as he had thought at first – not with so much self-assurance.

Disappointed, she made no attempt to hide the fact.

'My brother Bengt is not here,' she said, 'he has to travel for his job, but he will be back for the weekend I think. He is my lodger you see. He only uses my house now and again.'

'As a *pied à terre*,' suggested Ramsay.

'That's right,' she agreed, smiling for the first time.

'He said he would be here today.' He took care to keep the annoyance he felt out of his voice since he needed her co-operation. His chances of making contact with Smith were thin enough as it was. He would simply have to wait in his modest hotel until Winblad took it into his head to reappear.

'Bengt is not always . . .' she hesitated and did not complete the sentence, as if it was now her turn to go carefully. Then hastily she added, to catch his attention before he made up his mind to leave, 'there are more things upstairs as well. Would you like to see them?'

Of course he would. If he was going to have to hang around in Stockholm for a couple of days he might as well spend them usefully and anyway he liked the look of her and her house. As he followed her up the steep stone staircase to the floor above she chatted about herself easily – accepting this dark-haired young Englishman as an equal, someone she could trust.

Her father's mother had been English she said – had met her husband when visiting the Berlin Olympiad in 1936 – they had both been good amateur athletes. By profession he had been an engineer. After his death this house which had belonged to his family for generations had been given to her by her grandmother with its contents; for tax reasons it had been necessary to skip a generation.

Upstairs the furniture was just as rich and desirable. He eyed another walnut piece, a bachelor's chest which couldn't have been later than 1720, in one of the bedrooms, and an earlier oak chest in another. She saw him eyeing its handles for authenticity, the feet for signs of repair; he tried a drawer.

116

'That would make how much in London at auction do you think? Two thousand five hundred pounds?' She was very well-informed. Or was it no more than a lucky guess? 'And the other one, made of walnut,' she went on, 'more than sixteen thousand, don't you think?'

That certainly was no guess. This girl beside him had an expert's eye . . . and as he looked down at her in surprise he was certain that she wasn't as young as he had thought.

Seeing the look on his face she explained, 'I used to be a member of the fine furniture department at Ahlov's.' Ahlov's was one of the leading auction houses in the city, he knew that much. He didn't ask her why she no longer worked there but she told him anyway. She was forthcoming, factual – she had nothing to hide.

Sweden had gone through its own version of the eighties' boom. The young newly rich traders and speculators had spent millions of crowns on antiques in a fever to own, to invest, to buy and to be seen to be buying. The prices of Gustaviansk furniture – late eighteenth century – had reached stratospheric levels. A bureau signed by Georg Haupt, *ébeniste du Roi*, veneered in birch rosewood and jacaranda, had made six million crowns, she told him, over half a million pounds sterling.

Then the bubble had burst. The market had collapsed, and with it Ahlov's turnover and commission earnings. The firm had made her and many of her colleagues redundant – with the greatest of regret. She had been forced to retreat to one of the islands in the archipelago for the summer with friends of hers who were similarly placed. It was cheap to live out there.

No doubt that was why she was having to sell these well-cared-for pieces of furniture he supposed, and hurried to cover the awkward moment. At the beginning of his career he too had worked for a major auction house, he said

– Crowthers in London. It gave them something in common.

She offered him coffee and home-made biscuits heaped in a good Coalport dish, no doubt part of the legacy from her grandmother. She wasn't proposing to sell everything – just enough, she said. He took care not to ask her just enough for what; instead he helped himself to another biscuit and let her carry on.

Stockholm was obviously the wrong place to auction English furniture and she was reluctant to send anything to London in case it didn't make its reserve and she had to find the cost of shipping it back. Besides the commission rates in London were horribly high didn't he find? Hence her advertisements in the English press. She would let the buyers come to her.

'How many have there been?' he asked.

She gave him a candid smile, ready to answer the question because she liked him. 'Nobody yet.' She pulled a sad face. 'But we shall see.'

All the furniture had been preserved in this quiet house for nearly fifty years as though in a time capsule. Everything that he had seen was well cared for. It would be fresh to the market . . . and an added bonus was that if he bought something it would demonstrate to Julia that, whatever she thought, he did have the interests of their business close to his heart.

'What pieces did you have it in mind to sell,' he said tentatively, warning himself not to let himself be carried away because she looked vulnerable and seemed to be going through a bad patch . . .

. . .They agreed terms. Both businesslike, both knowing the form. It was a fair price for the items on the list that he'd drawn up. The total amount would be payable in Swedish currency, half of it down and the balance when he collected it all for shipment. He didn't want to delay, to risk letting somebody else in on the act or giving her an opportunity for second thoughts, not that she seemed the type.

'Now I need to find a bank. Can you direct me?'

'I will take you. It isn't far and I have nothing else to do just now.'

She didn't in the least mind leading him through narrow streets behind the Royal Palace down to the waterside and then over the bridge to the everyday heart of the city. The interesting man who had bought her furniture.

The bank had been built on a Wagnerian scale, presumably in order to impress its late nineteenth century customers with its stability. Now its peaceful and gloomy cavern was almost empty. Eventually a member of the staff appeared and led them to an office where she acted as his interpreter. After one or two telephone calls, some signing of documents, much tapping of keyboards and consulting of screens he was provided with the money he needed. All that remained was to hand it over to her – twenty-seven thousand pounds in Swedish banknotes. With quick fingers she counted every note under the impassive eyes of the teller – then paid almost all of it back into the bank with a certain flourish.

After that symmetrical transaction they felt more relaxed. Out in the daylight she became light hearted and offered him lunch, a modest lunch in a restaurant in Stortorget which lay on the way back to her home. It was a small place and crowded so that they had no option but to sit close to one another, almost knee to knee. Now and then one of them would be forced to bend forward into the other's territory by a new customer pushing behind, pushing, trying to find somewhere to sit. At first, self-consciously adopting the role of the hostess she made the conversational gambits, telling him the local folklore, anecdotes from her time with Ahlov's. Gradually he opened up – found himself ready to reveal more to her about his reasons for being in Sweden than he would have done to any other stranger met by chance, found himself hoping too that after lunch she might be willing to keep him company a bit longer, that she wouldn't have some other person to rush off to. A partner, there must be somebody. That provoked a memory of his own partner, of Julia's elegant and forthright presence which in turn made him feel not so much ill at ease as resentful that she had been so off-hand about the fix he was in over Bressemer and the muddle his well-meaning father had blundered into. This Swedish girl was more understanding, less aggressive. He felt not the slightest touch of guilt over his encounter with her since, he explained to himself, he needed to cultivate her in case she could smooth the way for him with her brother – when he finally made contact with him. He watched her as she took a ladylike mouthful of lager and then deftly attacked the assortment of smoked fish and potato salad in front of her. She would make a useful ally.

Although they had come to the end of the meal and the bill was paid they still sat in a state of indecision beside the wide window which gave them a view of the square. The waitress cleared their table unhurriedly because it was getting late for lunch now and the pressure on places was easing. There was space to relax, and time.

He would telephone the next day he said to find out if she had news of her brother. Was that in order?

'But of course.'

Small, straight-backed, in command of herself, she smiled at him conscious that they had reached a natural break in their short acquaintance but that she could take it further if she chose. It was up to her.

'What are you going to do now?' she asked. 'Return to your hotel?'

'I suppose so.'

The way he spoke the words made them an invitation of a sort, not much of one but she snatched at it.

'What a dull end of the day for you,' she commiserated, making a face, 'when there is so much to see in Stockholm – Skansen, the *Vasa* Museum.' He shrugged. Such 'musts' for the tourist weren't really on the agenda at the moment. Was he going to be boring after all? She decided to try again.

'Then if you want to do something more profitable with your time why don't you make a tour of the antique shops? This area is full of them. Come on, I know everybody. I'll show you round.'

Of course there wasn't much chance of finding anything, but he had nothing else to do.

By now the storm had passed over and it was summer again. With one firm hand on his arm she guided him into the narrow rain-freshened streets behind the square where they visited low-ceilinged shops, peering at expensive antique folk art – a brass candleholder with a simple reflector to be hung on a wall, a naïve pine cupboard painted with scarlet hearts and the date 1835, peasant textiles. It meant nothing to him. This was a way to pass the time, that was all. There were plenty of tourists milling around but not much business being done as far as he could see.

What about this window? A display of Chinese porcelain – a big *famille rose* punchbowl, a pair of brightly enamelled figures of parrots, two or three Qianlong plates. Converting the prices roughly into sterling, he discovered that they didn't constitute robbery – in fact they were almost enticing. Standing in his doorway with his hands behind his back the owner of the shop pretended at first not to register his interest; then just as he was about to speak, Ramsay turned away with a sense of dissatisfaction because, realistically, there was nothing there to warrant the trouble of shipping it back to London. Now the owner was looking nonchalantly down the street, his moment missed, feeling just as much frustration perhaps.

'Anders may have something to tempt you,' Jenny Winblad announced. 'We shall go and see him.'

It was because he was a serious dealer who wasn't targeting the tourist trade that business for Anders was less than brisk. It had been slack for months. In the centre of his otherwise deserted shop he and a couple of comrades in the trade were seated drinking coffee and gossiping, recounting past exploits to each other, trying to keep their spirits up until the tide turned in their favour or the bank pulled the rug from beneath them. They feigned indifference as Ramsay made his survey. On the floor in front of him stood a small urn, about a foot in height, made of polished dark red stone flecked with white.

'Lift it,' she whispered. He could scarcely move it an inch from the ground; it must have been denser than granite.

'Porfyr,' she said. Porphyry – it was new to him. Anders made some remark in Swedish which provoked a chuckle from one of the others. A joke?

'He says it is devilish heavy,' she translated literally. No, not a joke. Given the state of trade the dealer found it difficult to be comical.

On the wall above the urn was a collection of Russian icons, most of them smoke-stained, none of them obviously restored. As Ramsay examined each of them in turn Anders named their subjects as though reading from a script – St George and the Dragon, the Mother of God of Kazan, an icon of Christ Pantocrator with a silver-gilt *oklad* protecting all but the face. Those icons had been there for a long, long time. He had them off by heart. 'St Dmitri slaying the Anti-Christ.' He was asking six thousand crowns he said, as though inviting a counter offer – and one didn't need a geiger counter, he added. His two cronies exchanged a grin.

'A geiger counter?'

'After the Chernobyl disaster many of the churches in the area were ransacked for valuables – crucifixes, icons, robes,' she explained, 'but this one is clean.'

As though signalling that the coffee break was over and there was business to be done, Anders stood up smartly – a middle-aged man but still spare, and energetic. Did he dye his hair? It seemed darker than one might have expected from the age and condition of his skin. A wig perhaps? After his friends had taken the hint, given various foreign excuses and left, Jenny made the introductions. Anders and Ramsay smiled their goodwill at each other, rendered dumb by their lack of a common language.

She said, 'I told him that you had bought some good pieces of furniture from me. Was that all right?'

He replied that of course it was. It seemed to have convinced the Swedish dealer that he was a serious prospect. There was more Swedish talk.

She looked up at Ramsay. 'Do you buy pictures? Because he thinks he has one that might appeal to you. Topographical. I think that is the word.'

Pictures weren't his thing really but he had time on his hands and nothing to lose.

Anders led them down a passage to a small room which looked older than the rest of the building – it must have been there since the Middle Ages – a dim room with a single small window set deep into its roughly plastered wall. Only when the lights went on did Ramsay see the pictures properly, hung in two rows on white screens set against the walls. Eighteenth and early nineteenth century most of them

123

and good decorative subjects – the kind of thing that went well with the grand furniture which was going to be their speciality, his and Julia's. He glanced here and there trying to identify the artists and found himself out of his depth again – a still life, a couple of seascapes which were Dutch certainly, but that was as far as he could go. Where was this topographical picture?

Anders shook his head to indicate that these were not what he had brought him there to see; he conducted Ramsay to a single canvas at the end of the room and gestured proudly in its direction. It was a large painting – a view of the broad avenues of a city with figures dressed fashionably, in the costume of the eighteenth century. The buildings though were the real subject: Classical, lovingly painted; Ramsay tried to place the town but couldn't. It certainly wasn't London nor Paris as depicted in any of the popular views of the period. There were no open stretches of water or the islands which were the hallmark of Stockholm. It looked more like a landlocked city, somewhere in Central Europe perhaps.

No, Anders had no idea where it was. Nor did he know who the artist was. He had been asked to sell it for a client on commission, that was all he was giving away. No provenance.

'May we have it off the wall?'

Ramsay gave the back of the canvas a careful examination. There was nothing there to suggest that the painting was wrong. Nor right either. No signature, but a spidery note in one corner, in black ink: *Pirna – vue prise de la rive gauche de l'Elbe*. So it was Central Europe – somewhere in Germany by the look of it. No point in speculating, it wasn't his field. Best to find an expert and leave it to him.

'The price?' he asked as he helped the dealer to put the picture back where it belonged. Promptly Anders gave the figure in Swedish and the girl translated.

'Two hundred and fifty thousand crowns.'

Her voice was prudent and neutral. She was offering no opinion, no hostages – neither enthusiasm nor discouragement – not that either would have carried any weight with him since it was no more her field than it was his. It was a serious picture and the rate for the Swedish crown was lower than it had been for years.

'Tell him,' he said, 'that I shall want some photographs. Good clear photographs. Besides an overall view I shall need close-ups of this area, this and this. Would you ask him to send them to this person at this address as soon as he can?' He took out one of his trade cards and substituted Julia's name for his own. The prints would serve as part of the reparation that was due to her. There was plenty of time to fax her to tell her what to do when she received them.

After leaving the shop they wandered down towards Skeppsbron, skirting the edge of the island on which the old town was built. Looking outwards across the water she pointed out the sights to him – Skeppsholm, Skansen, with the tall cranes painted drolly to resemble giraffes which belonged to the amusement park – while he looked for the words he needed to thank her for her company and bid her goodbye.

Suddenly she called out, laying a hand on his arm, 'Look. Look there.'

High up, far beyond those tall cranes, sailed a tiny blue shape in the sky.

'A balloon,' she called out with delight, 'a huge hot-air balloon . . . like a blue pear drifting across the sky, isn't it?'

Yes, he thought tolerantly, it did look rather like that, and went on to wonder what that picture was really worth.

Hand on the rigging, Erik was explaining to the American

125

woman beside him, 'Down there you can see the Royal Palace and the spire of Storkyrkan. You see?'

'Isn't that really something,' she agreed absently – because she wasn't looking where he was pointing at all but was referring instead to a slip of paper which she held tightly in her hand against the breeze which flicked at its corners. He could see that paper was precious to her – she had brought it a long way. She was not a young woman and he hoped that she wasn't going to find this aerial journey too much for her.

'And where,' she enquired, 'is Fleminggatan? My grandparents lived there you know. At number 244.'

Erik surveyed the crowded panorama to the west with overused eyes and began, 'Do you see the tower of the City Hall . . .'

This was going to take some time. Was his other passenger going to feel neglected? Glancing sideways at him he saw that there was no risk of that. The same folded chart in his hand, wearing the same red sweater in grubby synthetic fibre, Vallin, the shabby man, was absorbed totally in what he was doing. Ignoring his fellow passengers, he raised his head and looked eastwards to the horizon. Again Erik wondered what could possibly be important enough to him to justify his spending another hard-earned wad of dollars on this second trip. But it was none of his business he told himself, looking down at the game American lady.

'. . . if you take two fingersbreadths to the right of it like this, that's Fleminggatan, running away from you . . .'

Doubtfully she looked at the far off mass of buildings, trying hard to see what she had come all this way for, from Minnesota, while Erik considered again the Estonian or Latvian or whatever he was. Could he do that too? – find what he was searching for – Erik wondered as *Isolde* glided

like a dowager along her accustomed and invisible path
through the air.

James Smith had never been one to stint himself when times
had been good and he was damned if he was going to alter his
ways now that the wind had changed. Had become more like a
gale, in fact, that had shifted halfway round the compass and
was roaring in his face now from the bloody Arctic – much
more like that. It hadn't happened all at once, but in stages. To
begin with it had seemed as though he might be able to turn
things round, find a way through his misfortunes – which was
how he thought of them – and emerge from the storm with a
little personal credit left to wrap around himself, enough to
enable him to continue with the life he knew . . . after making
amends for a sufficient period.

As one hammer blow had followed another it had soon
become obvious that there was no chance of that. Disasters
had happened which he could never reverse. The world he
had known was gone, irretrievably, and he had to turn his
face away from it and learn to survive in this colder, harder
reality he had been thrown into . . . by events, he asserted.
Although he could come to terms with the fact as it was, he
still had difficulty in seeing himself as its cause. That was yet
to come perhaps. Meanwhile he allowed himself to be as
much a victim of an Act of God as any unlucky client he had
insured against such an eventuality when he had been an
underwriter.

It was his father who had found the niche for him and
pushed him into it – he had known better than to argue with
the manic old man. A stranger whom he had addressed as
'Sir' until the day he died – a red-letter day for James Smith.
He had always watched out circumspectly before speaking
to the old bully, in case he had something he wanted to say
first. It was the discretion which the son owed to a father

who took pleasure in reviewing the provisions of his will from time to time.

James Smith had never married, though there had been a girl at one time. He had felt too much of a hostage himself to invite her to share his insecurity and he had been proved right by the disaster which had hit SJ Underwriting. Imagine being married with a family in his present predicament? The thought made him shudder. It was bad enough as it was – desperate. At least he was unencumbered, responsible only for himself. One way or another he would survive. He had told himself that a hundred times since he had left the Isle of Wight and then London, Heathrow.

Don't lower your standards, that was the first rule – which was why he had taken a room at the front of the hotel where they were more expensive. For him it had been a necessary extravagance and this year, even with the tourist season at its height, there were plenty to choose from.

He strolled to the window to enjoy the view he had paid for and it was at that moment that he caught sight of the balloon moving across the afternoon sky. He stood and watched it until the small frivolous shape had shrunk to a speck the size of nothing.

Then he turned away and began to unpack his luggage and hang up his clothes. Next he extracted the files at the bottom of the bulkiest of his bags and counted them. It had cost a fortune in excess baggage charges but that had been money well spent as well.

Spreading out the contents of one of the files on the bed, he began to go through it, checking off the papers on a list stapled to the front. Finding it difficult to relax and deal with the ordinary little task calmly. Outwardly, he might have been any one of thousands of businessmen in Europe that night making doubly sure of his facts, planning his strategy, preparing for a crucial meeting.

Chapter Nine

The Villa Johansson lay behind high walls in a secluded, exclusive neighbourhood. Like all the other houses nearby its privacy was shielded by a thicket of electronic beams, anti-bugging devices, the latest in automatic surveillance equipment. Johansson himself liked to think, although there was no way that he could prove it, that his mansion was as well protected from prying eyes and ears as the embassy which was its nearest neighbour.

There wasn't a security guard in sight not because he was a careless man but because he was a realist who didn't allow his arithmetic to be distorted by his feelings for the objects which he owned. However you felt about it, a thousand was a thousand, a million was a million – and while the Villa was a treasure house, the pictures, the furnishings and the rarities which it contained had a finite value which was properly insured and was a fraction of a fraction of the fortune which he might lose through the interception of a particular fax or telephone call. That was the risk which he had to minimise and the simple question was – what price did one put on the honesty of a security guard? Even in a country where standards of behaviour were as high as they were in Sweden the figure was small change to the corporations which his enterprises had to live alongside in the big jungle; organisations whose business practices were not on

129

the same elevated plane as his own.

Hence at the Villa there were no guards open to temptation, who could be suborned. People like that had their uses, and indeed he did make use of them from time to time, but he kept them on the periphery, the outermost circle of his affairs, right away from the sensitive heart. Secrecy was his surest ally.

The one confidant whom he permitted to come closest to the centre was Axel and he was late. Or was he? On top of the superbly fashioned commode by Molitor which had once belonged to Bonaparte stood a clock in bronze and marble; above its cylindrical body a golden *Directoire* goddess reposed calmly with a fragment of drapery fluttering out from around her shoulders, frozen in a wind which had never existed. That sight had often brought him ease at times of tension. He glanced at the dial beneath her for a second time and then at the watch on his wrist which was accurate to a second. The clock was fast by a minute and a half.

Such error was not 'the Johansson way'. Accuracy, absolute veracity were what he demanded from everything that he controlled – from his clocks, his staff, from the Johansson Bank, the holding company, the manufacturing interests all over northern Europe; their balance sheets had to conform to the strictest standards and be able to withstand the most searching tests his auditors could devise.

It was a tradition that went back to their founder, a 'wood baron' who had opened up the forests in the west of the country more than a century earlier. He had been a man of fierce and uncompromising honesty and had made sure that those who were to take his place followed his example. Soon although his surname was one of the commonest in Sweden everyone knew whom you meant when you spoke of the Johanssons in a particular tone of voice. It was why the family had never taken a more glamorous sounding name when that became the fashion later on. They hadn't needed to. A more important reason was that the 'Johansson way' had become a byword in the commercial life of the country much in the same way as the name Rolls-Royce had passed into the English language as a synonym for excellence in anything mechanical. The phrase had been a huge invisible asset to the business in many ways as its size and power had grown – not least, during what Johansson thought of as 'the long socialist years', in allaying any public concern about the concentration of so much influence in one pair of hands.

Nobody was more conscious of that than he was and nobody regretted more than he did the way his son Carl had demolished that asset which it had taken so long to build up – a huge and fragile thing like a house of cards and just as quickly flattened. His ill-timed venture into the Lloyd's insurance market in which he had involved so many of his peers, young men of his own age – greedy and inexperienced but convinced that they could make money five times as fast as their elders – had destroyed the fine image of the concern in the public mind in less than a week when the story had broken. By the time the press had finished gloating in moralistic fervour over their misfortunes at Lloyd's, those words had been turned into a sickly little joke – 'Make insurance pay, the Johansson way,' they sneered.

He flicked the side of his head with his hand as though trying to brush away the irritating memory. Sweden wasn't what it had been. The newspapers were no longer respectable – there were foreigners in the streets, strangers who spoke the language with an unexpected intonation and worshipped other gods, who drained the budget and mounted demonstrations about grievances which were beyond his comprehension.

Without his being aware of it, few of those ideas of his

were better than second hand. For he rarely saw such people, being insulated from them by the style of life which his wealth, his background and the past imposed on him. Occasionally he glimpsed a dark face in the polished granite entrance hall of the Johansson headquarters. Sometimes glancing out of the smoky glass window of his limousine he caught sight of a scribble of graffiti at the foot of a building which he remembered clean in its youth . . .

Axel walked into the room precisely on the hour. Knowing that there was no need to announce himself because J would be ready to receive him.

They seated themselves and got down to business with not a word wasted – so well attuned that much of the communication between them seemed to take place in the silences between the brief questions and equally brief replies.

As his *protégé* worked through the agenda on his knee Johansson observed him – in his forties, a spare casually dressed figure who had an aura of well-being about him. No doubt he would be spending part of his weekend pottering among the outer islands with his family in their big but less than ostentatious sailboat, making the most of the summer as a healthy man should. The product of the foremost business school in Europe, fluent in two languages besides his own, he could nevertheless relate to people at every level. Straight as one of the founder's fir trees, he had suffered from no traumas in his childhood and had no hang-ups. In short he was not damaged goods. Axel was the sort of man who made things easy – the sort of man he should have had as a son rather than as a second cousin.

It took them no more than an hour to clear the decisions for the week and when they had finished Johansson rose from his seat and strolled across the long Malayer carpet – one of his great-grandmother's wedding presents – which covered the oak parquet; as he did so he caught the corner with his foot and turned it over; unhurriedly he toed it back into place before continuing to one of the big plate-glass windows which her husband had installed because he believed in plenty of light. He looked down between the trees over to the place where his yacht was berthed. He had a question to ask, a question which even though it was at the top of his mind he had left deliberately until last because it was a discipline and in any case business had to be done in the proper order. He took care to ensure that his tone was casual.

'Have you found him yet?'

'No. We will.'

The younger man offered nothing in extenuation, made no apology. The question was of the same importance to both of them; he would have done everything that could be done and there was no point pursuing the issue with instructions or unsolicited advice, Johansson felt. Sooner or later his son would have to break cover, would be noticed in a shop somewhere, recognised by a filling-station attendant, and the story would explode in the media. For it had all the exciting smells the doglike public enjoyed – the aroma of money, the scent of scandal, a whiff of pathos. The young man was much too well-known a figure to be able to keep himself anonymous for ever. Unfortunately they didn't have as long as that to find him – to be precise they had until his birthday, which was only three weeks away.

He continued to look out of the window without giving any overt sign that he wanted to hear more.

Nevertheless as a makeweight to keep the tyrant happy Axel added, 'We are nearly there.'

It was almost five o'clock. As Axel took his leave and quit the room the *Directoire* clock interjected with its silver chime – a minute and a half too early.

Chapter Ten

'The photographs came this morning. I'll contact the man you said.'

Julia's voice was sharp in Ramsay's ear although it was at the other end of the line, probably a thousand miles away – a distance of that order.

'When?'

'Tomorrow. When I can get a moment.' Don't push me around, her tone said, I'm the one who's virtuously remaining on the bridge whence others have fled – fled being the key word, the one she would have mentally underlined in red ink.

'Anything else?'

'I managed to off-load the mirror.'

What did she mean by 'off-load?' The mirror had been a find, early Georgian, unrestored, something to be resold reluctantly to a well-established client, as a special sign of favour.

'Who to?'

'Ethelred.' She spoke the name airily, trailing it in front of him, baiting him lightly with it, knowing just how much he thought of Lewis and how little. He was no special client. Ramsay replied with as much indifference as he could scrape together.

'Really? How much?'

'Three and a half.'

Hell's teeth. They had agreed that four thousand was the absolute floor for that mirror; in order to spite him she had done her former boss a favour. Why? What was going on? He could imagine the scene. Lewis listening to her troubles, judiciously sipping Lapsang Souchong like some Chinese imperial eunuch, playing the wise adviser while she grew more and more indiscreet about the partnership, their disagreements; she, in exchange for his concern, selling him that splendid item cheaper than she should; a perky Lewis quitting the showroom with not only the mirror but a fat gobbet of gossip besides – to tell to his friends, such as he had.

Ramsay opened his mouth to argue and checked himself. He wasn't going to descend into a wrangle over that and risk the fragile truce he had achieved with her; getting an opinion on that picture quickly was far too urgent.

Going off at a tangent he remarked, 'It could be important.'

'What could?'

'The picture.'

'Yes, I did know that,' she said shortly.

There was a pause while each of them looked for something else to say and then he decided to opt out of the competition. She hadn't asked whether he had made contact with Winblad yet and if she wasn't interested there was no point in opening up the topic now.

In fact he was due to meet him in half an hour. What was the time? Still holding the phone to his ear Ramsay bent down to consult the radio clock beside the hotel bed. He'd already got some feel for the layout of the city. *If he left straightaway there was time for him to go on foot over the bridges to Gamla Stan and the house in Biskopstorget. The fresh air off the water would clear his head, make it easier to*

136

think out his approach to the man . . .

'Well,' Julia asked, 'Is that all?'

. . . There was the furniture to deal with too. Now that he'd found a firm to ship it to London for him all that was necessary was to fix up with Jenny Winblad a convenient time for them to collect it from her house.

'Think so,' he replied, 'take care.'

. . . He had to make arrangements too to get the balance of the purchase money transmitted from his London bank. That could be organised in the afternoon.

'You too . . . If you can't be good be careful.' The cliché was stuck on the end unthinkingly and frankly there didn't seem to be much point in it.

'Bye,' he said and put down the phone.

'Welcome, fellow Lloyd's victim from London,' intoned Bengt Winblad raising his glass of chilled orange juice in a courteous salute to his guest. He had an aversion to coffee of any kind and it was much too early in the day for alcohol, wasn't it?

He looked a lot older than his sister but that wasn't difficult – much taller, with fair hair pressed close to his scalp and pale blue eyes which seemed to have no reservations in them about the tale which he had just heard from his visitor. His English was more accented than hers but just as efficient.

He put his glass down, not on the mellow surface of the side table but carefully on the tray which he had just brought from the kitchen, beside the tall jug of juice, its glass sides beaded with condensation. Since that desirable table was shortly to become his property Ramsay found some satisfaction in the small action. It said that Winblad was a responsible type – candid too. In that he did resemble Jenny.

Where was she? Winblad looked as though the question was something he hadn't expected. Somewhere in town he thought, shopping perhaps – whatever it was, it wasn't important, his manner indicated as he waited for more to be said, something to the point.

'I was told that the head of SJ Underwriting was on his way here. To Sweden.'

'Yes.'

Winblad's voice was neutral – he was ready to hear more, that was as far as it went.

'I have to find him; it's why I am here. I was told that you would know where he was if anybody did. It is imperative . . .'

'Told? By who please?'

'Clarke.'

Winblad poured himself another glass of juice. Would his guest like one too? No, thank you.

'There are many people who would like to find him,' he said solemnly. Ramsay was about to come back on this glimpse of the obvious when the doorbell rang. Striding easily towards the window which gave on the square Winblad craned his head round sideways to see who was outside. With a muttered, 'Excuse me if you please,' he went to deal with the interruption leaving the door ajar. There was a rattle of Swedish in the passage, a pause for a few seconds, then a few sentences more. A head went past the window – it was Anders from the shop, the one with the interesting painting.

Although the incident was nothing it gave Ramsay a feeling all of a sudden that this, the most ancient part of the city, was a neighbourhood with a life of its own, rather like a village into which he had come as an interloper. They would all know each other – the dealers, the shopkeepers, the people who lived in the quiet tree-shaded square. They had common memories and interests, a common past. He was being fanciful because he didn't speak the language. Perhaps the dealer was Jenny's boyfriend and wanted to know where she was, or perhaps she had some deal going on with him. So what?

Winblad was back in the room; now he was even more intense.

'Before we discuss this matter any more I should warn you seriously about this James Smith. He is not trustworthy.'

'Why do you say that?' Ramsay objected.

'Look at this syndicate of his.'

'It may have been simply a question of poor judgement.'

'Do you think that even if you are . . .'

'I have no opinion yet,' Ramsay interrupted him. 'I have never met him. I shall make up my own mind when I do.'

'He has ruined us. Me and so many of my friends. We secured our guarantees on our property – land, houses, flats – at a time when the market was much higher than now. There has been a catastrophic fall in values. Much worse than in your country. They have halved . . .'

So when the guarantees were exhausted these Swedish members would be sold up – at the bottom of the market.

'. . . Do you know what one of those big insurance men is said to have called us?' Winblad demanded. His composure was beginning to go, shaking; it was going to crack. 'Sheep for the shearing. Sheep.' Against the low ceiling of the room his voice exploded with the enormity, the injustice, the impertinence of it.

'My father was one of the sheep. He was shorn too,' Ramsay reminded him, adding deliberately, 'Smith. Do you know where he is?'

Winblad didn't reply. Instead he picked up the tray to return it to the kitchen as if he was trying to find a way of closing the discussion.

'He is in Sweden, isn't he?' Ramsay hazarded urgently.

The other man hesitated, stopped still for a moment before he turned and put the tray back on the table. He sat down. 'Yes. But I don't know exactly where. I have a telephone number only. I am to meet him . . . to talk . . . There might be a way, I am not sure . . .'

'Meet him where?'

'Not here. Whatever you may think the man is . . . He must not see where I live. It would not be the right thing, not at all.'

'Where then?'

It was time for Winblad to make another decision and he plainly didn't like it much. 'He wouldn't tell me where he was staying so . . . we agreed . . .' At last he came out with it. 'The Crown. It is a small café not far from here, a rather ordinary place. Round the corner from Stortorget. I am to meet him there in seven days' time. Possibly with the other man, the Coathanger – Carl Johansson – but that is not yet certain.'

Two of them, one of Winblad.

'Let me come with you. I could back you up.'

That idea didn't seem to ring the bell. Ramsay pressed on. 'Your command of English is excellent but the Lloyd's insurance market has a complex language of its own. Explanations may be needed.'

'Johansson will be there. He will be able to . . .'

'Whose side is he on? Besides, you don't know for certain that he will be there.'

It took another five minutes of argument to persuade him. Yes, it would be useful to have an ally at the meeting he conceded in the end, but the meeting itself was crucial and might be his only opportunity to negotiate with them. He didn't want to see it taken over by somebody else's problem; in any discussion the interests of his members must come first and he must control the agenda. Yes, Mr Ramsay?

Very well, since those were the only terms going.

'Three o'clock at the Crown then, a week today,' Winblad said and got up to take him to the door.

'One other thing. Could you give your sister a message from me? It is about the furniture.'

The tall Swede looked mystified.

'The furniture I bought from her the other day. The table there, the long-case clock,' Ramsay pointed. 'I have arranged for the packers to come here to crate it – she suggested that – and we need to fix a convenient time for both of us.'

It took Winblad a moment or two to digest this. Then he spoke.

'I don't understand at all what you are saying. All this furniture belongs to me and the house too. Everything here is mine.'

It was a flat statement, allowing no contradiction.

'But she lives here?'

'Not any longer. I allowed her to stay here last winter after she lost her job – it would have been much too difficult for her out on the island. But now she lives out there with that colony of people she looks after.'

'Not here?'

'No, certainly not. That is the fact,' Winblad replied. The only thing that was certain was that one of them was lying and since the brother was his only means of getting to Smith he couldn't allow it to be him, not yet. Ramsay told him what had happened.

'A misunderstanding – a disappointment for you, Mr Ramsay, but I think that is all, isn't it? Jenny had no right to play such a joke on you.' Winblad was very much the censorious head of the family – the part suited him.

Perhaps one of them wasn't lying – perhaps they both

were. Ramsay considered the possibilities. He didn't know how bank guarantees operated in Sweden but banks every-where had one characteristic in common – they did like to have their money back. One thing he did know was that Winblad faced a devastating call from Lloyd's and if every-thing was in his name as he alleged, how much time had he left to enjoy it? – this elegant house, the splendid furniture? He was a tenant on a very short lease – in fact, legally speaking they might already be somebody else's property altogether – might no longer belong to either him or his sister. If so it would be an obvious temptation for them to extract whatever cash they could from the situation while they had the chance, then lay down a smoke screen of accusation and counter-accusation. What chance would their victim have of recovering his money? Charles didn't feel like tackling that question. Play it straight, that was the only way.

He said firmly, 'It was scarcely a joke. I paid her a deposit.'

'You did? How much?'

'About three hundred thousand kronor,' Ramsay admit-ted.

The other man's features relaxed. 'You will have paid by cheque of course.'

'No. Cash.'

Winblad was incredulous.

'So much money? In cash?' The hint of criticism in his voice was irritating but at the same time reassuring.

'It was the most convenient thing to do. I have no bank account here.'

No need to explain that he had completely trusted the girl and had been completely taken in.

Winblad went into action. She had to be found immedi-ately. He phoned round her friends updating Charles on his progress after each call. This one hadn't seen her lately – that one thought she was out on the island. As he exhausted the possibilities he seemed genuinely bent on getting his sister out of trouble, to clear the matter up before this visitor added to his burdens by calling in the police.

His obvious anxiety was reassuring too and it fitted Ramsay's preconception about Sweden. A country where financial probity was the norm – where people meant what they said and said what they meant. Except Jenny.

Now her brother seemed to be getting somewhere. He looked across and reported, 'A girl friend of hers says that she was staying the night over in Sodermalm. Jenny told her that she would return to the island on the boat this afternoon.'

Ever helpful, he hurried off to look for the ferry timetable.

Chapter Eleven

The boat was not one of the low-slung floating greenhouses, lovingly preserved, the antique ones with tall black smoke-stacks banded with yellow which he had seen sedately ploughing across the open water from the Deer Garden. Not at all. It was sharply modern and dazzling white, its low wheelhouse embellished with an array of aerials. Ramsay looked for her in the small crowd of travellers waiting to be allowed to board – elderly people in the pastel clothes beloved of Scandinavians in summer, children looking forward to the trip, mildly impatient but well behaved, their parents – everybody tanned, healthy, well dressed.

She wasn't there. A young man came forward and beckoned the queue to come on board. It began to move in its orderly way under the pale lifted elbow of the bow section – raised above like the bleached jawbone of a shark.

If he stayed behind on the wide cobbled quayside she would see him as soon as she arrived. Then she might simply make off into the town and he would have lost her. Board the boat, that was the answer and keep a lookout for her from inside the saloon on the lower deck.

He paid his fare to the young man, to Alvarö. That was where she was going Winblad had said – the name of the landing. He took the casually proffered slip of paper and seated himself beside one of the large square windows. The big diesels pulsed quietly. A small boy in the seat in front of him pushed towards the window, half-obscuring his view, calling out incomprehensibly to a young friend behind him. On the quayside one or two people were waiting to wave a farewell to family or friends on board; one of them called out a last question or reminder to someone on the upper deck and a woman took a sighting through the viewfinder of her camera, ready to take a picture of the boat's departure, to record the minor fact . . .

. . . and there was no sign at all of Jenny Winblad.

He glanced at his watch. The boat was due to leave in two minutes. What should he do if she didn't show? Go to this place Alvarö and meet her there when she arrived on a later ferry? How often did the ferries run? He went and inspected the blue and white timetable framed on the central bulkhead. One sailing a day and this was it. He had no idea what the islands were like but he doubted if . . .

He looked up and saw her. Walking along the quayside – a scarf round her hair, in dark blue leggings and a windcheater to match – purposefully, despite the rucksack on her back and the bulging carrier bags which she had in each hand. It looked as though she had been doing some considerable shopping. Hastily he climbed the stairs to the upper deck and went forrard to watch her from above making her way on board. Slightly stooped to counterbalance the weight of her backpack, she didn't look up towards him.

The bow section was lowered behind her making the boat into a neatly-closed trap, and the sound of the engines became more urgent as the vessel began to back away from the quayside. Give her time to unsling her rucksack and stow it away in the rack and to find a place for those heavy bags full of luxuries which his money had paid for. Let her settle down. Then go down and confront her.

As soon as she saw him she gave him a smile, a restrained

smile of recognition not a big hallo.

'Mr Ramsay. Good afternoon.' Neither pleased to see him nor annoyed. When he sat down beside her, she moved into the seat next to the window simply to give him a better view of the panorama of the city sliding now behind them across this open stretch of water which was called Saltsjön – that much he had discovered from the city plan in his pocket. Saltsjön – the salt sea.

'I have just come from the house.' *The* house. Not 'her' house or her brother's house; he wasn't committing himself on the question of whose property it was.

'House? Which house please?'

'Biskopstorget 42.'

She gave a little laugh. 'You don't say it like that. It's pronounced Biskops*toryyet*,' she said.

'Your brother was there.'

'Bengt. So you found him. Good.' She didn't look uncomfortable with the idea. 'Was he able to help you with your dealings about insurance and things?'

The travellers sat in peace on their new well-upholstered seats, each with its armrests and a small pristine head cushion inscribed 'Welcome on board', relaxing as though on a country bus. One woman nearby was reading a magazine, her eyes following the print, oblivious of the scenery unscrolling past the window. In front where there was more space an elderly man with cropped white hair sat with an accordion on his knee, fingering the keys, practising in silence to avoid disturbing the other passengers. Civilised people minding their own business.

Moving his face a little closer to hers, trying to create some privacy for both of them in that public place, Ramsay spoke unemphatically. 'He claimed that all the furniture in the house, including the pieces which I bought from you, belonged to him. That's what he said.'

147

Her adolescent face, mildly tanned by the northern sun, turned slowly towards him, frowning slightly in puzzlement, her eyes seeking more information. There was nothing overstated about her reaction – no open mouth, no exclamation, no vehemence.

'He told me that the house belonged to him as well, as a matter of fact.'

'No, fiction. A matter of fiction,' she said firmly. 'Just like him,' and she gave a half laugh – small and decorous though.

Ramsay produced the list detailing the pieces which she had sold him with their prices – the big total, the big balance still to pay, the big amount he had paid her in advance. He returned the receipt she had signed to his pocket – she wasn't going to get her little hands on that. His twenty-seven thousand pounds.

'Look, here is the list of the items we agreed.'

She glanced down at it. 'That's right,' she said, then took a moment to scrutinise it with more care. 'It is correct. That's fine.' Dismissively.

'So you don't deny that I bought them from you?'

'But of course not,' she answered, the slightest sing-song accent colouring the words. It was an attractive sound and that irritated him.

He kept his voice low. 'I bought them in good faith.'

She looked blank – it wasn't one of the idioms she had learnt at school. 'Good faith?' she asked. 'What does that mean?'

She might well ask.

'I bought them from you on the understanding that they belonged to you.'

'They do,' she said, 'they all do. Everything.'

'Your brother says that they don't.'

'And the house,' she added with finality, 'that's mine too. Everything,' she repeated with satisfaction.

'I'm not concerned about the house.'

She looked wide-eyed at him, indignant at this heresy. 'You aren't?' she exclaimed. 'I am.'

The woman reading the magazine looked up from it discontentedly.

'It's not what I meant. The furniture . . .'

'It's mine. I have told you that.'

'That's not the thing. How am I supposed to collect it?' he cried out in exasperation. Several heads turned. The man with the accordion looked back at them across the top of the seats, an uneasy look in his eyes. He preferred it to be quiet when he was practising.

'Easy. You wait until he has left the house – he is away most of the time – and then you go in and take it away. I'll lend you the key.'

The engines suddenly powered up into full throttle, as though going into overdrive. He had to speak more loudly to get above them, 'Look. I think it would be much better all round if you returned the money to me and I held it until this has been sorted out.'

Without a word she rose from her seat, glaring at him to let her pass; automatically he stood up to do so. Pushing past him she crossed the aisle to the door marked TOALETT. She had found sanctuary.

A boy, a child, kneeling on one of the seats ahead was watching him.

Another passenger came to the door and tried the handle. Waited.

Before long it opened and she emerged and, without looking at Ramsay, made for the stairs. He followed her to the upper deck.

The engines idled, then went into reverse because the boat was approaching a landing. There was a group of houses there, painted the restrained red colour which you

149

saw everywhere, and a shop, and in front of them a midsummer maypole crowned with swags and wreaths, dressed in foliage now brown and dead. As the boat reached the quay and the bow section was raised, the knot of people waiting there divided to let the passengers get off. Then they boarded themselves, the bow was lowered again, and the boat reversed out into the channel and was on its way – all within a minute or two. A bus exchanging passengers at a bus stop; as quick and casual as that.

She was sitting on a white bench seat facing aft, among the passengers who were out there to enjoy the peace, the sunshine, the fresh breeze from the open water as the boat accelerated. On either side was the shoreline, forested in dark green. To the right stood a house built on a granite bluff with a flagpole carrying the blue and yellow Swedish flag, a summer retreat. Down by the water a couple and a child wearing a life jacket were climbing into the family motor cruiser. It started up with blue smoke and a roar.

Braced against the guard rail he stood in front of her and demanded his money.

'Go away,' she burst out, 'leave me alone.'

Two girls seated on the other side of the deck looked at him in alarm as the quarrel between them built up steadily layer by layer.

She had been devious, he told her.

She had not, the furniture was hers – her brother never told the truth. Never had. She could tell him things about Bengt . . .

He wanted his money back.

Why should she return it? They had a contract, didn't they? That advance was part of it.

He wanted his money back.

He could collect the furniture as soon as her brother

quitted the house. He would only have two days to wait. No more.

No deal. She had to return his money.

She burst into tears. Out of the corner of his eye he saw one of the girls standing up, hesitating, wanting to speak but unsure of herself. Before she plucked up the courage, Jenny rose, turned and fled downstairs. There the argument burst out again. Louder and louder – they were both losing control – the altercation resounded in the confines of the saloon deck.

The other passengers were growing more and more uncomfortable. Such noise! Such emotion! The white-haired man laid aside his accordion, the magazine-reading woman put down her magazine. Ramsay could see her thinking, Who does this foreigner imagine he is? Harassing one of our own. A pleasant-looking young girl, scarcely more than a child. What does he want from her? The impressively built young man who dispensed the tickets and was the only crew member down there emerged from his small office. Then standing by, only partly understanding what was going on – not sure whether he would be justified in intervening – he waited for Ramsay to make some conclusive move.

The engine note dropped. They were coming to another landing. Hastily the young man went back into his cubby hole to be ready to operate the mechanism which raised and lowered the bow section.

Jenny Winblad demanded, 'Why won't you listen? Why are you so . . .'

Shaking her head in frustration because she couldn't think of the English word she needed, she stopped in mid-sentence. She looked back hurriedly towards the overhead shelf where she had stowed her rucksack and went to collect it. Putting her arms through the straps and heaving it on to her back, all at once she looked fragile bowed under its

151

weight. She found her bags – the big awkward carrier bags.

Instinctively Ramsay came forward. 'Here, let me . . .' he took them from her.

The vessel had come to a stop; somewhere a winch whirred as the bow section was raised. Three or four passengers were waiting beside them, ready to get off. As they did so she went with them, Ramsay bringing up the rear with the bags.

Turning she stretched out her hands for them. 'Thank you.'

Now the entrance of the bow of the boat was clear for the travellers who had been holding back on the quay.

Gallantly he demurred – he would carry the bags for her.

'Give them to me please.' Her voice was firm, her hands decisively outstretched. Unplacated, she gazed at him. She gestured with one impatient hand, 'Come. Please.'

Defeated, he handed them over. In a flash she pushed past him, hurried back on to the boat under the bow section as it came down and closed behind her. Two thin legs clad in blue was the last he saw of her. Then the white bow of the vessel was backing away from him.

He turned to one of the others who had just left it with him, the old man with the accordion. The instrument was slung over his shoulder, heavy in its case. 'Can you tell me please? Is this Alvarö?'

Gazing at him with pale blue eyes the man shook his head with a smile. What did that mean? – that he didn't speak English or that it wasn't? Why was he grinning?

Ramsay tried again, 'Alvarö?'

'Nay,' the man said – a negative word. Offhandedly he added something else in Swedish, pointing at the white streamlined form of the receding boat. He looked at

Ramsay again and gave a dismissive nod before trudging off up the path with his squeezebox banging against his backside. Obviously he wasn't minded to be helpful after what had happened on board.

Ramsay followed him, keeping his distance.

Out in the middle of the sound the engine of the little boat died. The man sitting in the stern spoke the incomprehensible words curtly, saying something Scandinavian and holding up his hands to display seven extended fingers. He proffered a palm as a convenient place for Ramsay to count out the notes. Folding them he leant forward, hand on the gunwale to steady himself, and thrust the thin sheaf of money into his back pocket. Restarting the outboard with a jerk of the cord he steered the boat, spray flying as it hit the current, onwards to the jetty.

'Alvarö,' he announced.

Ramsay stood up in the boat, balanced himself and scrambled ashore, thankfully.

'Hey,' the boatman said, waved a hand, and went.

Ramsay looked round. There was the jetty with a rubber tyre nailed to its side and a large fibreglass dinghy riding in the water, bumping against it. A small boathouse with birch trees behind it and an area of rough grass. That was all. There was a path, however, so he followed it and came to a low building constructed of rough-hewn logs, painted red and roofed with tiles of a paler red. There were other buildings nearby, purpose unknown.

A couple, man and woman, were spreading out a long tunnel net on the grass, cleaning away the occasional twigs and scraps of water-weed that had been caught in it. Presumably two of the lame ducks that Bengt Winblad had mentioned.

Ramsay approached. The fair-haired woman, thirtyish, looked up.

Did she know where he could find a Miss Winblad? Beckoning to him with a smile she led him to the entrance of the house, leaned in and called, 'Jenny' in a voice which was scarcely reticent. Giving him a brisk nod she rejoined her man and continued with her task.

He entered. Jenny Winblad was at the sink, scraping potatoes for the evening meal. She dropped another into the bowl of water beside her and turned towards him with dripping forearms, a small knife in her hand.

'You found where we live,' she observed. Evidently. She didn't seem much surprised. After all, twenty-seven thousand pounds offered him plenty of incentive to find her.

He glanced round the tiny kitchen. A sink, a draining board and a wood-burning stove. An oil lamp. It was two centuries behind the sophistication of Stockholm, the steel and glass functionalism of the office blocks on the way out of town. This was the simple life.

Pretending to ignore him she turned back to her potatoes and began to scrape fiercely again.

'You escaped,' he observed.

'Yes. That I did do,' she replied plopping another potato into the bowl, putting a neat full stop on the thought.

He began, 'You realise that I was quite . . .'

'If you are going to start a big argument again,' she said, 'you won't eat. That I promise you.'

He was very hungry, he realised. The open air had given him an appetite. He wondered where the nearest restaurant might be. Twenty miles as the crow flew at a guess, and he wasn't a crow. How often did the ferry visit the island? Once a day.

'What's for dinner?' he asked.

★ ★ ★

When he had demonstrated his good faith and domestic
sense by helping to set up the trestle table on the patch of
grass outside the porch, had collected chairs from indoors
and laid the table, she thawed a little. The house was what
was called in Swedish a *parstuga* she explained – a 'double
cabin'; built on the bedrock, it consisted simply of the small
kitchen with a living room to one side of it and a bedroom to
the other – where the couple, Lars and Gunilla, slept. They
were not well off, she confided. Misfortune had followed
misfortune. Lars had lost his job as an architect not long
after buying a larger flat in town when the market had been
at its peak, just before the collapse. He couldn't claim social
security benefits unless he sold it. If he sold it he would lose
a great deal of money. They were waiting with fingers
crossed – or 'holding their thumbs', as she put it – until times
got better.

'Just like me,' she confided as she handed him the large
bowl of salad. About to take it to the table, he turned and
found himself face to face with an old man, a tall skinny old
man with a small child on either side of him. He introduced
himself punctiliously, heels together, in the old-fashioned
way, a nod of the head held just long enough to make it
count as a bow.

'Ericsson,' he said.

Uncle Henrik, she said, too busy laying out the steaks on
the plates to tell him whose uncle he was. The old gentleman
eyed the steaks with approval. Mr Ramsay was an antique
dealer who had bought some furniture from her, from
Biskopstorget, she explained.

'Jaha,' he replied succinctly, with a smile towards their
guest, much as Tiny Tim must have regarded the bountiful
Scrooge. A benefactor bringing sizzling steaks, two each for
everybody – round, perfectly formed, lying in a little pool of

melted butter – salad with mustard sauce, petit pois, French wine. Such a feast tonight.

They sat down at the table – Jenny Winblad, Ramsay, Gunilla, Lars, Uncle Henrik and the two children – and devoured it. When they were replete – had eaten the marzipan cakes which came next and drunk the coffee which followed it, with cognac for the men – Jenny handed out the presents. Frugal presents. Something for the children first, tobacco for Uncle Henrik to smoke in his big hooked pipe, some pairs of tights for Gunilla, chocolates . . . Christmas in midsummer . . . God bless us every one.

As the most senior member of the group, Uncle Henrik turned to their guest and courteously toasted him. Skål. Skål to Mr Ramsay, the founder of the feast. Thank you so very much.

The key rattled in the door of the chalet. She threw it open. 'You can sleep in here. I hope you will be comfortable.'

It was clean and basic, with a scent of freshly sawn timber about it – a bed, a chair and a table, that was all. She sat down on the bed, on the worn, well-washed bedcover, and felt the meagre mattress underneath her, a thin oblong which scarcely cushioned the hard planks supporting it. Not much of a bed at all – it was all that she could afford. Ramsay sat down beside her and that flustered her.

'This simply won't do,' he said.

She misunderstood him, patted the bed defensively. 'I know it's not as comfortable as it could . . .'

'Not the bed. You know very well. You have three hundred thousand Swedish crowns of mine,' he insisted, 'and I want them back.' At least she hadn't spent much of the money yet as far as he could see. Surely, there would be stringent laws against fraud in Sweden. Otherwise he could bring a civil suit, he supposed. How long would that take to come to trial? In England the delay would be two years at least. In Sweden? He had no idea. He would need a lawyer; there would have to be trips, consultations, affidavits. What would it all cost? There had to be another way.

'They are so happy, the others,' she answered, flashing him a cheerful smile. 'It makes me feel, you know . . . *warm* to be able to give them something – a nice meal. They can't just live on fish and potatoes all the time and it will be winter before we know it. It was a horrible shock for them all when Lars lost his job . . . and the children are so nice, don't you think? So well behaved. But thanks to you . . .'

'I want the money back. All of it.'

She stood up with dignity.

'We shall talk about it in the morning, that would be the best. Not now I'm afraid. So, good night. Sleep well.'

She was already stepping lightly away down the steep path, arms outstretched to help her keep her balance.

'I tell you. I'm not leaving . . .' he called after her.

'In the morning,' she flung back to him over her shoulder.

He looked at his watch – there was still enough daylight to tell the time. It *was* morning in fact. Past one o'clock. He looked skywards. Still enough daylight? If anything it was growing lighter.

He was disconcerted to find that the little community on Alvarö accepted him as one of their number without the least difficulty. The fact that he was an uninvited guest seemed to bother nobody. So he had chosen to stay with them? That was OK. They saw to his needs, found him the everyday things he had to have – a towel, soap, a razor, a clean shirt. It soon became clear though that in return he was expected, as a fit young man, to do his share of the work. To draw water, find wood for the stove, help with the fishing. Since it was free they ate a lot of fish, Jenny explained briskly – it wasn't possible to have a feast like last night every day. Oh no.

By the end of the first day he felt much as a piece of grit must feel after being absorbed into the soft moist flesh of an oyster – not merely rendered harmless by it but made agreeable against his will. He now had five days left before the critical meeting with Smith and from the relaxed way he was treated by all and sundry it was clear that they were quite willing to put up with him for much longer than that. They could outlast him without any difficulty. He wasn't being unpleasant enough – therein lay the problem.

Before dinner that night when they were all seated, just as Uncle Henrik, spoon poised, was about to attack his soup, he laid it on the line. They did not understand fully what had been happening, he said – what had been done to him. The ownership of the furniture was in doubt. He would never have dreamt of paying over such a sum of money if he had known that. Three hundred thousand crowns – he pronounced each syllable distinctly, driving the impressive number home like a big nail. He appealed to them as fair-minded lookers-on – shouldn't it be repaid until the question could be resolved?

Uncle Henrik laid down his spoon, one of the children sat mouth open in an O, entranced by the novel language spoken by this stranger. Ramsay glanced at the friendly smiling faces of Gunilla and Lars and the truth came to him. Not one of them apart from Jenny had a word of English. Without a sign of reproach she began to interpret his speech for him, approximately no doubt. Her brother's name was mentioned once or twice – he caught that. Afterwards there was silence. At last, picking up his spoon again since his soup was growing cold, Uncle Henrik made a brief observation in Swedish.

'He says that Bengt always was a tricky bastard,' she reported back to Charles. This seemed to dispose of the thing to the satisfaction of everyone else around the table.

Chapter Twelve

Carl Johansson lowered himself into the bitterly cold water and allowed it to hide him as he did every evening, although evening was scarcely the proper name for it – it could have been noon on an overcast day. He let go of the wooden ladder which he had constructed to make his daily ritual of purification easier and groped with white feet among the peaks and valleys of rock down there for a comfortable place to stand. That was better.

In the mass of reeds to his right a brown duck surrounded by her brood was searching for food, ignoring him because she had learnt over the weeks since he had come to live there that he was not the giving sort.

He stood up to his shoulders in the water. Of almost anybody else in the country he thought one could have used the phrase 'up to his neck', but for him that phrase was – he searched for the right word – inapplicable.

Up to his neck. A neck. It was an ordinary enough thing to have but not one which had been allotted to him, that was all. He didn't possess one. And it wasn't something that one could pretend one had, like a missing foot or an eye because there was no room for a prosthesis. The thought of an artificial neck in pale plastic struck him as almost comical.

Closing his eyes he tried to imagine, as he often did, what it would be like to be able to move one's head freely . . . to turn it on supple vertebrae slowly to look at someone . . . to look at a girl for example. At a girl. Slowly, like this. He knew exactly what was going to happen before he slewed his shoulders round to make the water swirl, sending the ripples racing across the surface of the lake. Riding them, up and down, the mother duck was keeping a weather eye open now, not alarmed but cautious – one small round eye watching him. He leaned back and imagined what she saw, a face floating on the water like a mask, a face which must have taken some getting used to. He made a second attempt because unlike that duck he was not willing to learn from experience. That bloody duck with its long neck, capable of moving its head into any attitude – as flexible and graceful as a snake. Again he failed and again the bird rose and fell, regarding him unwinkingly. All of a sudden he roared a curse at her, waved his arms, slapped the water – anything to break up her disdainful elegance – and was disappointed by the result. Her maternal instinct was too strong to allow her to take flight. Instead she half-scuttled a short way across the water and then led her young with dignity away from the commotion. Silence settled once again over the lake.

Emerging from the water he pulled himself up the ladder and then rubbed his cold and streaming body dry with the towel he had brought with him – his body, such as it was. The one he had been endowed with.

As he pulled on his shirt and trousers he found himself unable to stop his mind from going back to the beginning, as though the machine in his head had reached the end of the cassette and was now automatically rewinding, taking him back to his earliest memory.

He was lying face down with a pain which he carried like an unbearable burden on his back, a pain which gripped and kneaded it – his screams his only means of communicating with the face which hovered beside him and then disappeared. A white face which murmured comfort but brought him none. Was it his mother, or a nurse? He turned the memory over in his mind like a much-used coin, trying to decipher its message. It didn't really matter now whether it was or not since she had left his father's household not long after his eleventh birthday after giving him reasons which might have been enough for someone older but were not comprehensible to him.

When he was small she had been his confidante and protectress, feeding to him, fragment by fragment, the details of the battles which she had fought with his father over him, keeping him away from that disquieting figure as much as possible. There had been other signs of those conflicts. Once he had been required to undergo psychiatric examination, tests of mental competence which he had passed without difficulty. There had been other tests of a medical kind which at the time he thought were just one more episode in his parents' long-running struggle to improve him – or rather it, the object which he had become. When she hinted that they had another purpose, something to do with whether or not he was his father's son, he was disappointed to hear that they had proved conclusively that he was. He wasn't greatly concerned about his father's motives. In the battle to make him presentable he had so much to endure that the reasons for two particular skirmishes out of so many scarcely mattered to him. What did matter was that she had not seen fit to take him with her when she left.

Nowadays he understood her motives well enough. His face at the dining table would not have helped to foster her relationship with her lover – a well-known artist who had an eye for symmetry – and she was no longer young enough to take any chances. In her situation he would have done the same he thought, although he had no experience of such matters.

So he had been left behind as a farewell present for his father who had dealt with the responsibility as he always did – as a problem which was capable of a solution in a rational way, if enough trouble was taken and enough money spent. The money had been his father's but the trouble had been only his.

He had learnt to fear the times when his father became friendly and went out of his way to find diversions for him. Those were the dangerous times when some new treatment or procedure would be proposed. Away at school he had been safer; he had been educated at one of the country's few private boarding schools – a progressive establishment for the children of diplomats and overseas executives – where despite his tantrums and black moods, the inevitable misunderstandings with his fellow pupils, the malevolent practical jokes he had sometimes played on them, despite all that, he had been well treated.

A sly smile puckered one side of his face. That had not been altogether surprising since the Johanssons had founded the place and owned the land, the buildings, the sports hall, the science complex, everything. There must have been relief all round when he left.

Before he went to bed he made an extra reconnaissance, concentrating all his attention on it, sweeping every familiar metre of the shoreline with his binoculars, every tree. Despite the extra measure of security which the absence of light gave him he found it impossible to get to sleep for hours and when he was woken up at seven in the morning his hunger for sleep was still unsatisfied. From the sensation in his eyelids he could tell that if he decided to look at himself in a mirror his eyes would be bloodshot; the flesh around them felt dry and puckered.

For a long moment he lay there listening to the thread of sound outside. A high noise like the buzzing of a fly against a window-pane but not altogether like that because it was continuous, persistent. All at once the artificial darkness in the room was no longer a comfort to him, the rag mat which he had nailed over the window a source not of security but of danger. A trivial anxiety touched him. The first thing he had to do was to relieve himself while there was still time – otherwise he would be at a disadvantage when the invader arrived. He scrambled out of bed, pulled on his clothes, and went outside to the place where he had made his latrine. When he returned, the boat was still too far away for him to see who the occupant was. It was no more than a rowing boat with an outboard motor, its bows cocked out of the water.

Hansson, that was who it was. That was different.

He loped clumsily down towards the jetty and waited for him to arrive, took the rope from him and made the boat fast beside his own. The farmer didn't leave it and climb up on to the jetty – he was behind with his morning routine as it was.

'I couldn't get the motor on the other one started,' he explained in the loud open-air voice. From his seat in the back of the boat, elbow still resting on the steering arm, he looked up towards Carl, looked at him frankly, with neither pity nor curiosity in his eyes, accepting him as he was. 'Somebody telephoned last night. An Englishman . . .' Hansson shrugged, at a disadvantage for once. He was a man with a good many strings to his bow but he couldn't speak a word of any language but his own. '. . . the wife got something down. Here.'

Kneeling down Carl took the scrap of paper from him and unfolded it. It was a piece of a supermarket receipt; on the back she had written down a number and the name of a hotel. He didn't know how much English she understood – maybe they were correct, maybe not. He wanted to put it to the test as soon as he could. Now that the message had arrived after days of waiting he felt a release of energy, an overwhelming surge of impatience to get things moving.

'Would you take me back with you?' He threw the question behind him already turning to go back to the house to get his coat, money . . . what else would he need?

'OK. You'll have to get a move on though. I'm not hanging around here all day.'

Hansson spoke to everybody like that, with the same brusque informality. It conveyed exactly what he felt about his neighbour – that he was no more and no less than anybody else he came across in his daily round. Sometimes a foal or a calf was flawed, sometimes a man. It was how the world was and nothing to get worked up about. It wasn't an attitude that Carl came across often and it made the man someone to be valued he thought as he hurried clumsily along the path. The best thing about him, though, was that he kept his mouth shut.

The crowd had gathered behind the Royal Palace to watch the morning parade, the band in blue uniforms and *pickelhaube* helmets looking like gentle Prussians, the ceremonial contingent behind – clean, smart and warlike, only in a stylised way. Vallin, the man in the red sweater and worn jeans, pushed his way through the assembly resentfully. They were too civilised, too peaceful, too rich, these people. How little they comprehended of the way things went in his country to the east, only three hundred kilometres away on the other side of the Baltic. Three hundred kilometres – it could as well have been three million. What did these people know of suffering? How could they ever understand what it meant to be occupied by the Reds, the Nazis, the

Reds again. To try to live, to survive through war, famine, oppression. Hundreds of thousands of his countrymen dispossessed by Russian incomers, land confiscated, families uprooted and transported to forced labour in Siberia. These people knew nothing, understood nothing of raw bloody life. He felt the bitterness rise in his throat as he made his way down the cobbled street towards Anders' shop.

He pushed open the door and found his way blocked by a thin customer, an American by the look of him, examining a brass wall-sconce decorated with hearts, made to hold a candle. It was the kind of thing that always sold well. Arching himself to allow the man to pass him, the customer gave Anders an enquiring look.

'Two thousand crowns,' he said. Objectively it was too much for a piece that was of no great age or merit, but it was the sort of thing that tourists liked and two thousand was the standard price. Anders was confident that such a thing couldn't be found any cheaper elsewhere in Gamla Stan and the customer must have done his own market research already and come to the same conclusion because he unzipped his back pocket, drew out his wallet and paid up without another word.

Anders accepted the money gratefully. It was quite like old times, pre-recession times, to have someone paying up without a murmur.

His gaze resting on the icons, Vallin listened to the exchange with a pang of rage which sent a shiver through his chest like a branch of lightning. Two thousand crowns was twice what his parents back in Zemgale had to live on for a month – for heat, light, food and a roof.

Anders turned to him. This inelegant man was no asset in his showroom and he wanted to see him out of it, particularly now when at last he had a genuine customer inspecting his stock, ready perhaps to dip into his wallet again and spend some more. It was just like Vallin to choose the worse possible moment to arrive.

Anders strode to the inner door, opened it, and ushered the outsider through it firmly. 'The picture I mentioned is in the other room, at the end of the corridor. I'll be with you in a moment,' he said.

When he joined him he found that Vallin had lit a cigarette, of a kind – a rough tube of paper and loose tobacco which had dropped a black fragment or two on the grey carpet. Anders knew it would take days for the acrid smell to disperse. It was a detestable habit which he had never once been tempted to indulge in himself. He was too intelligent, had too much respect for his body, unlike this regrettable Balt. Anders could scarcely understand how he had become involved with such a man. In his prosperous days when it had been possible to make a decent living in the antique business here he wouldn't have thought of it for a moment. He stared at his visitor. Vallin seemed to be diminished by the austerity of the room with its white screens, its plaster walls and shadowless light. A cold room.

'It is time to move,' he said.

From his trouser pocket he drew his much-folded marine chart and spread it out. He pointed with his forefinger among the thinly outlined islands, the grey shadowy depths between them.

'That's the place.'

'You seem very certain.'

Vallin looked knowing and shrugged. His small command of Swedish wasn't enough for him to embark on any kind of explanation.

'That's it. There.' He made a dismissive gesture which said 'take it or leave it'. He enjoyed putting the other man down, laying down conditions.

'When?' Anders asked.

'On Monday.'

At least, the Swede thought, he wasn't going to be made to wait for days like last time. Humiliated again. He nodded. 'I shall have the boat ready at ten.'

Vallin placed the palm of his hand on Anders's chest and shook his head decisively. 'No. That boat too small.' He turned over his chart and flicked an impatient finger for something to write with, a ballpoint, anything. When he had been found a pencil he made a quick sketch of a shape on the back, scrawling in the dimensions, the weight, and then scanned Anders's face with the impatience of a dumb man for confirmation that he understood his message. It was clear enough.

Taking the pencil and the sheaf of paper from him Anders went to the wall and leaning against it drew a boat. Neatly he added details of its beam and length before handing the chart back. 'That boat there. Monday night.' He paused. 'You understand?'

'Winblad,' the other man said.

'I will deal with Winblad,' Anders answered.

That wasn't enough to satisfy Vallin. There was something else he wanted. He jabbed his thumb towards the big painting on the wall, the townscape that Anders had offered to Ramsay for a quarter of a million crowns.

'You sell,' he said. His Swedish was so rudimentary that it wasn't clear whether this was a statement or a question, whether it related to the past or the future. Anders decided that vigorous affirmation was all that was required.

'Yes,' he nodded, 'yes. I shall sell.'

'For dollars. Dollars.' The thumb rubbed against the fingers in the universal gesture for money.

'Dollars. Crowns. Of course. Sell to the west.' Anders pointed in that direction. However, once again the visitor had not altogether managed to get his message across. He pushed up insistently against the dealer who caught his unwashed smell, a feral smell from a less civilised world.

'Dollars,' he repeated urgently. He rifled his right-hand pocket and displayed the result – a thin selection of loose change.

Anders understood. This wasn't a shakedown or if it was that was only because Vallin was down to his last few crowns. It wasn't greed but necessity that was making him so persistent. Money had to be found for him otherwise who knew what he would get up to – some incompetent burglary or mugging that would bring the police eventually to the door of the shop. There was no other choice – for the time being Vallin had to be subsidised.

'Dollars no. Swedish crowns yes,' Anders conceded. 'Wait.'

He went down the passage to the showroom, unlocked the drawer of his till, withdrew three notes adding a fourth after a moment's hesitation, then returned and handed them over to Vallin who, after checking it, stuffed the money into his back pocket. It took all of another five minutes to get rid of him.

When that had been achieved Anders did not experience the relief he felt he was entitled to. The grey confusion of spirit which had grown inside him ever since Winblad had inveigled him into this venture was a little more in evidence. He observed it as carefully as somebody with a progressive disease, watching for signs of any deterioration. Some days there was a remission and he almost felt he could live with it. At other times it was a pain, certainly a focus of physical discomfort. He longed to go back to the comfortable days, the days when he could afford to be above reproach.

For the first half hour of his car journey there was scarcely anybody on the road and with the forest protecting him like a dark wall on either side Carl Johansson did not feel threatened. When he reached the main road though there was more traffic. Occasionally a lorry or an impatient tourist would come up behind him; he would always let them pass. Now he found himself stuck behind a farmer dawdling home but he did not harass him. Keep a low profile, he thought, smiling sidelong at an irony which he had not consciously intended. Now he was past the narrow shelter of the forest and the country was opening out on either side of him – clumps of trees, open prairies of unfenced grass, with here on his right a herd of horses running wild in a burst of self-confidence which he envied. A massive vehicle swept down on him, passed him, with a string of frustrated cars in its wake. He suddenly sensed the cold investigative gaze of the drivers probing the interior of his car, one after the other as they passed him. The feeling of security which so far he had managed to keep in place began to slip from him like a single inadequate blanket from around the shoulders of a naked suspect. Perhaps this decision to drive to Stockholm in search of Smith had been taken too impetuously; after all he had only seventeen days left to wait before the situation shifted decisively in his favour. No, he decided, better to make sure of contacting Smith whatever the risk. He had to get to him before his meeting with Winblad – that man was the key to the whole operation. He calmed himself down; there was plenty of time.

The most powerful argument was the look he would see in Hansson's face if he returned today without a tolerable explanation. Instinctively he pulled the hood of his anorak around his face. As he did so his glance fell on the fuel gauge and he saw that the needle was hovering well below the refill level. He had to stop at the next filling station, whatever it was like. He couldn't allow himself to be choosy – there weren't many on this road.

Here was one. Modest, with a shop selling groceries, magazines, confectionery as well. Nobody about except a young couple just getting into their car.

He drew in and waited for them to leave. It was the girl's turn to drive. She asked her companion to hand her the map and studied it for a moment before returning it with a couple of businesslike words. Carl continued to wait. She pushed her seat forward to get more comfortable, adjusted the mirror above her head and began to move away.

As soon as he heard the burst of power from her engine, Carl got out of his own car and busied himself with the cap on his fuel tank, keeping his head bent, averted from the window of the shop. He unhooked the nozzle of the hose and filled his tank, squeezing in the ultimate drop of petrol. He checked the amount displayed on the pump and, still keeping his head turned towards the road, reached for his wallet, counted out the notes and felt in his pocket for the coins he needed to make up the exact amount.

He glanced in through the window and waited. It wasn't raining and he felt conspicuous with this blue hood pulled up over his head – more conspicuous by the second. It made it difficult to see the traffic sweeping past him on the road. Three vehicles went safely by in quick succession. Sooner or later one would stop.

The boy behind the counter seemed determined to stay where he was. Slowly he surveyed his stock, satisfied himself that everything was as it should be. Then he sat down. Surely he didn't stay there all day? Carl heard the sound of an engine slowing down behind him. Another customer was arriving to fill up.

He couldn't postpone the moment any longer. Pushing open the door of the shop he walked quickly inside, placed his money on the cashdesk and said, 'Sixty-six litres.'

The young man stood up, his eyes searching for the figure

on the pump outside. 'Wait a moment.'

Carl Johansson ignored him, turned and hurried straight into a customer coming in through the door – a tall rangy fellow, in cotton trousers and a T-shirt, his hair lightly touched with grey at the tips. Taken aback, his hand outstretched to fend off the collision, the man apologised automatically then looked away as though to avoid an eye contact which both of them might find uncomfortable. He didn't think to step aside; he was still standing in the doorway, barring the exit.

The voice of the boy at the desk came again. 'A moment please. I must check . . .'

The figure in the anorak groped in haste for his wallet. Without looking he scrabbled inside it for more money, then threw the crumpled handful of notes down. 'Have some more then. There. More,' he rasped out in a voice which seemed to come not from his throat but from the middle of his body, forced from the belly. Pushing past the tall customer he was out of the door and away.

It took a good many kilometres of uneventful driving before Carl settled down. Knowing while it happened that the outburst would draw attention to him, he had been quite unable to suppress it. Why should he be forced to undergo the scrutiny of such people for a moment longer than he wished?

He was hungry now. He slowed down suddenly, drew into an empty lay-by, and brought out the lunch that Hansson's wife had found for him as he was leaving. Processed cheese, a tub of margarine and a packet of hard bread; a chocolate bar; a bottle of diluted fruit juice. It was enough to keep him going until his rendezvous with Smith that evening. It would have to be – he could not risk going to a restaurant nor to his apartment in Strandvägen.

Before he started off again he sat for a minute or two running over in his mind his choice of routes into the city, considering which car park would give him the least obvious access to the hotel. At the same time he kept a weather eye on his wing mirror. As soon as he had the chance he turned off the main road and made a long detour, driving almost at random for an hour over country roads which were new to him. He couldn't be certain whether that precaution was effective or not but it made him feel better.

It was after six by the time he reached Stockholm and it was already quiet – most of the commuters and shoppers had gone and the tourists were back in their hotels.

As he got out of the car he found that it was raining. This was an unlooked-for bonus because it justified his anorak, and it gave him new courage when he came to the unforgiving space in front of Slussen and found himself right out in the open. When he crossed over into Skeppsbron he would be within sight of Smith's hotel – only a few hundred metres more.

He turned the trunk of his body awkwardly round to the left, looking out for traffic, then the other way as a gust of rain hit him full in the face. He brushed the water away from his eyes sensing that he should have waited to check again but willing in his haste to sacrifice that extra fragment of security. A moment later he was over the broad street in safety and had reached the heavy plate-glass doors of the hotel; he pushed his way into the pastel-coloured space of the reception area towards the smartly uniformed girl at the desk. Her head was bent; she was filling in some details on the room list in front of her.

A man in a dark blue suit, correctly dressed, had got up from the banquette beside the door. The voice was quiet, almost deferential. 'Mr Johansson?'

The figure in the anorak stopped and listened, with his gaze elsewhere.

'Mr Johansson. I come from your father. He has asked to see you.'

Carl took a single step forward, the pressures on him exactly in balance as he made the calculations forced on him by this new situation. Could he afford the luxury of ignoring the order? The girl at the desk looked up, ready to deal with his enquiry whatever it was. Although her eyes were dismayed by what she saw she was too well trained to allow them to register anything but a cheerful welcome.

The man said, 'The car is not far away.'

Turning, Carl followed him outside into the street.

The incident resolved, the girl's gaze returned to the guest list in front of her. There had been no cause for concern.

Chapter Thirteen

Charles Ramsay was not going to give up; he wasn't the type. The only answer was no co-operation. To stay as a stranger amongst them, a living reproach in the midst of the little community on Alvarö. He withdrew his labour – stood watching with arms folded while others dug those eternal potatoes or fetched wood for the stove, pretended not to understand when help was needed with manhandling the boat. While they were simply puzzled at this apparent eccentricity at first, he sensed soon enough that he was stoking up their resentment. The steam was building up nicely.

Not with Jenny Winblad though, whatever he felt about her, and he didn't bother to keep his dislike of her to himself. That would have been too much to expect when she was so much of an obstacle to him. While he had to cope with reality she didn't seem to think it mattered. She was fey, gamine, quite happy with herself as she was – unaware of the total nuisance she had become – and it infuriated him that she got away with it. Oblivious to his frustration she handed him his plate at mealtimes promptly with no shadow of contrition in her small face, nor any sign that she disapproved of his behaviour. However, after he had withered one or two of her attempts at conversation she gave up trying and soon she wasn't speaking to him at all. She smiled at him from time to time to show that there was no ill feeling.

The others boycotted him. At mealtimes the children stared at him silently until he stared fiercely back at them, the others pretended he wasn't there – at least not present enough to be spoken to. It was stalemate – and he was due to meet Smith in three days' time. Should he capitulate? He was damned if he would. He was immovable. A rock.

Nor did he slink away to his cabin in the evening. No. He remained obstinately in evidence at the *parstuga*. When, after the meal, they all sat outside – Uncle Henrik with his pipe, the others rereading the magazines which Jenny had brought them so thoughtfully from Stockholm – he lay on the grass. A silent presence, always there. When the twilight came they lit the lamps and went on reading, mostly in silence, and he continued his vigil, watching the moths fluttering as close to the heat as they dared. It was very boring.

But next morning, after he had washed and shaved by the water's edge, he walked down to the house expecting to meet a thick glass wall of disregard and it wasn't like that at all. Jenny was all vivacity, full of talk, as though those two sullen days had never happened. As she poured his coffee for him from the dark red enamel pot, she announced, 'I have to go out to set the eel net today. Would you like to come and help me? That would be nice, wouldn't it? It is a fine day. We could take some lunch.'

A picnic. He ought to have asked himself where this charm offensive was leading but her eagerness to please touched him and the truth was that he hadn't much enjoyed being sent to Coventry. If she was allowing him to rejoin the human race why should he make difficulties? Perhaps he hadn't behaved too well – not childishly but not well . . .

and one could say that the problem was one which they shared. Something which they had to solve between them. It did look indeed as though the furniture might belong to her – Uncle Henrik certainly seemed to think so.

The eel net was really a tunnel supported at intervals by U shaped lengths of cane with lead weights to keep them upright on the bottom. Open at one end it had a sleeve which allowed the eels to swim into it but trapped them when they tried to get out. The local fishermen caught a good number every year and sent them in to Stockholm to be smoked she said as he helped her to fold the long net, section by section, and lay it in the bows.

In minutes they were out in the channel in the sunlight. Sitting opposite him in the boat she pointed. 'Over there. We are going out quite a long way,' she called over the roar of the outboard motor, the wind blowing her hair about, snatching the words away. 'It's the best place for eels.'

Soon they were into more open water. There were islands still, mostly uninhabited. Here and there Ramsay saw the occasional shed or boathouse but there were no longer any smart weekend houses with flagpoles and motor cruisers.

As the first hint of the open sea hit the boat, making it buck and rear, she throttled back the outboard and let it idle into the lee of one of the larger islands.

'Here,' she said, 'take the oars.'

He did as he was told and steadied the boat in the water as she stepped deftly past him into the bows to set the net on the bottom, dropping each half hoop in its proper place.

'There we are.' Triumphantly she laid the big lead weight which anchored the end of the net to the bottom. 'Row in,' she ordered. 'We can tie up here.' She scrambled ashore and made the boat fast.

'Lunch,' she announced. While he spread out their blanket on the rock she opened the tidy packages she had brought with her – handed him a napkin, a knife, a mug.

Screwing up his eyes against the sunshine flashing off the water he lay on one elbow and looked to the horizon. One of those immense ferries was heading out towards Finland; otherwise the sea was empty – and the islands deserted too as far as he could tell.

As she poured the coffee from the flask she said, 'Now I am going to tell you about Bengt and me, so listen.'

Her parents had idolised her elder brother. Precocious as a young child he had managed to keep himself in the centre of the stage from then on. They had been almost intimidated by his brilliance as a student – had found it difficult to deny him anything he asked for. Immensely confident in his own ability he had persuaded them to back him in a number of ventures – a car dealership, a restaurant. These had paid off, or so he said; everything he touched seemed to turn into money. The evidence was there – the large flat in town with paintings by Liljefors and Zorn on its trendy pale brick walls, extended holidays abroad on warm and exclusive islands.

The one member of the family who refused to take him at his own valuation was his grandmother. Because she was English, an observer from another country, she took a more dispassionate view. She weighed what she saw of his businesses against what she saw of his expenditure and came to the unshakeable conclusion that one could not support the other. She mistrusted him – which was why her house and its cherished contents had been made over to her granddaughter. When the family protested she overrode their objections. Bengt was doing so well one way and another, she said, that he scarcely needed anything from her, did he? His modest little sister loved beautiful things, had made her career in that world, would look after them properly. She should have them. Within a week the deed was drawn up, signed and witnessed, and that was that.

At first Bengt had pretended not to mind that he had been bypassed, that the gift meant nothing to him. His sister needed it, he did not – he could make his way on his own. He did make his way – into the well-heeled circles where the richer pickings were, cultivating people who had much more money than he had in the hope that some of it would come towards him; which was how he had fallen in with Carl Johansson, a man whom Jenny knew only by reputation, and had become involved in this insurance thing – which she didn't really understand, she admitted, cutting Ramsay a slice of cheese to put on his rye bread and handing him a tomato to go with it.

Munching it, he pondered. It sounded plausible until he tried to match the opportunist she painted with the man he had met at Biskopstorget. A prim type, no extrovert – not his idea of a car dealer or a restaurateur. Could he believe her?

Having pared and quartered an apple she held a section of it between thumb and forefinger and inspected it with satisfaction.

'I don't know what Bengt is up to now. Some wrong business I should think.' Reflectively she bit into the pale flesh, giving him a sidelong glance – relieved that he did not see it because each time she looked at him she felt her need for him growing a little more, moving up a notch. She could not allow him to guess that.

'Why should he claim the house and furniture are his if they aren't?' he asked.

'It's just the thing he would do,' she shrugged, as though that was an explanation, wishing that he would stop drilling away at the subject like an over-enthusiastic dentist.

'I don't see how he could gain from that.'

Her head turned and she gazed, unbelieving, at his naïvety, 'To make me give some of the money to him, of course. What do you think? He always needs money these days.'

A kind of blackmail? Ramsay wondered – it didn't fit his picture of her brother at all but he had to admit he'd only met the man for less than an hour.

He helped himself to more cheese. It wasn't bad. 'I am not a suspicious man . . .' Why was he so pompous, she asked herself. '. . . You must see this from my standpoint.'

Why? What was so special about him? That was the question, of course . . . what was so special! Looking at him again she tried to decide what it was about the obstinate young man lying on her own picnic blanket that excited her. She was aware of the exact distance between them, how she only had to put out her hand a few centimetres and she could touch him – draw the back of her hand across his cheek. There was silence except for the tiny splash of wavelets against the smooth bank of granite at the water's edge. For a moment it seemed to her that the air between them was so heavy and highly charged that it was a miracle that she could breathe it in at all. Of course he was quite unconscious of anything like that as he bit tidily into his tomato.

There was a great deal more she wanted to tell him but he was so locked up in his own troubles that she doubted if he would listen and besides she wasn't sure that she could explain herself clearly in English. She was liable to sound ridiculous. She looked at him again and tried again to decide what it was about him. Plenty of dark hair, good teeth – you could see that when he smiled which wasn't often – but as soon as he opened his mouth again she knew he would be talking about his stupid money or his father's big house that meant so much to him, that had to be saved he said. He had to be stopped – and she felt aggrieved too, as though it was he who owed her something and wouldn't pay.

She busied herself with the remains of the little meal, brushing crumbs into the grass beside them. Avoiding his eyes, not daring to do otherwise in case he read her mind, she put the hard bread back in its airtight container, snapped the lid shut and picked up the napkins and carefully smoothed them – they could be used again. Holding up his mug – half a mugful of undrunk coffee – she asked, 'You have finished with this? Yes?'

When he nodded she flung the dregs into the undergrowth nearby with a nervous jerk of the wrist. Then she went to the water's edge with her own mug as well to swill them clean, swinging them afterwards to throw the surplus water off them. He called after her, 'I can't leave it like this. You haven't given me enough to . . .'

I, I, I – me, me, me. She turned on him. 'I have told you everything. All about Bengt. More than you deserve to know really. I have told you lots of things. Private things,' she said in a stubborn voice which imitated that of a child and irritated him as she could see. Good.

'I need evidence.'

'Evidence? I won't discuss it.'

'Come on, a fact. A simple fact in my hand that I can touch and see. The deed that your grandmother signed for example. That would be quite enough.'

She burst out with indignation, 'That is an absolutely personal matter. My business. Who are you, the police you think, that you demand to see my private papers? I am not a criminal. You can't make me do that.'

Of course he couldn't, not without going to law, and if he did he guessed she would fight a rearguard action inch by inch to the very door of the courtroom producing the deed with a flourish at the final minute. He would regret it.

She threw a glance at him, to size up his reaction, while she rummaged around in her bag for something. Then she extracted a plain glass bottle from her basket, the sort that might have contained a soft drink once – something she had bought for the children – but now was full of what looked like water. It had a screw-on metal cap which she couldn't easily shift. She gave it to him to deal with.

'You look as though you have strong wrists,' she said. 'You open it.' He did so. she handed him one of the mugs, still wet. 'Try some,' she said, pouring for him before he could refuse.

Suspiciously he peered down into the white interior of the mug. 'What is it?'

'Schnapps,' she said. 'Lars made it from his potatoes.'

What was she up to now? Still, he was in need of a drink.

The liquid caught the back of his throat and a thin stream of fire glowed under his breastbone as though a miniature furnace had been tapped inside there. Taking the bottle from him she tipped her head back and opened her lips for a neat little swig before wiping them with the heel of her hand.

She gazed around her at the grey rocks and dark water. The island was completely deserted with not a boat in sight but it wasn't enclosed and golden like her imaginary bedroom, heavy with the warm animal scent of furs and spicy perfumes from the south. The hard flat rock underneath her wasn't right either. Nothing was as she had imagined it. Still the wind had dropped so that it felt like summer and she was flushed by the schnapps besides. She reached out a thin hand again for the bottle but he had it – was pouring himself another drink. The fact that he hadn't asked her permission was a sign that his inhibitions might be dissolving.

She got to her feet.

'Move please,' she said. Taken by surprise, he stood up awkwardly, still clutching the bottle, searching for the cap so that he could screw it back where it belonged. Picking up the blanket by two adjacent corners, she shook it, flapped it out and laid it again carefully on the unyielding rock so different from the large and commodious bed she sometimes imagined in the night when she found it difficult to get to sleep again because of the all-pervading midsummer light.

She had no idea where this was going to lead but she had no intention of retreating now. She lay down on the blanket, feeling the warmth of the schnapps inside her, the sun outside, and observed him, unable to think of the English words she needed. Then he lay down beside her.

A few minutes later she remembered something. Sitting up and searching her bag of worn reindeer skin she produced a small square paper package and handed it over. 'You will need this, I think.'

It was not a gift he could refuse without humiliating her and besides, he told himself, adjusting to the new situation he had created, they were both adults; they knew what they were doing – she knew.

As she reached her climax she gave a great cry of ecstasy which echoed across to the other island lying deserted in the sunlight. To him it seemed a wonderful sign, a mark of reconciliation.

Now he was asleep and it was peaceful. The sun was beating down on her face and she was content, every nerve alive, remembering a pleasure which she had only half dared to expect. That at least had been right. All at once, feeling the weight of his sleeping head on her shoulder, she knew that she wasn't going to be able to face him when he awoke. For a few moments she put off the decision, then easing him

185

slowly, carefully, away from her she got up and quietly collected the things she had to take with her.

He stirred and opened his eyes. Where was he?

Looking round he slowly reorientated himself. On an island in the skerries outside Stockholm, that was where he was. The view hadn't changed a lot, in fact not at all, although there was something different going on. What was it? The noise of an outboard motor. Somebody out fishing he guessed. He glanced at his watch – he'd been asleep for longer than he thought. Then he remembered what had occurred. The girl wasn't there beside him. Where had she got to?

He stood up and called out, 'Hallo. Are you ready to leave now?' Trying to make it sound as though nothing had happened.

No reply; not a word. It was understandable perhaps – he was unsure of himself as well. Not altogether comfortable in fact. He took two more tentative paces but the branches still obscured his view. She had to be over there somewhere.

'Isn't it time we were going back?' he called. Louder.

No response.

Where had she gone? There wasn't a sign of her. No Jenny Winblad at all – and no personal blanket. He glanced down towards the water – the boat had gone. Nothing there except the little orange float which marked the location of the eel net. Shading his eyes against the sun he stared across the dazzle off the water, searching for her. Her boat had gone out of sight past that headland. Could he still hear, far off, the sound of it heading back down the channel to Alvarö? He imagined that he could. No point in looking for her on this uninhabited island because she had deserted it and him. Both. She had marooned him, that was what.

His blue waterproof jacket was still lying where he had

abandoned it. She had also left behind a bottle of mineral water and the plastic picnic box which was thoughtful of her. What was there inside? He pulled off the lid. Half a packet of Ryvita-style hard bread, a tub with a bit of margarine left in it, a chunk of hard cheese and a banana. It was something. Not to be eaten now though; he would keep it for later. He didn't know how long it would be before she relented, got over her embarrassment or whatever it was that had prompted her departure, and came back to fetch him.

She was going to come back, wasn't she? She hadn't simply panicked and fled, had she? There was no note though. Yes of course she would come back – she was a sensible girl. All he had to do was to wait. Meanwhile perhaps he could attract the attention of a passing vessel, a fisherman or one of those summer sailboats. However, if all he did was shout and wave his hands they might take it merely as a salutation, a cheery sign of summer, and serenely pass him by. He needed a flag to wave, a flag of distress – his shirt would do. He went back into the woods, found a suitable branch and began to strip it of its dark green needles. A flag. There, he had one.

Waiting. It was quite pleasant at first, waiting – sitting in the sun with his home-made flag ready beside him on the rock. An hour went by, two hours. There had been another ferry boat going past but a long way off; not within signalling distance and he didn't suppose it would have come to fetch him off the island if he had hailed it. Long after it had gone past the waves created by its wake hit the bluff below him as though teasing him. The sky became overcast and the air grew chillier. He decided to keep himself warm by climbing right the way round the coast of his kingdom. It might be a useful exploration, one never knew . . .

It wasn't a big island – a mound of rock rising out of the water thick with trees, scarcely larger than his father's garden at Bressemer. It didn't take him long to get to the other side and find the opposite coast, another warm grey slope of granite worn smooth by sluggish glaciers a few thousand years earlier. He looked round for some diversion and there wasn't any. Trees, rocks, sunshine, very much like the other side.

No, there were no surprises. No hut or other dwelling, no boathouse with a convenient boat in it. This place was exactly what he had thought it was in the first place – an outcrop of granite sticking up out of the Baltic, with trees on top. Where the hell had she got to?

Back at his starting point he ate three pieces of bread and a mouthful of cheese washed down with a swig of water. He eyed the banana.

It looked as though she was determined to push this test to the limit, that he was faced with an overnight stay. There were plenty of fir branches to use for a mattress. Back to nature.

Although it was still daylight, it was ten o'clock in the evening now and it seemed less and less likely that he was going to be rescued by a passing boat, so he dismantled his flag and put his shirt back on again under his jacket.

He ate the banana – it had to go sometime.

Settling down among the boughs, he tried to get some sleep. Although he thought otherwise it was not the flat twilight that kept him awake, the half daylight that seemed to wash the colour from his surroundings and invest them with a mystical Nordic meaning which he couldn't penetrate. In marooning him she had left him with all his problems for company as well. Now that he was vulnerable, they swooped down on him – the dispute with this eccentric

Swedish girl was merely the last of the series. He went through the others. The outcome of the inquest on Barbara Russell – he still had no idea what had happened there. His quarrel with Julia was not yet resolved. A threat was still hanging over Bressemer – one which he couldn't bring himself to spell out in detail. He remembered his father standing in front of the huge façade of the house, which still seemed so solid, waiting for his son to produce a miracle for him. As Ramsay lay head back, forcing his eyes to remain closed against the light, the arguments surrounding each of the problems, pros and cons, downside and upside, became so entangled in his head that he couldn't follow any of them to a clean conclusion.

Was she going to come back and fetch him in time for him to make his crucial rendezvous with Smith at the Crown Café? If she didn't he was finished.

He couldn't sleep. He sat up and stared across the water.

Something out there caught his eye. A sliver of white. A white sail – twin sails – half a mile offshore. It wasn't a yacht, more like a small schooner with a square wheelhouse aft, its sails bellying in the light breeze, sliding silently through the grey dawn like a phantom. Coming slowly round, it was making towards him now. For a second or two he thought it was a dream. It wasn't until two members of the crew emerged from the wheelhouse and began working the boat, lowering the sails, that he woke up to the fact that they could take him back to civilisation. The ship was still a long way off. Probably too far for him to catch their attention.

Nevertheless he shouted, and waited. With the vessel bow on, it was difficult to make out what they were doing. If they had seen him. He pulled more of the chilly dawn air into his lungs and bellowed some more. He took off his shirt again, tied it to his branch and waved it about, feeling Crusoe-like . . . ludicrous.

189

No, there was no sign that anyone on the boat had seen him, no answering shout, no arm waving back at him. Then he heard the muffled beat of an auxiliary motor and the boat began to turn away in a wide arc towards the open sea. As it drew away he saw that the crew had left a pale blue buoy bobbing on the surface of the water in its wake. He watched it until it was obscured by trees at the water's edge.

He might as well try and get some sleep.

'Hey.'

Jenny's animated face was above him, her eyes watchful. The sight was almost welcome.

'Wake up.' She shook his arm impatiently. 'I'm back.'

'Like a bad penny,' he muttered.

'Bad penny?' she frowned.

'An idiom.'

'An idiom? What is that?'

'Forget it,' he said.

At least she had come back to fetch him, she thought. Obviously it had to be done but it had cost her an effort. Now that he was awake she looked hard at his face to see what he was thinking – what he thought of her after the . . . adventure of yesterday afternoon – whether it was more or less – and saw nothing there.

For a moment she hesitated, uncertain what to do next and he did nothing to help her. Then she opened the bag slung over her shoulder and produced a razor, some shaving cream, a towel. That was something. Then from another came a loaf of bread, cheese, butter, a flask of hot coffee. Even better.

He looked at her suspiciously. What was the purpose of these timely offerings?

'I shouldn't have left you here I suppose but you deserved it,' she observed, handing him the towel when he came back dripping from his ablutions at the water's edge.

'Leaving me here like that was the act of a child,' he muttered as he dried his hair. 'What did it achieve?'

He spoke as if nothing of note had happened the previous afternoon – nothing worthy of comment.

'It made me feel much much better,' she replied, more than ready to punish his indifference. If indifference was what it was. She started to speak again. 'Yesterday afternoon you know . . .'

He interrupted her. Wanting to change the subject – that above all. 'There was a boat out there this morning. I almost escaped in it.' He told her about the schooner and pointed out the buoy – 'There.'

Humbled, she narrowed her eyes. Her mind busy, she tried to follow where his finger was pointing, 'Yes, I see it. When you have finished your breakfast we shall go over and inspect it,' she announced.

'Why?'

'Because I want to,' she replied.

When they reached it the blue buoy was larger than it had seemed from a distance. As Jenny pulled on her right oar to bring the boat up close to it he stood up and grabbed the handhold at the top of it. As it swung over he almost lost his footing.

'Good. Hold on.' She called out. With his other hand he clasped the gunwale on the far side of the bow, keeping boat and buoy together, while she reached underneath it for the mooring rope. She called out, 'I have it. I have the rope.'

She yanked at it healthily, panting. The boat heeled over and he glimpsed for a moment the blue nylon rope, taut in her hand. It disappeared as the boat righted itself and she was pulled further out, dangerously, over the water.

'Let go,' he shouted. For once she did as she was told and just managed to recover her balance.

Whatever was on the end of the rope was much too heavy to be pulled up off the bottom like an eel net. If they tried that they would swamp the boat.

'There is probably nothing down there except a block of concrete,' he said. 'Just a weight to keep the buoy in place.'

'If so, why put a buoy here? It must be to mark something,' she insisted.

'So?' he asked.

'A schooner. A sailing boat with two masts?'

'That's right. I told you.'

'I'm going down there to see what it is,' she declared.

No she wasn't, he decided wearily, it was his job. He pulled off his shirt reluctantly – a cold bath would wake him up he supposed.

He plunged over the side, then surfaced to see her startled face looking down, above him. Cold was the word. Taking a deep breath he dived again.

Underwater he could see the pale rope snaking down towards the bottom. Quickly he pushed himself with his legs down from the light at the surface towards the darkness below. He put out a hand and caught the rope to guide himself to whatever it was at the end of it. His other hand brushed the granite shelf at the bottom, located . . . what was it? A rectangular shape. He could just make it out when he opened his eyes. A black cube. He felt it – not a rough surface like concrete nor hard like metal – a yielding surface. Now his pulse was thudding in his ears and he felt his chest dragging for air. He rose towards the pale surface, towards the light with the shadow of the dark underside of the boat lying on it.

'Mind the rope,' Jenny called out as he thankfully gulped in air. 'Don't get caught in it.'

He went down there again. This time he knew where his target was and he had more time to explore around it. Here he could feel something – it felt like the straight edge of a sheet of thick plastic film. Lower down there seemed to be a net containing it. He opened his eyes for a moment and glimpsed the rope, divided, dragging at it, held taut by the pull of the buoy on the surface. Motionless for the moment.

Back up to the boat. Grasping the gunwale he called out, 'I'm coming in.' Awkwardly he pulled himself up and she helped him over, watchful to prevent the boat from shipping water. Since there was no towel she bunched up his shirt and tried to dry him with that while he brushed the water out of his eyes and heaved to get his breath back.

'What was down there? What did you see?'

'Something square, held in a net.'

'How big?' she demanded.

'A metre or more each way. Wrapped in heavy plastic sheet by the feel of it.'

'So maybe it is a block of concrete?' She sounded cheated.

'A cubic metre of concrete simply to anchor this buoy?' He nodded towards it. 'That's scarcely necessary. And why bother to wrap it up?'

That cheered her up. 'A crate perhaps?'

'Something of the kind.' He said, 'It's not merely a weight, I'm sure of that.'

'We must report it to the police.'

Why was she panicking?

'Hold on. There could be a perfectly innocent explanation.'

Contacting the police would mean getting involved, giving a statement, making a fool of oneself perhaps.

'The nearest telephone is on Elvö. Not far. We must go there,' she insisted, turning behind her to start up the outboard motor. He had forgotten how law-abiding they were in Sweden.

★ ★ ★

193

One of those ubiquitous blue and yellow flags flew from the pole outside the general store on Elvö. Jenny, ahead of him, shouldered her way into the interior smelling of newly sawn pinewood and fresh bread in an earnest search for a telephone.

When she had finished her call Ramsay managed to persuade the shopkeeper to let him ring London. He'd been out of touch for days. The Swedish girl stood and watched him speculatively as he listened to the ringing tone.

Julia's first words were: 'Are you still there? In Sweden?'

'Yes. On an island in the skerries,' he replied.

'The what?'

'The Stockholm archipelago.'

'What are you up to out there?' It wasn't the time for an explanation and he didn't offer one. After a moment's silence Julia went on, 'There's one piece of news.'

'Which is?'

'The police rang the other day. They were surprised that you had left the country without informing them.' She spoke lightly, making a joke of it. 'I did my loyal best to defend you. It doesn't look good though, you know. They've had the inquest by the way. On Barbara Russell.'

'What was the verdict?' Because of the tinge of hostility in her voice he found it difficult to ask the question.

Before she answered it she paused, almost deliberately it seemed, as though she didn't want to make it too easy for him.

'It was adjourned,' she said at last.

'For how long?'

'Don't know. Didn't ask. What are you going to do now?'

He scarcely heard the question – his mind was too busy. 'Stay here. I have other things to see to – other business. A meeting.'

'How long. Two days, three?'

'I don't know yet,' he replied sharply.

'You've got to come home sometime. There's a business to see to over here. Don't forget that.'

'I haven't forgotten. What was the verdict on the photographs I had sent to you?'

There was another moment of hesitation. 'Nothing yet,' she said.

'You should have heard by now. What's holding things up?' he asked impatiently, feeling himself at a disadvantage, trying to reassert his authority.

'I'll follow it up,' she agreed, a tinge of resentment in her voice again. It was all very well, him issuing orders from over there.

Jenny Winblad was still close to him, eavesdropping and making no attempt to disguise her interest – soaking up as much of their conversation as she could hear. He felt he had to allow her a certain intimacy because of what had happened the previous afternoon.

Julia continued, 'By the way, I nearly forgot, your father rang the other day. Wanted to know if there was any news. What do you want me to tell him?' Perhaps the old man, seeking reassurance in his isolation, anxious to talk to somebody – to her because his son wasn't there – had taken up too much of her time.

'Say that I haven't met Smith yet but I hope to very soon. Say I'll be in touch as soon as I can.'

'Is that all?'

'I don't want him to be disappointed.'

'Very well. Are you all right?'

She was doubtful, puzzled. He wanted to say something reassuring but how could he with Jenny Winblad standing at his elbow? It was not a time for endearments.

'Fine . . . I'll be in touch as soon as I can,' he repeated, and put the receiver down.

Jenny Winblad felt a little measure of relief. The aftermath of her escapade did not feel as bad as she had thought it might. On the other hand she had a feeling as she watched Ramsay paying over the money for his call, frowning as he scrutinised the unfamiliar banknotes, that she might have gambled more on him than she had meant to. Only time would tell how much she might have lost.

Chapter Fourteen

The elder Johansson nodded towards his blue-suited employee. 'Tell my son we are ready to talk now.'

He gave the order with the self-confidence of someone who, so his employees said, had been born with a chequebook in his hand – a chequebook giving him the right to draw on an immense, an inexhaustible, family fund of money and influence. He was not as others were.

The man left, his shoes clattering on the oak parquet. His position in the hierarchy dictated formal clothes for him, a white shirt, feet encased in hard brown shoes, whereas Johansson himself was dressed casually – soft-soled shoes which fitted as easily as gloves, dark blue slacks and a polo-necked cashmere sweater to match – the perquisites of his rank.

As elegant too in his own way, Axel sat in one of the fine but unyielding Gustaviansk chairs as apparently composed as if he were relaxing in a deckchair outside his own porch at home on a Sunday morning. He had a gift for making everything look easy; even if it was only to appear comfortable in a chair that patently wasn't.

But they were strung up, both of them. Like partners at bridge picking up the cards they have been dealt and putting them in order, each examined the deficiencies of the hand he had been given to play. This interview was going to be as crucial as any negotiation they had undertaken in the past couple of years. Much more difficult than the last round of wage negotiations. Far more difficult than that. More fraught than the restructuring of their Danish container subsidiary which had involved days of closed meetings, fighting to grind away their bankers' objections millimetre by millimetre amid a fog of fatigue. In the end their persistence and stamina had eroded their opponents' position, despite the strength of its logic. Sometimes it was not reason but sheer cussedness that won the day.

The big door opened and Carl barrelled into the room. He was dressed in a pair of worn Levis, and a lumberjack shirt in a harsh red check. Without his anorak his disabilities were more conspicuous, more blatant, and the sight of him touched off the sort of despair in his father which nothing else could. His son came to a halt in the middle of the room and looked first at him then at Axel, swinging round from the waist with his legs planted wide, turning the whole of his torso because nature had given him no choice in the matter. From the chest downwards his body was normal enough – there was nothing to find fault with there – but higher up it was different. He was a joke out of an animated film, a child's cartoon. His head seemed to have been squashed down by some tremendous hammerblow at birth so that his shoulders, if those unlikely arrangements of bone and tendons was what they were, seemed to begin at the level of his coarsely shaped ears, sloping downwards only slightly on each side where his neck should have been. His tormented head was everything that was ugly, something which might have been dreamt up by a Roman sculptor to set off a perfect masterpiece, the triangular face of a satyr set askew, drained of any dignity and made to look still more ridiculous by the lapels of his shirt which because of his lack of a neck were stuck out halfway up his cheeks, like some red appendages decorating his ears. Above the pointed chin, a lopsided smile, a flat snub nose, and slanted eyes which were incapable of looking directly at either of the others in the room for more than a fraction of a second. The gaze would stop for a moment then slide off sideways to fix on the ceiling or the fireplace, as though the owner of the face was absent with his thoughts most of the time, trying to avoid their pity or distaste or whatever else was in their minds.

Observing him dispassionately Axel thought the head, with its roughly cut hair looked more like that of some less-than-holy idiot from a Russian folk tale. A squat and deformed Rasputin.

Johansson wasn't given to flights of fancy like that. After he had got over the shock of seeing his son as he actually was and not as he remembered him he even congratulated himself. When he recalled what Carl had looked like at birth, when his wife had brought him back to Stockholm half in trepidation, half in triumph, he reckoned that his insistence on treatment, repeated intervention by the most skilful plastic surgeons, had paid a dividend although one could scarcely call it a handsome one. Carl should be grateful to him.

However that wasn't a helpful thought at the moment so he suppressed it. He had to move delicately, knowing that the least word out of place would cause his son to slam out of the room and bring this critical meeting to an abrupt and probably permanent end. The recollection of those improvements which he had endured when he was young could still make Carl behave like a child, choke him with resentment. The memory of his original shape and his earlier faces had never been displaced by what the mirror showed him now – something which it was at least possible to look at.

Of course his son ought to be thankful, thought Johansson,

but apart from his disabled body he had a warped and enfeebled soul which made it impossible for him to feel anything as sane or normal as gratitude. In a sterner and more practical age such an infant would have been left out in the bitter snows of midwinter to take his chances. An altogether cleaner and more natural solution. Better for the race. Like a breath of cold air touching a sensitive tooth a pang of regret bothered Johansson. If only he had accompanied his wife to Switzerland for her confinement this problem would never have happened. It would have been dealt with there and then. Strangled at birth. He put the tantalising thought out of his mind. He never allowed regrets to linger – they were a waste of thinking time.

Carl asked, 'Why have I been brought here?'

His voice always came as a surprise at first hearing. Although it issued from a larynx buried somewhere in his chest it was a pleasant baritone.

The father answered, 'Carl, you were not brought. You were invited and you accepted our invitation because you were a sensible fellow who knew that this meeting was necessary. Whatever is decided.'

Axel added, 'We didn't know where you had got to. We had a job finding you.' He had meant to sound friendly but couldn't manage it. This damaged creature had always meant trouble.

Carl swivelled round, was about to speak and then decided not to waste his energy arguing over the impertinence. Instead he took refuge in a long, sidelong stare at the ceiling.

Now the father had to suppress his annoyance at both of them – at Axel's tactless intervention as well. It wasn't like him to make a false move, particularly when one considered the position that Carl might occupy if they couldn't reach an accommodation with him very soon. Didn't his deputy realise how finely balanced this situation was?

Johansson spoke softly, almost apologetically. 'Surely it's not unreasonable? As chairman of the company and head of the family I have to know your intentions.'

'Why?'

It was a deliberately provocative reply because all three of them knew the answer to the question perfectly well.

His father shrugged. 'Because your thirtieth birthday is less than three weeks away.'

For years the date had represented no more than one more neatly written item on the action list which he kept in his mind. In recent months it had emerged as a threat and when Carl had gone to ground and they had been forced to adopt extraordinary measures to locate him the threat had become suddenly urgent. Johansson's plans for dealing with it had been thrown out of gear. Now the day was approaching as inevitably as the final emptying of an hourglass. He couldn't stand and watch the grains of sand subsiding, falling away. He had to act.

Conscious that while he was standing up he was at a psychological disadvantage, Carl sat down in one of the delicate, antique *fauteuils*. 'My great-great-grandfather laid down in his will . . .' he began.

'Not in his will,' Axel interrupted, 'but in the trust deed.' Johansson shot another irritable look at him but he didn't retreat. 'The trust deed,' he repeated. 'The facts must be correctly stated at the outset. Otherwise we won't know where the hell we are.' It was unusual for him to employ even the mildest oath. It seemed to Carl that their customarily relaxed mode of doing business had suddenly become embrittled. Hairline cracks were showing in the enamelled surface.

'Very well. If you want the facts why don't you state them,' he said carelessly, his gaze wandering off again; this

201

time towards the Molitor commode in the corner and the clock with its golden goddess dressed in her floating, immobile drapery.

Axel's next words were spoken without hesitation, as if he were reading from an autocue. 'The trust deed signed in 1874 by Arne Johansson states that the son of the head of the family shall, after reaching the age of thirty years and provided he is mentally competent, take an equal share with his father in the running of the company. The manner in which this is to be accomplished is laid out in detail in the deed.'

Still staring at the clock, as though he couldn't drag his attention away from it, Carl said. 'That seems sensible to me. It gives the heir time to develop the wisdom he will need when in due course he has to take over. It ensures continuity. He is able to benefit from his father's experience. What's wrong with that?'

The silence which followed was complete. Had something gone amiss? Normally his father and Axel operated almost as one, their plan worked out in advance, their tactics fully co-ordinated – like a pair of lions stalking their dinner on the veldt.

Finally Johansson said, 'I am mindful of your welfare – that is all.'

Axel put in, 'As one of the leading figures in the commercial life of Scandinavia you would be exposed to unremitting publicity. Paparazzi outside every restaurant, outside your flat. Your photograph bought and sold by the European press as a tradeable commodity. Is that what you want?'

Not in the press or in the streets but in the circles close to him the envious had sneered at him, called him 'the Coathanger' behind his back. The nickname had spread; neither of them spoke it but both remembered it. Carl replied, 'It is nothing new. I have been there before.'

Couldn't they do better than that?

'You disappeared so we thought that you had grown tired of all that . . . pressure. Understandably in my view,' murmured Axel.

'It is absolutely straightforward. We simply need to know what your wishes are,' his father put in.

'So you said. I had got that far.' Had they nothing else to add?

'There are other facts,' Axel began.

'Such as?'

'The good reputation of the company is vital. You agree?'

'Of course. So?'

Axel glanced at his chief for guidance. Should he go further along that line?

Johansson said softly, 'If you hope one day to become the head of a company like ours you should not need to have such matters spelt out to you in words. However, I will give you a clue. A single word. Lloyd's.'

Carl's gaze went wandering again. 'I am dealing with all that – the process is in hand.'

'How?'

'Why should I tell you that? What I will say is that your own handling of the Danish restructuring didn't do much for the company's reputation either. Look at what has happened to the share price since March.'

'We had the banks eating out of our hands in the end,' Axel protested.

'Considering that you virtually gave them the container stock, that comes as no surprise.'

Johansson broke in angrily, 'We merely adopted a prudent valuation. There was going to be no second chance.'

'You capitulated to the banks,' Carl shot back maliciously.

'We did nothing of the kind. It is the Johansson way. You know that very well. Nothing dubious, no adventures in our accounting practices.' Axel half rose from his seat and subsided again. It should have alerted the older man to what would have been obvious to an outsider – that his son was out to provoke him. It didn't. He went on, 'Because your antics in the London insurance market did so much damage to our name we have had to be more careful than ever.'

Carl retorted, 'All forgotten, months ago, by the public and the press, both.'

Johansson exploded. 'Never! Absolutely not.'

Axel was in despair. The interview was sliding into chaos simply because of the size of the father's ego, the old man's need to prove himself right. There had to be a way of restoring the status quo. He tried to draw Johansson's fire on himself.

'I think Carl may be right. The public memory is very short,' he ventured and found himself ignored.

'Why was it necessary to involve yourself or anyone else in that business? That is what I don't understand. You have no need to make a few extra per cent on your capital by gambling with it. The whole thing was unnecessary.' Carl made no reply. Thinking he had an advantage, his father blundered on, destroying all hope of a reconciliation. 'Unlimited liability. You backed your syndicate with everything you possessed and handed over the management, the underwriting, to somebody else. What sort of commercial judgement is that? Our shareholders won't thank us for importing such expertise into the company. And you involved so many others. The Lundberg brothers, this man Winblad who made all the trouble with the press, young Engström. Have you any idea what that did to our relationship with Engström Shipping?'

Carl swayed from side to side with frustration, trying to break in. At last he managed to say, 'I told you. I am taking steps to resolve the problem.'

Johansson was no longer listening. By now he had become completely reckless – his voice was unrelenting, cutting through the space between them. 'Carl, you have always been a liability to the family. A burden which we did not deserve. Now you are proposing to make yourself an encumbrance to the company which it has taken four generations of effort to build up. Go back to wherever you have been hiding and leave us to manage the business. Just be thankful for the money and power it gives you.'

His son looked slyly at him, then he spoke. 'I give you notice that on my thirtieth birthday I intend to take up the responsibilities laid on me by Arne Johansson's will.'

'Trust deed,' said Axel automatically again. 'Not will. Trust deed.'

'I shall fight this,' his father announced.

'On what grounds?' demanded his son.

'On the grounds that you do not conform to the conditions laid down in the deed.'

'How is that?' Carl enquired.

'You are not mentally competent. I regret to say it, but there is no doubt about it in my mind.'

Axel sat stock still and considered. There was nothing to be done. Their position was hopelessly compromised now. The old man hadn't the faintest hope of proving that allegation in court; the question had been resolved years ago when he had insisted on having his son examined by psychiatrists in an earlier attempt to stop him from qualifying for his inheritance. It had been a miserable failure. Not even the most compliant of the specialists had been willing to testify that Carl was mentally unfit.

Axel knew that they had lost game, set and match. He felt betrayed by Johansson's inability to stifle his own feelings and make the special effort that was needed to resolve this crucial difficulty. At the moment of crisis his chief had allowed himself to wallow in a self-indulgent anger. The man didn't deserve his position, he hadn't the self-control, the sheer guts that were necessary to win this kind of battle. Axel wondered if perhaps the time had come to switch sides – although he had to admit that allying himself with Carl, that monstrosity looking so incongruous in the elegantly fashioned eighteenth-century armchair, wasn't an attractive alternative. The monster seemed to have withdrawn into himself, to have switched off his attention. Then he began to laugh. Oh God almighty, thought Axel, perhaps he really was round the bend. Perhaps they both were, father and son. He had a sudden vision of the big ship *Johansson* heading for a black reef, with J in the grip of a manic rage shouting orders from the bridge and Carl in the bow laughing uncontrollably as the rocks came nearer and nearer. Things must be bad if they provoked such images in his well ordered head.

He heard Johansson repeat, 'You are not mentally competent,' and watched, frozen, as Carl rose from his seat and went over to the Molitor commode. Approaching the clock which seemed to have fascinated him throughout the interview he dragged it up and, hoisting it above his head, advanced on his father. It was heavy, the gilded sculpture hard and jagged, capable with enough energy behind it of inflicting a terrible wound. Johansson stood up, unafraid or apparently so. Carl had raised the clock at full stretch above him, had drawn it back, almost off balance, ready to bring it down on his father's head. The movement had taken Axel by surprise. It wasn't until that second that he woke up fully to what was happening; he exploded into action, launching himself at Carl, charging at him shoulder first. The moment he made contact, Carl lost his footing as the rug he was standing on slid along the polished parquet. He fell to the ground, his head just missing the marble surround of the

206

fireplace. The clock slipped from his hands, skidded across the floor and hit the skirting.

In the silence that followed Axel picked himself up while Carl lay where he had fallen, under the humiliating gaze of the other two. It was his father who spoke first, his voice more or less under control. 'As I have just said. Neither mentally nor physically competent. You have made the case for me.'

That was nonsense, Axel thought, as he went over to draw Carl to his feet, realising, as if the thought carried some significance, that he had never touched him before. When he did so he found that it was no different from touching the skin of anybody else. The fact surprised him.

For the time being neutrality was the best course. He hoped that Carl would recognise that he had saved him from himself and give him credit for it. The son showed no sign one way or the other as he went and picked up the clock and put it back where it belonged as though the episode meant nothing, as though they had been rehearsing a play.

Johansson had picked up his mobile phone and summoned the man in the blue suit who was now in the doorway, alert, waiting for Carl to make another move. Instead the son lurched past him, pushing him aside. The man glanced towards Johansson for instructions, and receiving no sign stood back, his heels clattering on the floor.

Axel went over and checked the clock for damage. The glass had been smashed – there was the streak of a fresh and unsightly crack across the marble base, tiny chips of marble missing and the gilt surface of the goddess had been scraped here and there. It could be repaired of course but it would never be its pristine self again. It glared its reproach in the otherwise perfect room – an exact symbol of their failure.

Johansson seemed to be oblivious to what had occurred. He said, 'I was right of course. He isn't sane.'

Axel felt a stab of hatred for the stiff-necked old man. Couldn't he see what a mess he had made of all this?

'He has to be stopped,' Johansson continued obstinately.

There was no point in trying to humour him; he needed to be brought back to earth. 'Not feasible. That objective is out of sight.'

Johansson was still absorbed in his own line of thought. 'He is the end of our line anyway. Can you imagine any woman going to bed with that – having it on top of her – producing its children? The time has come to find new blood. You must take his place.'

Nobody was more conscious of his own virtues than Axel, nobody more aware of how well qualified he was, but he was a realist. It was a daydream.

'He must be removed from the scene.' Removed? 'It can be done.'

Of course it could be done, thought Axel. What was the going rate? Ten, twenty thousand dollars perhaps? That wasn't the point. There were implications . . . the inhibitions which were bred into one.

He looked at Johansson with a kind of respect. Nobody could say that he wasn't capable of thinking the unthinkable.

Chapter Fifteen

Bowing gallantly the tall blond police officer handed Jenny into his launch offering some small joke or compliment in Swedish as he did so. When she smiled back almost with complicity Ramsay was taken by surprise by a twinge of jealousy. The policeman was cheerful – probably glad to be taken out of the office by an investigation in the skerries.

Sending spray flying out sternwards the launch bounced and swayed across the water. She seemed to be exhilarated – facing forward into the wind, a tendril of hair whipping against her cheek – still glancing now and then with an indulgent smile at Persson, the policeman. The slipstream did nothing for Ramsay except make his eyes water.

It didn't take long to reach Elvö. He recognised the shop – the old man hadn't bothered to run the flag up the mast today – and as they roared past the point he saw the island where she had marooned him. That was it, wasn't it? Yes, because on the other side lay a broad vessel painted a smart dark blue, at anchor – there were anchor chains at either end. Amidships it had a squat black crane which was not yet in use. Over his shoulder Persson spoke a couple of sentences to Jenny and leaning back she relayed them to Ramsay in English. Only one or two words reached him above the noise of the engine.

'Necessary . . . solid platform . . . a big lift.'

They seemed to be making a meal out of raising the crate or whatever it was which he had discovered down there on the bottom, beneath the buoy. Admittedly it had felt solid, enormously dense to him. Feeling a misgiving, he shouted to her, into the wind, 'I hope I didn't exaggerate the weight.' She grinned and wagged a finger at him in mock reproof.

Once they had scrambled aboard the vessel they were introduced to two frogmen, ready and waiting to make their first exploratory dive. While the arm of the crane was swung out over the water, Jenny briefed the first of them. He flashed a smile at her – she seemed to be popular today – before pulling on his mask and checking it. Then he rolled backwards into the water close to the long blue rope snaking down from the buoy into invisibility below. The other followed him.

On board, they waited for one of them to break the surface again. But when the black head with its facemask appeared, instead of signalling for the crew to lower the cable the diver swam to the side of the boat; climbing inboard he gave some rapid instructions to the crew of the crane.

'He wants a net to be lowered,' Jenny reported. A net? There was no need for that. The crate, box, or whatever it was already had a net around it. He knew it had; he had felt it. All they had to do was to secure their hawser to it and hoist the whole thing up. Besides, they wouldn't be able to get another net underneath it. It was too heavy – he was equally sure of that.

He saw the police officer glance at Jenny with a look that was more professional than hitherto – a look that had a touch of doubt in it, or concern perhaps. Ramsay wasn't sure which.

The crew had rigged their net, half of it hanging free to make the job easier for the men down there. The winch whined as the net was lowered smoothly into the water. Then there was silence except for the lapping of the water against the hull.

Jenny looked towards him, covertly, as though hiding her glance from Persson, almost as though she feared that something was amiss and was seeking reassurance from her confederate. Ramsay sidled over to her. What was the penalty in Sweden for wasting police time? Not much. They could live with it.

'Why did the frogman need a net? Did he say?' he murmured.

She shook her head.

'Didn't you hear what he said?' he insisted, as if the second question might produce a more helpful reply.

'Don't know. He just asked for it. That was all.'

'But they don't need one,' Ramsay protested.

He felt himself wanting to move away from her, to put distance between them as though somehow that would restore their innocence. No, that was too strong a word. Their respectability rather.

Perhaps someone had already been and collected the crate – drugs, arms, whatever it was those men were smuggling. Or suppose he'd got the whole thing wrong, suppose that rectangular mass he had located down there was no more than a home-made weight for a fisherman's buoy and he had involved Persson and his team in a wild goose chase. No, neither was likely since there was obviously something on the bottom which they wanted to retrieve.

Otherwise they wouldn't have asked for a net. Why on earth did they need another net?

The winch jerked into life, but a second later someone shouted a sharp warning at the operator and halted it. A voice barked a hoarse comment and somebody chuckled; to them it was just a job of work. Then they all settled down to wait again.

One of the frogmen came to the surface again, making it boil and swirl as he did so. Then one black arm sent a signal to the operator and the winch began in earnest.

When the dripping net came into view Ramsay couldn't see exactly what it contained. It was just a large black mass silhouetted against a background of scintillating water and then the bright sky. What he could see, though, was that it didn't look like the square-sided object he had glimpsed underwater – it didn't have the same edges. The arm of the crane swung it slowly inboard – gently, almost reverently – and lowered it on to the scrubbed deck. An elongated shape with a bulbous mass at one end, patches of white against the black net, glimpses of cloth. Two of the crew moved forward to unhitch the bundle and open it up to expose what lay inside.

The flesh of the face was bluish white. Water streamed across the pale blue eyes staring upwards and through the blond hair darkening it, spreading in a slowly enlarging stain on the deck. It dribbled from the slack open mouth, then, as somebody tugged at the edge of the net, gushed in a sudden spurt as the head fell sideways.

Jenny's jagged scream tore the air, startling a clutch of gulls on the shore of the island opposite, sending them soaring above the dark firs. She stood with her fists clenched, trying to prevent the next outburst, then clutched in desperation at Ramsay's arm, her fingers clamped on it, tighter and tighter as she fought to contain herself.

It was the corpse of her brother.

Ramsay looked down at it helplessly, at its legs. Where the feet should be was a metal drum – it looked like the bottom half of an oil drum. With one arm round Jenny whose face was buried in his jacket he leaned forward slightly to get a closer look. The drum was filled with a grey mass of what looked like cement or concrete. Bengt Winblad's feet disappeared into it as though they had been cut off at the shins – they were encased in it. It was incongruous, an old-fashioned mobster-style killing. But this wasn't the East River he had been fished out of; they were in law-abiding Sweden not many years short of the twenty-first century. His hands had been tied behind him. Whoever had done it would have had to gag him while the concrete was setting around his feet. The gag must have come adrift while he was struggling down there in the water, and that was no surprise. Ramsay wondered what had happened to the crate, his crate – he felt a certain proprietory interest in it. Gently he patted Jenny's back, heaving with long automatic sobs. He too was shaken, and sorry for her – that was as far as it went.

One of the crew shrugged as though to say 'nothing to be done'. There was a hiatus for a moment – nobody seemed to be clear what should happen next. They stood and waited for the captain to come down from his little bridge to consult Persson. The two men spoke in solemn official voices, each sounding conscious of his own responsibility and its limits. With Jenny out of action Ramsay had no means of knowing what had been said. When and where would the two of them be required to start explaining themselves? There was going to be a lot of that to do. How long would it take? Would they be detained? He was due to meet Smith tomorrow.

When the body had been taken away and they had completed the cheerless journey back to Alvarö, Persson was distant but sympathetic. He would have to question them both but was prepared to delay the interview until Miss Winblad was in a better state to talk. No, she shook her head decisively; she wanted to get it over while she still remembered the details she told him as she led the way to the *parstuga*. Uncle Henrik came to the door – he was alone. Lars and Gunilla were out in the woods and the children were with them, he said. It took a moment or two for the story to register with him. But as soon as he realised why the policeman was there he bustled about clearing the dining table of the mugs and plates from their breakfast, helping Ramsay to find chairs for them, while Jenny waited, isolated in the centre of the room, with the policeman. When Ramsay followed Henrik into the little cubicle of a kitchen with the crockery in his hands, Henrik muttered something to him in Swedish in a whisper nodding his head portentously. Ramsay didn't need a phrasebook to get the gist. Bengt had it coming to him, the other man was saying.

When Ramsay went to sit down at the table Persson looked at him sharply. 'I will speak to this lady in private, so you will go somewhere else please. You will not be required to wait long.'

Ramsay went outside and sat on the cement step listening to the rise and fall of the two just-audible voices inside. A short singsong question in the policeman's light baritone followed by a longer more hesitant reply from Jenny. Sometimes there would be a pause while she seemed to be straightening out her thoughts – then a quick rush of words. Was she keeping close to the truth? How close? He had no idea. Now and then he thought he caught the word Bengt – that was all.

After about twenty minutes she was released, pale faced, her eyes still tearful, and Ramsay took her place. A cassette recorder on the table between him and the policeman, Ramsay told the exact truth. He wasn't the kind of man who in this situation would do otherwise. If there were discrepancies between his story and Jenny's because she had omitted or fabricated anything Persson would have to make up his own mind. The policeman fussed with the machine. No, Ramsay confirmed, he had no objection to their conversation being recorded.

Persson glanced at the series of questions he had jotted down in English on the reporter's notebook in front of him and fired off the first of them.

'How did you come to be spending the night on that island?' With the point of his pencil he indicated a small elliptical shape on the mariner's chart in front of him. He spoke a few words into the recorder – to identify presumably the island in question.

Ramsay was chary. He needed to orientate himself.

'Where was the wreck found?' he demanded. Persson made a faint pencil cross on the chart. Yes, that was it. Ramsay tried to make his explanation sound convincing. '. . . I daresay Jenny Winblad has told you how it happened?' he concluded. Persson made no comment but ticked off the first of his questions.

'Miss Winblad has identified the dead man as her brother Bengt. Did you know him?'

Ramsay nodded.

With his pencil the policeman indicated his black box. 'Say so, please,' he said. 'The recorder does not have eyes, you see.'

Of course the bloody thing hadn't; Ramsay cleared his throat and said, 'I had met him once. Yes.'

'How did that come about?'

'Do you want the whole story?'

'Please.'

So Ramsay gave it to him. Lloyd's, the London insurance market, the Names Association. He spared him nothing. That didn't bother Persson who seemed to welcome the wealth of detail – obviously he liked amassing facts. Giving

215

Ramsay an encouraging smile, he gravely ticked off the second question on his list.

Then he took him stage by stage through the arrival of the schooner, the dropping of the buoy. He was asked to repeat his description of the container, the crate or whatever it was, that he had found beneath it, lying on the granite bottom of the sound. He was not asked to speculate on how it had come about that the weight on the end of the line had been switched in such a macabre way. Nor on the odd coincidence that the dead man's sister had been involved in the events leading up to the discovery of his corpse. Persson was a methodical man who began with the simple information. There would be plenty of time later on for them to fit it all together into a story.

When he had squeezed the last fact out of Ramsay he wrote down his name and the address of his hotel on a slip of paper and placed it carefully with the cassette of his evidence.

'Am I free to leave?' asked Ramsay.

'Why not?'

'I may wish to return to London before long.'

Persson scribbled a number on another slip of paper and handed it over. 'Please telephone me on that number a day or two before your departure. We may need to have another talk with you.' In their leisurely and civilised quest for a solution to this unusual puzzle.

That was all.

It was Uncle Henrik who accompanied the policeman to the landing and saw him off, leaving Ramsay on his own. Jenny had disappeared, presumably in search of Gunilla and womanly comfort. Perhaps she was right about her brother – that he had been involved in some dubious business with the East. Anders's dealings with him, and the kind of stock that he held in his shop pointed to that.

Another thing. The two underwriters of the SJ syndicate would no doubt feel easier now that Bengt was out of the way.

Why had he been killed in such a theatrical fashion though? Why moor him to the buoy when simply by tipping him over the side anywhere else in the Baltic the murderer could have prevented his corpse from ever being found? Who would want to draw attention to Bengt's departure from life, and why? Perhaps he would get the answer to that question when he met Smith tomorrow, Ramsay thought.

When he told Jenny that he had to return to Stockholm, she asked to come with him. She didn't want to have to go back to the house she had shared with her brother to face the traces of his recent presence on her own.

Since seeing his body, his face flabby, streaming with water, on the deck of the recovery boat, her behaviour had appeared mechanical, action and reaction costing her a disproportionate effort. Now, on the ferry from Alvarö into Stockholm, she brightened up a little, tried to take an interest in Ramsay's affairs – because of what he meant to her now.

Her feelings towards him had been transformed by that episode on the island so quickly. It was strange. A few minutes on her back, a few moments of ecstasy, and now she found she could scarcely drag her gaze away from him. She was intimidated by the risk she faced now – by the price she would probably have to pay. Still she knew that she couldn't have survived the stress of her recent trauma without him and at least her feelings demonstrated that she was still alive.

She asked him dutiful questions about his forthcoming meeting with the underwriter, trying to tease out the links between the three of them – Smith, her Bengt, her Charles.

She did her best to follow when he explained, with patience yet again, the workings of the Lloyd's insurance market.

'Excuse me,' she said penitently, 'but what is reinsurance? Remind me, please,' and sitting beside her on the long seat next to one of the windows on the lower deck Ramsay did his best to tell her, losing confidence as he found himself exposing gaps in his own knowledge – making her confusion worse, he thought. She was clear about one thing, however. That this man he was going to meet had ruined her brother. Therefore he was an enemy. Dangerous, irresponsible. How could it be otherwise when he had put the fortunes of so many people into hazard?

He glanced at her white face, the face of a shaken schoolgirl, and he wondered whether her judgement was any more mature. Perhaps murder was too rare a crime in Sweden for her to understand how strong the motivation for such a premeditated killing had to be. On second thoughts, did he himself have any better idea of how strong Smith's motive might be, especially when behind him stood that partner of his, Johansson, the one with the slightly sinister nickname – the Coathanger. He was a completely unknown quantity, merely an outline, waiting to be filled in.

'You must beware of the man you are going to meet.' She gestured with one slight hand towards the landscape outside the wide window beside them. 'Look out there. How empty it is. How few people. How few police. Most of Sweden is like that. When you meet him don't let him persuade you to travel anywhere with him away from town.'

Only her desolate look stopped him from laughing. Yes, he agreed hastily, Sweden must be an ideal place for getting rid of a body. It was just as well that her countrymen were civilised, because the whole place was ideal for corpse disposal. All the more odd, he thought again, that whoever had done away with Bengt Winblad had left his weighted remains tied to a bright blue buoy – advertising it to any passing boat.

'This man Smith. He may have killed my brother,' she insisted in a fierce whisper, afraid of being overheard by one of the other passengers. She went on, 'I suppose if he did kill Bengt he won't be at the café this afternoon. He wouldn't go to meet a person he has just killed.'

That, thought Ramsay, was exactly what he would do. In some ways she was an innocent.

He had time to accompany her to the house in Biskopstorget. When she unlocked the door and led him inside he found that nothing had changed – the Chinese Chippendale clock was still there, the rugs.

Seeing him looking round she said hastily, 'It is all here, your furniture. You can make arrangements for it to be shipped now, can't you?' The death of her brother had resolved their dispute.

Moving closer to him, bringing herself into his ambit, she stretched out a hand and touched his arm. It was not the gesture he expected from somebody as aloof as she had been. The hand lingered there awaiting a response from him, asking for comfort because she had nobody else to turn to. It was the penalty she paid for her self-sufficiency, her fierce independence. Rising up on her toes she kissed him on the cheek, her face wet with new tears against it. He held her there, feeling her small shoulder blades under his hands, and heard her voice close to his ear saying solemnly, 'You must be very careful.'

Begg stood in the half light near the entrance of the *Vasa* museum, huge as a hangar. Behind him loomed the wooden hull of the pride of Gustavus II's navy, the warship which had heeled over and sunk on her maiden voyage in 1628 and which had been recovered from the bottom of the sound thirty years earlier and restored. Unique. On her high stern castle the baroque carvings designed to overawe her enemies were back in place – a lion's head grinned from above each gunport. The rising ramps which surrounded her enabled visitors wandering along them to inspect her from stem to stern, from any height or angle.

Because he was unsure of himself in a strange city and he was determined to avoid giving Quist any cause to complain, Begg had given himself longer than he needed to locate the museum. With time to spare he had already carried out his own inspection of the vessel and the artefacts which she had contained and had read the story of a hand-to-hand encounter between Polish and Swedish ships during the Thirty Years' War. That had caught his imagination because it had the smell of blood and smoke about it. Loitering by the door waiting for Quist he thought of it again and it made him hanker again for a bit of action.

Quist came in briskly through the entrance, dressed in a dark blue suit, swaying to avoid a couple of tow-headed children. 'You are here. Good,' he said to Begg without pausing, walking straight past him, expecting him to follow on, towards the exhibition area. Obediently Begg fell in behind him. The man had been generous with expenses if with nothing else – now that he had got this far and the end of the job was in sight he wasn't going to give his employer any excuse for ditching him.

Quist had halted, his attention suddenly taken by a showcase containing the remains of crude surgeon's instruments which had been salvaged from inside the ship after it had been raised from the bottom of the sound. The light spilling from the exhibit caught the man's thin face – intent, unemotional. Begg waited.

220

Quist looked at him and said, 'I do not need you this time.'

'This time' – what did he mean by that? Begg asked himself what had changed. Was he going to be sidelined? It had happened to him before. Ditched in a foreign country.

'Wait a moment,' he said. 'Just you wait . . .'

'No. It is for you to wait,' Quist replied pedantically. 'The next task is for only one of us. Me.'

'It won't make any difference to the money? My money?'

Quist shook his head.

The tension in Begg's arms and hands relaxed a little as the danger that he might have to return to 27 Freshwater Walk receded.

'So what do I do?'

'I told you. Wait,' Quist replied impatiently, reaching into his inside pocket for a slim black wallet, producing a neatly folded slip of paper from it. He handed it over. 'This is the time and place for our next meeting. Do you think you can find it?'

Begg looked down at the paper, the name of the rendezvous indecipherable in the half darkness. 'I got myself here, didn't I?' he asserted. 'On time.'

Quist didn't argue. 'Just be there,' he said.

Chapter Sixteen

There were cafés in Gamla Stan which boasted silver coffee
kettles and serving tables laden with regiments of delicate
pastries attended by pretty and amiable waitresses, but the
Crown was not one of them. It was not at all like that.
Although it was in a good trading position it still lacked the
one essential item for success – customers. Except for
Ramsay, of course.

He ordered a cup of coffee and finding a trace of purple
lipstick on the rim he pointed to it mutely. Wasting no words
either, the woman behind the counter poured the rejected
coffee away and gave him a fresh cup. She did not bother to
apologise. He could see for himself what the place was like –
a café which had given up the struggle. She went back to
primping her faded sandwiches and rearranging her maz-
arins, her Danish pastries and cinnamon buns – moving the
stale ones to the front again in an attempt to maximise their
sales potential. A vain attempt because there was nobody
there to buy them. Except Ramsay.

He took his coffee and sat down on one of those bentwood
chairs which belong in cafés all the way from Scandinavia to
the Mediterranean. The decor had the same ubiquitous
quality to it. A false porthole in the wooden panelled wall
with a maritime scene painted behind it – the sea too bright
a blue. A pair of reproduction brass candlesticks. A curtain,

which could have been cleaner, guarded the private spaces behind the counter. The proprietress went back there and left him to himself.

Ramsay wasn't late. The clock in its cheap pine frame hanging on the wall told him there was still a minute to go before three o'clock and his watch said it was correct.

He was facing towards the street. A man with his hands in his pockets strolled into view but his attention seemed to be caught by something in the window of the next shop and he passed on.

As Ramsay was taking a sip of his coffee somebody else appeared. Because the cup was half obscuring his view he put it down, feeling the hairs on the back of his neck rise as the man peered in. Was it an English face, one that might belong to a man called Smith? It was difficult to tell. Brown eyes, a carefully shaved chin above an open-necked candy striped shirt and a loose fitting linen jacket. He gave a sharp push against the café door and walked in, ignoring Ramsay as he went up to the counter. The chair of the owner scraped as she shifted on it and got reluctantly to her feet. The newcomer glanced round at what was on offer and instead of speaking, pointed at a can of some local soft drink; then his finger stabbed at a pastry dark with raisins and cinnamon. Having progressed that far without speaking a word he produced a handful of loose change from his pocket and invited the woman to take her pick. Only then did he turn towards Ramsay. However, he didn't speak but instead he sat down at the next table, the expression on his face hard to make out because the strong light from outside laid it in shadow. He set down his plate and glass and pulling at the ring on his can of drink he peeled off the triangular aluminium seal and put it down beside them. Each movement was deliberate, almost as if rehearsed. After inspecting the glass to make sure it was clean he poured the lime green contents of the can into it. A fastidious man caught out by his surroundings. Yes, an Englishman; it had to be Smith. He seemed ordinary enough – the man whose incompetence or worse had brought despair and ruin to so many. I ought to be feeling dislike for him, Ramsay thought. Animosity, indignation, a flush of aggression, but there was nothing there except a sense of arriving. Was that it?

'Herr Winblad, I believe. This is an unusual place for a meeting. I would have preferred somewhere more conventional. However, it will have to do I suppose.' The voice was high which was a surprise – almost a flute of a voice – and so artificial in its tone that it made even that straightforward statement sound false somehow.

Ramsay said, 'I am not Bengt Winblad.'

The other man didn't reply for a moment. Then he said, 'But you must know him otherwise you wouldn't be here. Did he send you?' The words sounded just as one might have expected they would – wary, as though the speaker imagined he had been tricked; as if, contrary to the ground rules already agreed for this meeting, he was being confronted now with an agent whom Winblad had sent in his stead. A lawyer perhaps. Somebody he didn't want to meet at any rate. There was a nice touch of anger there as well, alongside the suspicion, thought Ramsay.

'No,' he answered, 'he didn't.'

'In that case who the hell are you?' demanded Smith. He looked at his cinnamon bun with discontent, seeming to have decided that it was better left alone. Still not convinced by what Ramsay had said, he added, 'What standing do you have? Are you a go-between of some sort? I agreed with Winblad that this should be a private meeting on neutral ground. A meeting of principals. I made that crystal clear to him.'

'He didn't send me,' Ramsay insisted. 'I am Charles Ramsay.'

'So?'

'My father, Ernest Ramsay, is one of your Names.' He corrected himself, '. . . was one of your Names. He has resigned from your syndicate – all his syndicates.'

Who the hell was Smith to lay down conditions? Of any kind? To anybody?

The man gave out an ostentatious sigh, thrusting his arms wide in exasperation. 'Why am I being pursued like this? Why can't you people be patient?' His counter tenor's voice became suddenly businesslike. 'I've heard that story before. When did your father resign?'

Ramsay hesitated. It would save time to be candid. 'The date's uncertain, or to be more exact, I'm not certain about it. He maintains that he wrote to you and we have a note that says he did.'

Smith scoffed. 'Really. Did you consult our people?'

'Yes I did. At Lloyd's – and in Ventnor I saw Barbara Russell.'

'The super efficient Barbara. My right hand. She would know. What did she have to say?' Smith asked.

A drunken woman in a deserted office, whirling on an office chair like a child, a grey-haired child, an infant in late middle age. Surrounded by steel cabinets full of records which by now would be vulnerable to any prowling vandal.

Ramsay chose his words with care. 'She wasn't able to help me this time. She seemed to have troubles of her own.'

'Stewed was she?' Smith asked in matter-of-fact tones.

'Very,' Ramsay agreed. 'I couldn't get any sense out of her at all.' Smith appeared not to know that she too was dead. Was there any reason why he should? Ramsay went on, 'So that's why I'm here. To try to establish whether in fact a mistake was made. That's why I contacted Bengt Winblad – to get to you.'

Smith burst out, 'Winblad's the head of the action group. He ought to be here himself. Why isn't he?' On the point of speaking again he subsided as though ashamed of his petulance.

Ramsay shrugged his shoulders, still waiting for Smith to betray that he knew the answer to his own question.

There was a noise from the recess behind the counter and the face of the café owner appeared for a moment between the curtains, discontented because their conversation was too loud and too long for the modest number of crowns they had spent in her place.

Smith ignored her. 'So you thought Winblad would lead you to me? Why should I have the answer?'

'I was told that the syndicate records were incomplete and that you had taken most of the key documents with you.'

'Who told you that?' Smith asked.

'Clarke.'

'Scarcely one of my friends.'

The other man's gaze wavered and left Ramsay's face. He glanced away towards the street outside. Clearly his interest was waning. It was the mention of Clarke's name that had done it. Ramsay realised too late that he shouldn't have revealed that he had approached the organiser of the UK action group as well. His only hope was to try to engage Smith's sympathy before he decided that he was wasting his time and left. Smith got up from his chair. Ramsay hurried round to place himself between the man and the door.

'Look, let me tell you how my father became involved with SJ Underwriting,' he said and launched into the story. How the old man had trusted his bank, had accepted its advice without comprehending the risks he was taking at Lloyd's – the meaning of the two words 'unlimited liability'.

But now that he had the chance to put his case to the man at the centre of his problem he felt his confidence seeping away as he spoke. It sounded unconvincing, inconclusive.

Perhaps the truth was that there had been a clerical error – nothing more than that – thought Ramsay, calling to mind Barbara Russell's erratic behaviour at Avalon, remembering her on her hands and knees outside the back door of her home, then rising up in muddy disarray. It wasn't an encouraging picture.

SJ Underwriting had handled the affairs of hundreds of Names – he was looking for a needle in a haystack. Besides, why should Smith bother himself with the complaint of one obscure East Anglian landowner when he had such devastating problems of his own?

Ramsay stood in front of him, his statement made, trying to think of something else that would hold the man's attention, swing it his way. 'Clarke was right about the syndicate's records, wasn't he?'

Smith made as if to push him to one side.

'Let me examine them,' Ramsay requested.

'It would take too long and there isn't time. I have a journey to make – four hundred kilometres. Since Winblad isn't here I shall have to go without him.' Smith muttered the last words to himself.

'Where are you going?'

'Egnaby. It's inland. I have to meet my partner there. I have to go now. If I don't make the rendezvous I may lose touch with him altogether.'

'I could come with you,' Ramsay said on the spur of the moment. He had nothing to lose by the suggestion.

Smith looked him up and down, weighing up the choice between confrontation and co-operation – whichever would get him on his way most efficiently. He had that instant in which to make up his mind.

'Very well, why don't you?' he said. 'It's the only way you'll get anything out of me.'

Jenny Winblad cautiously opened the door of her brother's bedroom to see how it felt. So far there was no extra pain; the same numbness, that was all. She went into the low-ceilinged room. There was a shirt thrown on the bed and her foot knocked against something underneath it. She bent down. A shoe. She groped further to find the other one. That was unlike him; he had always been a tidy man – well organised in that if in nothing else. He must have been in a hurry when he had changed into the clothes he had later been found drowned in. His drowning clothes – clinging to him as he stood upright on the bottom of the fjord in the deep cold water with his feet weighted like one of those old-fashioned dolls that always sprang back upright however hard you tried to make them lie down. She shivered.

Her face felt frozen, like a stone mask drained of tears. She had not wept again since Charles Ramsay had left her. If he could have stayed it would have been better.

She had to concentrate. What was she going to do with all her brother's things? She pulled out the drawer of the walnut bachelor's chest – one of the pieces that she had sold. The runners were smooth but it was loose because over more than two centuries the wooden frame had shrunk a little. It would have to be emptied but she didn't need to do that job today. At least everything laid inside it was freshly laundered. Most of the shirts were almost new. Perhaps the Salvation Army could make use of them. As she closed the drawer she thought she heard the single beat of the telephone downstairs. Perhaps it was, perhaps it wasn't. Anyway it was a good excuse to get out of his bedroom.

Yes, it was the telephone.

'Winblad,' she announced.

'Charles here.' The voice was friendly. She felt some barrier break inside – a barrier which she had put in place after the body had been found – and now she felt the tears ready to come. Waiting.

'Did you meet him? Your man? Where are you?'

'At his hotel on – what's it called – Skeppsbron.'

He pronounced it with a hard k – mispronounced it – she didn't correct him.

'That's only a short walk from here. You haven't gone far.' It was commonplace but all she could think of to say. Then she added, off-hand, 'Why don't you come back here when you have finished your business? For supper? Something simple.' She tried to think what she could give him to eat. She had cleared out the refrigerator before leaving for Alvarö but there would be something in the freezer. Then there was no problem because he had solved it for her.

'Thanks but it can't be done, I'm afraid . . .' Although it wasn't a snub – his voice wasn't dismissive – the disappointment made her grip the telephone more tightly. For a moment she had felt the fire that had warmed her on the island begin to glow inside her again and before it had even had a chance to blaze up and take hold he had put it out. She wanted to see him. Apart from that undeniable need of hers she would have welcomed his company because somewhere in this house there was still a ghost.

'. . . I'm going out with Smith to the country to meet his partner, a man called Johansson,' Ramsay went on.

'In the country? Where?'

She had tried already to warn him of the danger without sounding too protective and he had ignored her. Why didn't he take any notice? Why was he so arrogant?

'A place called Egnaby,' he replied.

She nodded vigorously as though he was there in the room with her, as though the gesture would conjure him up. 'Yes.

230

I know it.' She felt a rush of concern for him, on his own in a strange country, too ready to be taken in by its safe, unthreatening air – at a disadvantage because he didn't know a word of the language. She wanted to tell him again but didn't know how to put her warning into the kind of words that he would accept. It was difficult because he was a foreigner. 'It's a long way,' she said doubtfully. 'Are you sure it's . . .' and already he was saying something else.

'So I'm leaving now. I don't know how long I shall be away. Two or three days at a guess. The collection and packing of that furniture will have to wait until I get back to Stockholm. Is that OK?'

'OK. Yes, OK,' she agreed readily.

'It won't inconvenience you?'

'Not, not at all. That will suit me well.'

'You're sure?'

Why did he have to keep asking? Couldn't he think of anything else to say?

'Yes. Sure. Really.'

'There is no telephone but if you need to get in touch with me, there is a neighbour.' He gave her a telephone number. Feeling that number was something intimate, that he had trusted her with something of himself, she made herself write it down with care and repeated it back to him. A man called Hansson, he said.

Why had he done that? Perhaps it wasn't so significant after all. Perhaps it was merely that he wasn't as confident as he sounded and wanted to tell somebody, anybody – her, since she was the only person available – where he was going.

'You need someone to interpret for you,' she said as brightly as she could. 'Why don't I come with you?' But he had already replaced the receiver at his end and she had lost him. Without thinking she stretched out her hand to dial him back. What number? She didn't know, of course she didn't know. He was out of reach. Why had she taken him with her to the island? She knew the answer to that very well. It was too late to regret it.

What was she going to do about all Bengt's clothes? Bengt and Smith – Smith and Johansson. It occurred to her that those were two of the commonest names in their respective countries, two anonymous, rather obvious names. Smith, he was certainly not safe. What about the other one? Johansson. Who was he? Perhaps that was his real name? A memory moved for a moment at the back of her mind, something she couldn't quite get hold of – like trying to pull the end of a thread through the eye of a needle. There was a connection. Johansson and insurance. There had been a fuss in the newspapers, hadn't there, but she couldn't remember much about it – these stories in the press passed by so quickly; flashed for a moment and disappeared. Perhaps Anders would know more since he and Bengt had been very close. Bengt often up there at his shop – involved in activities that she hadn't really wanted to know about in case the knowledge put her relationship with her brother under an even worse strain. Now that he was dead she was free to run her own check on what he had been up to.

She was glad to leave the house, to breathe more freely outside. Locking the front door she hurried up the narrow cobbled street towards Anders's shop. The tall tawny houses on either side seemed to bear down on her, shutting out much of the summer sunlight. She reached Stortorget – the ancient square where she and Ramsay had lunched the day she had met him first.

She didn't know the girl who was minding the shop. A new one with honey-coloured hair, a teenager who stood up, attentively.

Anders was upstairs the girl said, sitting down again,

disappointed because this wasn't a customer for her to practise on.

Jenny looked into the gallery where Anders kept his stock of paintings but it was in semi-darkness with no more than a glimmering of light from the small window. She called out and waited.

When she switched on the light she noticed that the big topographical picture which had been hanging on the end wall was no longer there – the painting of a town scene in Central Europe that had caught Charles Ramsay's eye. Had he bought it? He hadn't mentioned it.

She called out again and heard Anders's voice erupt suddenly behind her. 'Why have you come?'

The question was rough, discourteous. She wasn't going to answer it. Didn't he realise that her brother was dead? – that she was grieving for him? When she turned she found he was standing at her shoulder, almost brushing against her. She caught a scent from him – perhaps it was fear – and saw how pale he was, the shadows of his face washed out by the harsh white light reflected from the white walls and the screens where his collection of pictures hung in rows.

'You should have stayed away,' he complained.

'You know that Bengt is dead and what was done to him?'

He turned his head away in a kind of spasm as though shying away from the image.

She made herself sound vulnerable. 'Now that he is gone I feel that I never really knew what kind of life he led. I want to understand. There are things I need to know. Help me.'

The plea meant nothing to him. He went back to the door and pulled it open.

'I can't talk now. Too much to do.' He was trembling and she had a sudden feeling that if she touched the lever handle of the door after him, the old yellowed brass handle that was never polished, she would find it damp with his sweat. Yes,

Anders was afraid. Was it a guilty fear? Yet he wasn't the kind of man who would be able to risk engineering a death by drowning in broad daylight. Anders, with his neatly printed price tickets on every piece of stock, his obsessively tidy workroom where he framed bland prints for American visitors. He might be capable of one of the more genteel and bloodless crimes. Falsifying his sales-tax liability or dealing in goods without enquiring too thoroughly where they had come from – like the collection of icons downstairs, she suspected. An old-fashioned gangland killing was another thing altogether. She couldn't imagine him sitting waiting for the cement to harden around her brother's ankles while he moaned beneath his gag and squirmed like a cat trying to escape drowning. That wasn't Anders.

What was he afraid of then? That next time it would be his own feet which were going to be encased in cement? She looked down at them, concealed now in nicely polished loafers. Comfortable feet – unready for such a brutal change in their circumstances. From what she had read of the former Soviet empire in the newspapers there were plenty of gangsters over there who were quite ready to drown a man like that. Glad of a chance to show what they were capable of doing – to demonstrate their masculinity.

Yet she doubted if Bengt's death had anything to do with those dealings of his with people from the East. The men who had a real reason for wanting Bengt out of the way were up near Egnaby somewhere and Charles Ramsay was with them. She had to protect him if she could. Without protest she walked through the door which Anders was still holding open for her – he had nothing to tell her that was of any use. Once outside she started down the worn stone steps at a run.

Chapter Seventeen

The boat churned heavily through the water, overladen because apart from the three of them it was carrying provisions from the supermarket in the town and Smith's heavy bags in the bow as well. Sitting amidships, feeling cramped after the long journey up the lake – it seemed longer because it was unfamiliar – Ramsay couldn't think why the man needed to bring so much baggage with him.

His first sight of Carl Johansson, his head half hidden by his anorak, standing in the car park in Egnaby had been a shock. To begin with he had found it difficult to look at Carl when he spoke to him. He felt as though his own straight back and passable looks were almost an affront to the damaged figure in front of him – that he had to tread with absolute care not to offend him. His tone of voice, a gesture, a smile, everything he did was loaded with potential for misunderstanding. Now after a couple of hours he was, gradually, getting used to the sight of Carl and could look him in the eye, although whenever he did so the other man's gaze had a habit of slipping away from him, sidelong. Evidently it was just as hard for him to look at Ramsay, his grudgingly accepted visitor, there only on sufferance, shifting on the wooden plank seat.

They were ill-matched, the other two in the boat. Smith, overdressed for those surroundings making the occasional

sharp remark in that high-pitched voice of his, and Carl
Johansson at the stern, arm along the tiller – careless,
untidy, saying little. When he did speak in his firm baritone
his English was faultless, unaccented. A man of some
education but scarcely the sort one expected to find as a
working partner in a management syndicate at Lloyd's of
London with its self-conscious traditions, its pink-coated
waiters.

Carl Johansson's house wasn't impressive either. More
basic in a way than the *parstuga* at Alvarö, stronger and
more primitive. It too had been built on a platform of
pieces of stone roughly mortared together but the structure itself was more like a log cabin in the wastes of
Canada than one of the traditional houses painted dull red
which one saw everywhere else in Sweden. The timbers of
the walls were massive – roughly hewn to fit together at
the corners and painted with tar centuries ago. The
oblong windows were shallow, many-paned, and the roof
was covered not with tiles but wooden shingles, some of
them lying awry.

They went inside. With a grunt Smith dropped his heavy,
sagging bag in the living room, heavily impregnated with
years of woodsmoke. Carl made no attempt to make his
visitors feel at home, simply called on them to help him stow
away the groceries. They could sleep in the living room he
said, and then disappeared into his own bedroom in a hurry,
as though he found their company painful and couldn't bear
it a moment longer – as though he was addicted to solitude
and needed another fix straightaway. Before he shut the
door behind him Ramsay caught sight of the thick rag mat
nailed over the window to keep out the light. The man
seemed to live like a derelict, someone who had given up
hope. His losses at Lloyd's couldn't have brought him as low
as that so fast. A young man – in his late twenties so Smith

had told him – a little younger than Ramsay himself.

'Some welcome,' Smith complained when they were alone, less put out, though, than Ramsay might have expected. There was still a kind of satisfaction in the way he spoke. 'Which bed do you want?'

They looked equally uncomfortable but clean enough. In choosing the one nearest the window, Ramsay's eye was caught by the coverlet; then he gave it a closer look. It was an antique Kurdish silk embroidery, embellished with silver thread. No, he wasn't mistaken. It was puzzling to find such a thing in this neck of the woods. Then Carl emerged from the bedroom with a pair of binoculars in his hand – expensive German binoculars. They too were at odds with everything else – the paintwork laid waste by the freezing it received every winter; the makeshift bookshelves; the neglected streaks on the windows – the house was his hiding place, that was all.

'I am going out,' he announced off-handedly. 'Have something to eat if you want to.' He made a stiff gesture towards the store cupboard which they had just replenished. 'The stove needs a fire in it if you are going to heat water for coffee.' An awkward man, addicted to solitude, who disliked having them there, having his privacy invaded – resented opening his bedroom door to find strangers inhabiting his living room, strangers whom he had forgotten for the moment.

There might be those who could come to terms with being encased in that grotesque body, Ramsay thought to himself – one or two people who were exceptionally saintly and secure. Not many. He imagined how a young man like Carl would feel; how he would have felt himself – meeting girls, watching them trying to keep the pity or dismay he awakened in them from showing in their eyes, making an effort to treat him like anybody else.

Guardedly, Smith asked the monster, 'When do you want to talk?'

'Have you brought everything we need to have in front of us?' Carl answered, his glance resting on Ramsay for a moment. 'I hope so.'

Ramsay interposed, 'Do you want to speak in private?' and was ignored.

'We'll talk when I return,' Carl told his partner.

While he was out they pulled together a meal of sorts, the need to help each other find their way around Carl's domestic arrangements creating a sort of empathy between them.

Encouraged, after a smoky and lukewarm cup of coffee, Ramsay made his request. Could he go through the records?

To his relief Smith was amenable. It seemed to make sense to him to get it dealt with before Carl came back and they got embroiled in the affairs of the partnership. He went to his heaviest bag and took out a number of files, spreading them out fanwise on the bed. They were in chronological order he said, taking the first of them and handing it over before disappearing outside. 'I'll see where Carl has got to.'

Ramsay got down to work, going methodically through it, page by page. He didn't expect to find his father's letter. That, if it existed at all, was probably buried somewhere in the range of steel filing cabinets in the office in Ventnor. Somewhere though, in these interminable lists of SJ Underwriting's clients and their interests, there might be some clue, a note about his father's status.

He dropped the first file on the floor beside him.

When the others returned, he had been through them all, scrutinised every page, tracing from year to year the changes in his father's syndicates – the gains and losses he had made. Nowhere could he find the least evidence to support his father's story. If the old man had sent the letter either it hadn't been received or it had been ignored.

'I can find nothing,' he admitted. Carl seemed not to hear. He went and put some wood in the stove.

'You might have been better off staying in England, waiting for Barbara Russell to sober up,' said Smith carelessly. 'Why didn't you?'

It was something Ramsay didn't need to be told, sitting in silence, feeling nothing but a sense of anticlimax. After a long and eventful search he had completed the task he had come to Sweden for in a couple of hours. His objective had arrived and, almost without his realising it, had slipped behind him into his past. The job was finished and there was nothing else to keep him there. It was time to go back to the UK and see what steps he could take now to protect his father and save Bressemer. It would be a difficult fight and he wasn't looking forward to the journey.

He turned to Carl. 'I can leave whenever you like. I need your help to get back to Egnaby though.'

The other two exchanged glances. Carl said suddenly, 'Do you have to go straight away? Can't you stay here for a little while? A day or so.'

Smith chimed in, in his high, precious voice. 'We've only just got here. It's a tiresome trip. One of us has to go into town the day after tomorrow anyway. Can't you wait until then?'

They weren't being unreasonable – Ramsay took the line of least resistance. The delay didn't really matter now and he had nothing to gain by making an issue of it.

That evening, before Carl and Smith shut themselves in the bedroom with the files, Ramsay watched his host go out once again with those binoculars of his, the case slung across his chest. He stayed outside for forty minutes or more. Why? Ramsay asked himself. Was he a keen watcher of wildlife? Standing by the white painted wooden windows, he caught sight of him, squat and solitary, sweeping the panorama of the lake in front of him methodically from side to side, seldom pausing, or showing an interest in anything in particular. No, he didn't seem to be on the lookout for birds or animals. At no time did he stop to observe anything with the intensity that one sees in the dedicated naturalist.

Chapter Eighteen

There was a small crowd on the edge of *Isolde*'s customary landing ground. Apart from the four who were next in line to take to the air there was a woman with two small children in tow, waiting for her husband to return to earth. Sitting at the door of her caravan, Karin Andersson eyed her with sympathy. Obviously they had felt that the journey was too hazardous for the two small ones and the wife had been left behind to look after them. It was always the same – the excitement for the men and the routine tasks for the women. Beside them stood a Danish couple who had decided to treat their teenage son to a trip but had stayed grounded themselves – from prudence, financial or otherwise. An outing with *Isolde* didn't come cheap.

Karin looked up at the sky over the trees in the park, her eyes watering slightly because of the glare. There was no sign of Erik yet. It was always the worst moment, waiting just before the balloon was due to return. It was impossible for her husband to time the journey exactly. Sometimes *Isolde*'s blue pear shape arrived over the trees before she was expected and Karin was spared the worst of the nervous moments. Sometimes she was late and the uncertainty was harder and harder to bear.

A late customer. Karin flashed her white teeth in a

bigger smile than usual because this man had arrived providentially to keep her mind off the bad five minutes. She was most deliberate in collecting and counting his money, keeping her head down, making the most of the distraction he offered. As she handed him his ticket she saw that his eyes had taken in the bottle of champagne in its bucket of ice.

'Not for you yet,' she chided him waggishly. 'You must complete your journey first. Then comes the champagne.' She giggled and out of politeness he smiled a limited smile. She looked Quist up and down. Better turned out than that Estonian standing next to him – that shabby Estonian again – but still he didn't look quite right. Not relaxed and casual as most of her customers were but urban, like someone who had escaped from an office for that morning and seemed to be feeling guilty about it. He caught her look and as though he read her thoughts, removed his jacket and hung it loosely behind him over his shoulder with one hand and then loosened his striped red and white tie, trying to make himself a little more like a holidaymaker.

With a small intake of breath, Karin looked up across the trees again for a sign. And there she was, *Isolde*, hanging in the air above their green heads. She glanced at her watch – only four minutes late.

A shiver of excitement rippled through the group. One of the children called out 'Daddy' and was hushed by his mother. The Dane muttered an appreciative word to his wife. Smiling she grasped his arm a little tighter. The morning's experience had been worth every krona it had cost.

Isolde crossed the clear morning air towards them, losing height with a stately lethargy. The well-behaved little group stood well back, the mother taking a firm grip on the child on each side of her, one of them squirming to be free. 'Daddy,' he called out again.

With a gentle roar as Erik gave her a burst of fire to lift her gently at the last moment, her grey wickerwork basket kissed the grass in a perfect landing. The watchers by the caravan relaxed.

While Erik made the balloon fast and helped the passengers to climb down to mother earth, Karin emerged to do the honours with a dewy bottle of champagne in one hand and the beribboned cavalry sabre in the other, taking her station beside the folding table – five champagne flutes arranged upside down on its gaily embroidered cloth. A good housewife to her fingertips she picked up one of them with a smile and gave it a wholly formal rub with a napkin, turning it flashing against the sunlight to make sure it was crystal clean before handing it to the first of the newly qualified balloonists. Catching sight of his parents the Danish youth clasped his hands over his head in a gesture of triumph before taking a glass sheepishly from her.

Meanwhile her husband was shepherding the next group of passengers to the basket in single file with Vallin first in the line and Quist immediately behind him.

Karin laid the blade of the sabre against the neck of the bottle just below the rim and the wire. With a well practised jerk of the wrist she flicked it off – cork, wire, golden foil and a neat ring of glass – the whole of the top of the bottle. The wine foamed over the sliced off neck into the sunlight as she poured it, with a wink of complicity, into an outstretched glass.

Vallin climbed up the neat white steps into the basket – this was the third time he had taken an *Isolde* trip. Where did such a man get the money from? Was he developing some dangerous obsession, some strange addiction to ballooning, Erik asked himself, looking up into the man's face from his position beside the basket, observing it for signs of mania. A madman breaking loose in mid air wasn't at all a comfortable thought. Quist, his jacket still slung negligently over his shoulder, was next to take his place. He looked a safer type, Erik thought. Dependable. Swedish of course.

The little boy was growing more and more frustrated. There was his father, back towards him, waiting glass in hand for his helping of champagne, ignoring him – he needed his attention, wanted to chatter to him about this wonderful balloon, the flight. The child pulled away from his mother's restraining hand and rushed with his arms outstretched towards the man, determined to get him to acknowledge him. Karin was leaning forward bottle in hand. Although its neck wasn't jagged, the rim had broken off cleanly, it was nevertheless lethal, a circle of glass with a razor's edge to it.

She smiled her professional smile and brought the bottle close to his glass to pour.

'Daddy!'

As the child cannoned into his father's back like a small blue panzer the man's head went forward and hit the neck of the champagne bottle. He cried out. It wasn't a loud cry – more a cry of surprise than of pain. That wasn't the sound which clutched at Erik's attention. It was Karin's high-pitched shriek as the blood spurted from the gash and began to stream, mixed with the champagne which had splashed into the man's face, down across his eyes. Erik hesitated, torn between his responsibility for *Isolde* and her passengers and this sudden emergency on the ground. Now he saw that the injured man had his hands to his right eye. What had gone wrong? How bad was it? He wasn't blinded was he? Trying feverishly to recall the terms of his insurance policy,

Erik quit his post beside the basket of the balloon and hurried over to the group to support his wife. Scared by the bloodshed he had caused, the little boy began to wail, his voice rising and falling. His mother ran towards him, scolding.

'Nisse! What *have* you done?'

With all eyes on the casualty it was then that Quist ran lightly up the steps and jumped into the basket of the balloon. Casting off the moorings he pulled at the control to give *Isolde* a bellyful of flame which began to lift her skyward. Erik turned, bewildered.

'Hey. No. Not yet,' he shouted. 'Wait,' holding up a hand as though to halt *Isolde* in mid air. He glanced back anxiously at the victim whose face now had a scarf of blood flowing down it. That moment's delay was fatal – when he looked back she was fifteen metres up, her mooring ropes dangling too far away from him for there to be any hope of reaching them.

He watched helplessly as Quist took a blackjack from his trouser pocket and slammed it down on Vallin's bewildered head. Then the flame roared once again and *Isolde* bobbed up obediently, gathering speed to clear the trees, making towards Gamla Stan. When he reached a height of about a thousand metres Quist cut the heater and in the sudden quiet that followed he propped Vallin against one side of the basket, arranging his head and arms so that they dangled over the edge, keeping him hooked there with his centre of gravity lying high to make the next task easier. Then Quist pushed the big balloon up to her normal cruising height to allay any suspicion on the ground that anything was amiss with her – the big blue hot-air balloon that was an everyday sight over the capital. There was a stiff west wind blowing and it didn't take long for *Isolde*, the fire in her belly renewed now and

245

then, to sail down Kungsgatan – high above the busy department stores and banks, the market stalls under big yellow umbrellas selling T-shirts and folk art to the tourists – towards Gamla Stan.

The cold air rushing past his face began to bring Vallin back to his senses. His body twitched, he groaned, and he began to roll over on the edge of the basket. With one hand on the control of the heater, Quist silenced him with another blow from the blackjack in the other. Then dropping it he grabbed hold of Vallin's legs and tucked them under his arm before easing upwards the unconscious man's body – the head first, then the shoulders – the wicker of the basket clawing at his cheap red sweater. In a couple of seconds Quist had him almost balanced on the edge. With a single heave he pushed his burden over just as *Isolde* passed over the spire of Storkyrkan.

Vallin landed plumb in the centre of the light and airy space which is Stortorget, next to the ice-cream kiosk. Lighter for his departure *Isolde* rose buoyantly, pushing up through the air vigorously like a fisherman's float rising to the surface of a pond. Quist let rip with a gasp of flame as an added incentive. He took much better care of her than he had of Vallin, gave her an altogether easier and slower descent on to an open space on Djurgarden. When Erik reclaimed her, after some serious discussion with the police, he was relieved to find that she wasn't in bad shape at all. It was compensation for the loss of a regular customer. Truthfully he'd never much cared for that scruffy Estonian or whatever he was.

By that time there was no sign of Quist, of course. He'd probably just walked over to Skansen and lost himself in the summer crowds in the amusement park – that was what the police thought. When they questioned the people who had witnessed his sudden departure with *Isolde*, someone said he was of medium height, of stocky build. Yes, said the Danish mother, he was thickset but exceptionally tall she thought. Karin remembered that he had blond hair. When she said that, her husband nodded – but on reflection thought it might have been dark after all. One glance from her and he decided that he was mistaken. One way and another they gave the police a whole lot to go on.

Chapter Nineteen

Smith was at the table marking up a computer sheet, verifying figures from a list at his elbow, too engrossed to notice Ramsay as he brought in the two large polythene canisters that they used for carrying drinking water from the pump and put them down beside the sink. Ramsay was doing the job for the last time since he was leaving in the morning. They would take him in to Egnaby, they said.

Relieved of his burden he straightened up and observed the other man, head bent over the folded sheets of paper, a thin silver pen in his hand, ticking a total here, making a note there – a costly pen, whose nib slid smoothly over the paper, the ink flowing easily. A leftover from his high-living past. He was beginning to be in need of freshening up. He had swapped his linen jacket for a sweater but he hadn't changed his brightly striped shirt since leaving Stockholm and it showed. A lock of hair fell out of place on his head and he brushed it back irritably. When he became conscious of Ramsay's presence there it seemed to bother him, because he stopped work suddenly, slipped the cap back on his pen and laid it down on the table.

'Ramsay you are a remarkably incurious man. Hasn't it ever occurred to you to ask what all this effort of mine is for?' he asked, his tone patronising.

Ramsay wasn't going to let himself be provoked. 'None of my business.'

'You must have given it a thought, once or twice,' Smith insisted.

'I can't say that I'm much interested. You have your problems, I have mine,' Charles replied. His problems – all of them – were down to Smith and his partner. It would have been satisfying to say that, to have made an issue of it, but it wouldn't have served any useful purpose. He simply wanted to make an exit now with as little fuss as possible, return to the UK and leave this incongruous pair to their own devices. There was nothing they could do for him or he for them. Both of them were defeated. Two defeated men in this isolated hideout almost at the edge of Europe – you couldn't get much more remote than this place – shuffling around the evidence of the disaster they had themselves created. Whatever games they played with the figures they couldn't disguise the enormity of it.

Ramsay looked round the room, at the cheap varnished cupboards and bare boards, the elbow chairs dating from the 1950s, the varnish worn bald on the arms, the material of the cushions faded. It all smelt of failure, of unwillingness to face reality, still less to try to do anything to change it.

Smith asked, 'Have you seen Carl?'

'I guess he's out there somewhere,' Ramsay answered. Sensing that the man was looking for a break from his task and wanted to talk, he searched for something harmless to say. 'He doesn't live here all the year round does he? Not in winter?'

'Carl Johansson? Of course not.' Smith spoke the name loudly, his tone scoffing at the idea. Carl Johansson? It touched no chord with Ramsay, had no resonance at all for him. He waited to be enlightened but before Smith had time to explain, Carl himself pushed open the door and shambled into the room. He sat down abruptly in one of the chairs, the top of his head falling weirdly short of the upper edge of the back cushion, creating a distorted composition that cried out to be adjusted somehow.

Glancing at each of them in turn he said, 'Did I hear my name spoken?'

'I was about to explain to him,' his partner replied, turning to Ramsay. 'I have examined our records and established that the extent of your father's loss for the 1988 year of account is £174,126.

'I don't need to be told the figure.'

Twisting the knife in the wound Smith went on. 'Also, part was left open because of the syndicate's exposure to Personal Stop Loss insurance. Correct?'

Indignantly Ramsay leaned forward. 'Yes it was, and whose fault . . .?'

'Wait a moment,' Smith said. 'I am trying to be helpful.'

Ramsay turned to Carl, seeking his support. 'How can it be helpful to go over all this. I know the position exactly. Every detail.'

Carl was looking at him directly, intently, for once, and there was no lopsided smile on his face. It improved his appearance Ramsay thought – but not by much. What was going on? Why had they started this interview? What right did they have to take this high-handed line with him?

Carl asked, 'How do you think of us? As adversaries or allies?'

Ramsay glanced from one to the other and shrugged. Two broken men – the deformed unfortunate who had just spoken and the slightly grubby underwriter beside the window. Friends or enemies? What did it matter which they were?

Smith said, 'Make up your mind.'

'Why should I?' Ramsay shrugged.

'Simply because if he manages to survive the next ten days, Carl over there will become the fourth richest man in Scandinavia.'

Ramsay had to get a grip on himself to avoid laughing out loud. It seemed improper somehow to mock their fantasies.

'We have an idea, you see,' said Carl. 'A very simple plan and my partner James Smith has come here from London to help me execute it.'

Ramsay had never had to cope with anyone who was mentally disturbed before. What was it – mania? he asked himself. It was easy enough to understand how Carl had become unbalanced given the burden of anger and despair that he must have carried since he was a child. Say nothing Ramsay, he counselled himself; the best thing is to let him say his piece.

Carl looked across at his colleague as though seeking his sanction for what he was about to say and received a nod of approval. 'When I do take my place beside my father I must make sure that this Lloyd's matter is settled properly and our name, the Johansson name, is restored in the eyes of the public. Not only is this the right thing to do but it also makes commercial sense.' Carl's voice became more formal as he announced, 'Therefore I am going to pay the losses of all the members of our syndicate – and this includes your father, of course.'

'A great gesture. You are to be congratulated,' Ramsay said carelessly and smiled. He had always found it difficult to play the courtier.

Carl Johansson kept his eyes on him, trying to decide if he was sincere. Or had there been disbelief in that reply? Whilst he was capable of this act of good sense and enormous generosity he was not a man who accepted a slight easily. Ramsay was never to know how close he had been to destroying his father's chances of saving his estate.

Chapter Twenty

Carl Johansson had enjoyed his breakfast. The scent of coffee, the warm sweet rolls they had bought in Egnaby with fresh butter, almost white, spread on them. It was an ordinary enough meal but uncharacteristically he had taken more pleasure in it because he hadn't had to eat it on his own, and he was looking forward to the trip in the boat down the lake that morning. He wasn't altogether pleased that Ramsay had refused to stay on for a day or two, that having got what he wanted – and it was a great deal – the man couldn't wait to get back to Stockholm, Arlanda, London, and that mansion, wherever it was, that his father lived in, to take him the good news . . . Then he remembered the boat's fuel tank – that he hadn't checked whether he needed to refill it.

That was vital. The boat was his lifeline, their route to the outside world. How had he allowed himself to forget? He couldn't and wouldn't trust anyone else with the job – only he understood exactly what had to be done. He had to check the starter, that the fuel line was clean and clear. He would deal with it straightaway, while he was out on his morning reconnaissance.

He went to the big black-painted tank beside the house and filled the can he was accustomed to use, then began to make his way along the track to the jetty. After a short

walk through the trees it opened out and gave him a view
of the lake – it was the first stopping point on his habitual
round. Setting down the can on the grass beside him he
put his binoculars to his eyes and surveyed the edge of the
shore where any danger was most likely to be. It was
improbable that anyone would try to fight his way up
through the dense forest which covered the steep slopes
on either side of the water. It was a calm dull morning and
the surface of the water was as smooth as dark glass,
almost without a ripple. Now Carl looked at the other side
of the lake, his gaze inching down methodically towards
the jetty. There it was in sharp close-up – the grey
timbers, the water lapping around its heavy supports.
There. The movement of his glasses stopped. Something
had caught his attention.

He walked deliberately into the shelter of a clump of
spruce next to the path, then put the binoculars to his eyes
again in order to concentrate on the area around the jetty.
Emerging from cover he went slowly back along the path
until he was sure he was no longer visible from the lake. He
began to hurry back to the house, his gait made more
ungainly by the burden of the can he was carrying.

'You're back quickly,' Smith observed off-handedly, setting down his second cup of coffee. Ramsay was looking
through his bag, making sure he had left nothing behind. He
zipped it up.

'When we arrived here, you saw me tie up the boat, didn't
you?' Carl demanded.

Only half listening Smith answered, 'Yes. Why?'

'I did it properly, didn't I? Made the rope secure?'

'Yes, I think so,' Smith said. How should he know? It
wasn't the kind of thing you remembered.

'The boat. My boat. It's not there,' Carl announced.

'Perhaps the knot wasn't well tied. It must have drifted

off.' So what? It wouldn't be difficult to find it and recover it.

'It's not there,' Carl repeated. 'It's nowhere on the lake.'

Would they have taken it away? That was unlikely. 'They must have sunk it,' he said aloud.

'Who?' Smith demanded. 'Who must have sunk it?'

Carl rocked from side to side with frustration. He couldn't go into that now. There wasn't time to lay out in a convincing pattern the tangle of ill-defined suspicions in his head. It would have been easy enough to smash a hole in the bottom and weight it down with rocks. They must have dragged their own boat up out of the water and hidden it somewhere among the trees along the shore.

'I'll have a look,' Smith volunteered.

'No. Don't go out of that door,' Carl ordered him sharply.

'Come on now,' Smith answered in his high disdainful voice. 'Don't let's be paranoid about this. The boat's slipped its moorings, that's all.'

'I'll come with you,' Ramsay offered, also calling Carl Johansson's courage into question, or his judgement. The idea that suddenly there was an armed enemy out there was nonsense.

'Wait,' Carl called out, in desperation, as they both made for the door.

Now that the operation was underway Quist allowed himself a pang of resentment. It was all very well for his bloody employer to lay down this or that condition in theory but this operation wasn't straightforward. On the ground it wasn't easy, not at all. For one thing there was scarcely more than an hour of darkness at this time of year and for another the only way to approach the house was by water because the forests behind it were impenetrable – thousands of hectares. He hadn't been given enough time to do his planning. In an unwonted burst of lateral thinking he had thought of using a helicopter – the funds would run to it – but the next moment, feeling foolish, he had rejected that idea as hopelessly impractical. It would have scared off the quarry immediately.

So they had to come by water and in silence or as near as they could get to it, which meant rowing the last three kilometres or so in the early hours.

Begg was all for rushing the house and getting it over with, but Quist had quickly stamped on that idea. There was no need to take even that extra fraction of risk. They didn't know what weapons Carl Johansson might have in there, what security systems might be installed. There was no power line to the house. However, there was a fuel tank beside it – there might be a generator somewhere.

When they had observed two extra people, unexpected people, in the house Quist's mind had been made up. The best tactic was simply to stand back and pick them off when the opportunity presented itself. That was what they would do. He was the paymaster and he was in charge.

To get a clear view of the house he had to climb this damnable hillside. He pushed onwards parting low branches which sprang back in his face, stumbling over a thick carpet of moss which now and then collapsed treacherously under his boots, slapping at the midges from time to time. Eventually the climb got easier, the slope gentler and he arrived at a vantage point above the tops of the trees giving him an open view of the house below, a thin trail of smoke trickling up from its chimney.

He took the hunting rifle out of its case and lay down on the thick layer of moss behind a boulder, sighting experimentally along the barrel. A new rifle with its black metalwork unscratched; with the stock against his cheek he could smell the fresh varnish on it and a hint of new oil. A hunting rifle needed no explanation in this part of the world.

He felt a discomfort around his ankle and bent down to unharness his little friend, the ten-centimetre sliver of steel in its sheath which he kept strapped to the outside of his right calf under his sock. It had a ring for a handle so that it could be plucked out of its hiding place with his forefinger when the need arose. Although the need had never arisen yet it was an exercise which he practised every day. Bending down as though to tie his shoelace, then springing up from the ground with the tiny weapon in his hand, his thumb braced along it, ready to drive it into the heart of his assailant. It wouldn't be needed today however and it was in his way. Unstrapping it he tucked the sheath and its contents into his rucksack.

There were one or two branches lying across his front. Taking a claspknife from his pocket he laid down the rifle and crawled forward to cut them away, then moved back, lay down and waited.

It was a simple thing he had to do. When the right man came out of the door he had to kill him. It was an endgame at chess with checkmate very close. He had the three of them bottled up in there – the king, solidly in check now, a rook and a spare and solitary pawn – their space to move diminished now to a couple of squares. No room to retreat behind them, no way out ahead now that he had destroyed their boat. That had been a more difficult task than he had expected and Begg had grumbled. They'd lacked the right tools. What did Begg expect given the time they'd been allowed?

He looked across to the opposite bank and could see no sign of him. Unable to communicate with the man – not a man whose judgement he could rely on – he wished he had had the foresight to bring a two-way radio with him, some means of communication. Communication. The thought

257

inflicted a plunging sense of uneasiness on him. How had he missed that most obvious of possibilities? How? There was no point in seeking a justification for the omission now. Suppose they did have a generator, a source of power in there, and a transmitter of some kind? Or a battery-powered set. That would cut down the time he and Begg had available to beat their retreat by a factor of five. Get down the hillside, make contact with Begg – and how long did it take to get to the other end of the lake? They would need an hour at least which might bring them straight into the hands of the police from the town, who would have plenty of time to locate their car. Easy enough to kill and easy enough to get caught. And if he were caught he knew that he faced a death sentence. Not from a judge – there was no capital punishment in Sweden – but from his employer. That had been made clear right from the outset. There had to be nothing to give the least clue to that man's identity. He was hard, remote, shielded from the reality of his actions by distance, able to avoid guilt by avoiding the images of it. The blood. Like a general far behind the lines in the Great War he made his dispositions and left the risks and the guilt to others. He would have Quist snuffed out without a second thought. Better not to complete the job than to be caught.

At that moment he saw down there the tiny figure of Carl Johansson emerge from the house, fuel can in hand and make his way down the path towards the jetty. Quist watched him through his telescopic sight – the stunted dummy with the abnormal torso, almost headless. Something ludicrous in a carnival parade.

Should he cut him down now? Having reached the point of decision Quist found himself only half sure. Reluctantly he pushed a round into the chamber and curled his forefinger against the trigger – and hesitated.

No. He rolled over on his back and unloaded, the round bouncing against his chest and landing among the moss and twigs on the ground beside him. Taking out the magazine he pressed it back where it belonged. Then he watched his target retreating slowly towards the house until he moved past the cover of the dark branches down there.

He shook his head. Better to wait until all three came down to search for the boat as he had intended that they should, until they were out in the open well away from the house. That would give both him and Begg more killing time. He reloaded and bringing the rifle back up to the firing position he squinted again through the dark rubber eyepiece of the telescopic sight and waited.

Presently he saw the door of the house open, presenting a slot of dark shadow outlined by the white doorframe. His mouth slightly open, he ran the tip of his tongue along his dry top lip expecting a figure to manifest itself in that empty space. The first man. He was there. In his shirtsleeves, ambling out into the open. Where was the next one?

Begg's shot split the silence, echoing and reechoing, its sound bouncing down the valley from one side to the other, and the figure fell to the ground. Quist cursed his associate with sincerity, more than once.

Chapter Twenty-One

Hansson looked down from the top step of his house with interest at the girl standing in front of him, her grey dusty car behind her. Not a new model he noted, not at all. For a moment he thought she was a teenager, too young to drive, and that confused him. He looked round for the adult who had driven her right up to the door of his farmhouse. There wasn't anybody else around.

It was when she said, 'I am looking for Carl Johansson. Do you know where I can find him? It is an urgent matter,' that he realised that she wasn't as young as she looked. A journalist probably. Carl had warned him that this would happen. Those people ought to leave him alone.

He made a doubtful face, turned and called behind him, 'Ulla.'

His wife appeared at his shoulder, dressed in freshly pressed cotton, pressing up against him from behind because of the narrow doorway. The gaze of her pale blue eyes took in the strange young woman, the car. Mrs Hansson was a practical woman. White hair pulled back from her wide brow. A pale, candid face.

'The young lady is looking for a Carl Johansson. We don't know anybody round here with that name do we?'

Ulla Hansson felt her husband's shoulder tensed against hers warning her. 'It's a common enough name but – I don't believe so,' she managed. Lying wasn't her style and it was too difficult to go the whole hog and say no outright.

'Are you sure?' Jenny persisted. 'This friend of mine, an Englishman, was going to visit him.'

She made her little girl face hoping to provoke some sympathy in one or other of them. While they thought she looked decent enough they couldn't be sure. Perhaps she wasn't a journalist, thought Hansson, shifting his feet because he was getting bored with this. There was a cow that needed to be seen to and he'd been told to telephone the vet before ten, otherwise he'd miss him. Jenny could sense his impatience, that he wanted her to leave so that was the last thing she would do. She closed up on him, invading his territory – placed a small intrusive hand on his arm.

'I have to find him, this friend of mine. He may be in danger,' she went on. She was in his way and he wanted her out of it. Hansson's hand went up and stopped short because he didn't dare to push the girl away, not with his wife standing right behind him, at his shoulder. She didn't sound like a journalist.

Jenny put her other hand on his upper arm and put herself within an inch of him. He looked down and wanted to back away but he couldn't because Ulla was there behind him. He could feel her there, warm and solid against his elbow.

The girl produced a slip of paper from her pocket and thrust it in his face. 'Is this your telephone number?' she asked.

Looking over his shoulder Mrs Hansson inspected it and saw that indeed it was. Who was this girl from the city who looked younger than she had any right to? Where had she got her husband's telephone number from and why? He wasn't that sort.

Since he had got to ring the vet, was pinned between the women, Hansson capitulated. 'My neighbour Carl Johansson doesn't like visitors he doesn't know . . . but since you are a nice girl . . .'

Mrs Hansson reserved judgement. She wanted this woman under her eye, where she could see her. She was going to be motherly, she decided. That would be the best thing.

'Come in and have a cup of coffee,' she said tautly. 'You look very tired. Have you come a long way?' And she led the way to her kitchen with its elegant linen curtains which she had woven herself in open work to let the light through – so that visitors could see how well kept it all was. Except that the Hanssons rarely had visitors, living as far out in the country as they did.

There was a small red wound low down on Smith's right shoulder. He bent his head over to inspect it, his hair flopping over his eye.

'It doesn't look too bad, does it?' he asked, suppressing his anxiety as well as he could. 'It felt just as you imagine it does. Like a great thump on the shoulder.' He sounded satisfied that his preconceptions had been borne out in practice.

Ramsay waited for the shot that was meant for him, that might be going to kill him, and managed, to his surprise, to keep his voice from faltering. 'We'll get you back inside.'

When they started to lift the wounded man, his blood was pumping out on the grass beneath him. Ramsay bent down to look at the scarlet exit crater which the tumbling bullet had torn in his back.

'It could have been worse,' he said, as calmly as he could.

'That's good. I can't feel anything. Not a thing,' Smith said.

Carl Johansson had grabbed his legs at the knees and lifted him right up.

'Move now. Together with me. Now,' he ordered Ramsay. It was then that Smith screamed aloud. Half crouching they hurried crabwise for the open door, doing their utmost to keep his sagging back from touching the ground as they did so. Two shots whiplashed the air above them.

Once inside they laid Smith face down on the bed. Something had to be done even if it was only a token. Carl soaked a hand towel in the warm water from the saucepan on the stove and laid it over the wound but that wasn't going to staunch the flow of blood and there was nothing else to hand.

His face against the pillow, Smith smelt the scent of bog myrtle and heather in the shabby bedding beneath, the smell of resin in the rough wooden frame of the bed. It had been a peaceful room. His body had become suddenly lighter and he felt that if he could manage to make the least physical effort he could push himself up and turn his face towards them to see what was going on. Somehow though the effort was beyond him. If he could have had his life over again he would have done most things differently. For a start he would have married and taken a job which was within his ability instead of allowing his father to bully him into becoming an underwriter. A failed underwriter. He had been a waste of everybody's time. What were they doing to his back now? It was becoming more and more difficult to concentrate on what was happening but he ought to be helpful if he could.

'Shouldn't you be trying to clean the wound?' he enquired in that high fastidious voice of his and thereupon died.

A shot broke the window and singing off the black iron flue of the stove embedded itself in the floor. Smith's blood was still flowing into the wet pad of material which they had used to hide the gaping wound in his back. It grew pink – then darkly red. There was a double bang on the wall of the house as though it had been struck hard with a fourteen-pound hammer. Instinctively Carl and Ramsay both dropped to the floor.

As far as they could judge the shots were coming from low down on the bank of the lake to the right of the house. They needed to put as much cover between them and the marksman as possible which meant getting into the bedroom. Carl crawled clumsily across the long rag mat on the floor smeared with blood, with Ramsay behind him. Then Ramsay remembered the case containing the syndicate's records and slid round on hands and knees on the floor, to look for it.

'No time,' shouted Carl. 'Move now.'

'Don't bloody order me about,' Ramsay shouted back.

Feeling the adrenalin washing through him he caught up the heavy bag by the handles, lugged it round in front of him and pushed it towards the doorway of the bedroom. Another shot thumped against the heavy wooden wall of the house. Carl lifted up the stool beside his bed and smashed it through the frame of the side window, still covered with paper to keep out the light, then wrenched the woodwork inwards, the splintered double layer of glass cutting his hands, grazing his forearms. He smashed again at the jagged ends of the remains of the frame, hauling and pushing at it alternately as he tried to loosen it. When the whole of the bottom edge came away, he hurled it aside and dived through. Ramsay threw the case after him and then followed himself, feeling a spar of the smashed frame tear at his sleeve as he went over. Now they had a more effective shield from their attacker, Ramsay thought, feeling relief – a momentary euphoria – at the moment's respite they had earned themselves.

It was then that Quist began firing from the other side of the lake.

'A second marksman,' Carl declared.

That's bloody obvious, Ramsay thought, as half crouching he chased after him, stumbling towards the corner of the house. Somehow they were together, both labouring for breath, dragging it in in great spasms, leaning with their heads bowed against the blank back wall of the house. Ramsay could smell its faint scent of ancient pitch. All at once it was quiet, except for the sound of their breathing.

Carl spoke first. 'There are two of them out there I think.'

'Yes indeed,' said Ramsay curtly.

'Some way up the valley. You notice? After the bullet arrives there is a small delay before you hear the gunshot,' he went on methodically. Usually twitchy, unpredictable in his behaviour, Carl Johansson was now as calm and painstaking as a judge. How long had he been expecting this attack – going out morning and evening to reconnoitre? Why had he said nothing to either of his visitors? Ramsay felt angry at having been pitchforked into this situation without warning. One minute he had been checking his luggage, making sure he had left nothing behind – the next he was an assassin's target, without any kind of warning whatsoever.

He said. 'There must be one of them on either side of the lake. How long will it take them to get up here?'

'Who knows? Fifteen minutes, half an hour I suppose. It's heavy going through the woods.' Their progress would be slow perhaps, but inevitable. A few minutes of safety and then the two men sent to kill them would have worked their way in their own time around both ends of the house until they were in a position to take them out behind it – to execute them in that open killing ground at their leisure. 'We must get into the forest,' he announced. There was nowhere else to go. But how long would they be able to keep ahead of their pursuers? And once they were deep in there how would they find their way out?

Ramsay shrugged and started to push his way through the underbrush.

'Stop,' shouted Carl. Why did the man always assume that he was in charge?

Impatiently Ramsay turned to him. 'Don't hang around. We've got to move.'

'We will get lost in there. I have to warn Hansson so that he can alert the police.'

'But there's no way of warning him. Will you move?' Ramsay shouted again. The man was a mental cripple as well it seemed. He spoke English well enough but he didn't seem to understand it. Even at full volume he couldn't take it in.

'Fire,' announced Carl. 'We must set fire to the forest, the house, everything – to make smoke.'

It seemed a drastic solution. Being burnt alive wasn't much of an option, Ramsay felt, until he heard another shot thump against the front wall of the house. On second thoughts perhaps the idea did have some merit if they could keep ahead of the flames. There was no wind – that was a help.

'A fire? Will he see it?'

'Somebody will,' said Carl, 'sooner or later.'

He's too optimistic. Ramsay thought, would it be soon enough? 'Matches or a lighter? Where?' he asked.

'Matches. In there beside the stove. And bring a jug.'

'A jug?' Ramsay queried, at a loss for a moment and not at all convinced that he'd volunteered to go.

'A jug, a saucepan. Anything!' Carl roared back with malevolence. 'Don't you understand your own language? Get me a container.'

'I'll go,' said Ramsay to confirm that he went of his own free will, rather worthily he thought, remembering the raw bloody chasm in Smith's back. He would have to trust that at this precise moment the rifleman on his side of the lake was on the move. Should he crawl round the corner of the house? No, it was better to go upright and move as quickly as he could.

He had reached the window and hadn't felt anything yet. No hammer blow. He grabbed the splintered window frame and facing inwards pushed himself up with both arms. It was difficult to get a perch for his feet because the window sill was much higher to reach from the outside. Then he was up and over bundling himself inwards clumsily, any way he could. Keeping his head low he scrambled through into the living room. Where the hell were they? The matches? There. He snatched up the box and shook it. About half full. OK. And the saucepan. On an impulse he snatched the pillow from the bed he had slept in the night before and approached the smashed window. He pushed the saucepan into the opening, swung the pillow up and over on top of it and waited. It was a neat little problem. Assuming that the marksman wasn't on the move and was watching that opening the question was – could he see that it was a pillow? If he couldn't he might take a shot at it. On the other hand, if he could he might very well be waiting for Ramsay to follow it. He waited for a second or two, then plunged out through the window headlong. Picking himself up outside he ran for the corner, back to the transitory safety of the rear of the house. There was silence when he reached it and he felt foolish, standing there listening with that saucepan in his hand. Still it was better than being dead. He smelt of sweat – could feel it running down between his shoulder blades like blood, as though he'd been hit without knowing it. Concentrate on this – staying alive. Deliberately he took deeper and slower breaths. Nothing had happened, no shot from the other side either. Both of the marksmen were on the move then.

Edging round the corner of the fuel tank, Carl had opened its brass tap to let the diesel fuel flow out and soak into the ground. He had taken off his shirt and was using it to sop up the fuel – the huge irregular scar visible on his back.

'Saucepan, good,' he grunted, inching round the edge of the tank to put it under the tap and let the fuel patter into it. There was no other sound except his breathing as it gradually filled up.

His head and shoulders swivelled round towards his companion. 'This is going to take all day. Why didn't you bring something else?'

'If you want another pan you can go in and get it yourself.'

Carl Johansson's clumsy shoulders shook with laughter. He was enjoying himself. A shot clipped the fuel tank and whirred off into the undergrowth – covering fire for the rifleman approaching on the other side presumably. Carl pulled the full saucepan from beneath the tap and began to swing it from side to side, sending the contents shooting out in a great golden arc over the undergrowth, the pale grey moss under their feet, the young trees on the edge of the plantation. He sent the last of the contents of the pan swirling up the side of the house drenching and darkening the timbers.

Screwing up his shirt, squeezing the diesel fuel out of it, he doubled back uphill towards the trees calling out to Ramsay to follow him. Finding a dead branch he tied the shirt roughly round the end of it, his hands, arms and naked chest glistening with the fuel.

'Get away from it. I'll light it,' Ramsay shouted at the wild figure – a demon out of a painting by Hieronymous Bosch – who capered out of the way after laying the branch down on the ground at his feet.

'Get on with it,' Carl ordered.

The first match went out. When the second was lit Ramsay threw it down on to the makeshift torch and it went up on the instant like a smoky orange flare.

'Keep away.' Ramsay pushed it unsteadily towards the pool of diesel fuel underneath the tank then made for the forest after Carl. Turning back he saw the soft pink and yellow explosion of flame billow out from beneath the tank and race up the side of the house, rivulets of flame flaring up in the dead grass and weeds surrounding it, joining each other in a bright circle which spread wider by the second. Now the side wall of the house was already well alight as far as the roof. Then the fuel tank exploded sending burning fuel out to a radius of thirty metres. They were both on the ground, pressing themselves down into the carpet of moss and loose twigs jabbing into their skin, afraid that the flying gobbets of oil would reach them. Ramsay jerked in a spasm of pain as one splash of flame landed on his shirt. Slapping at it to put it out, he was up in an instant and making with Carl for the cover of the broad belt of trees behind the house. Those nearest the blazing tank were already alight, sending up a widening plume of smoke into the clear sky.

They heard no more shots. Either the attention of the marksmen had been distracted by the explosion or they were still moving into position.

Carl and Ramsay began to force their way through the forest, cursing the brown skeletal lower branches catching at their faces, their eyes, arms, hands. Soon they were in a quiet world. A wall of smoke like a fog crept slowly after them, eddying and swaying as it advanced slowly between the trees. There was silence in the empty forest in front of them except for the distant crackle of the fire.

'Let's hope that Hansson has his eyes open,' Carl said, 'or the forestry people.'

Only then did Ramsay remember that he had left Smith's case behind with the syndicate's records in it. He turned and stared behind him at the smoke enveloping the forest, making it doubly impassable. There wasn't a hope of finding it.

There would be another complete set of the syndicate's accounts somewhere else surely? At Lloyd's or at the office in Ventnor. Wouldn't there? Doubt crept over him like the oncoming smoke.

Chapter Twenty-Two

'You will have another cup of coffee,' insisted Ulla
Hansson, putting out an implacable hand towards her
guest. Neither she nor her husband had told Jenny
anything about Carl Johansson beyond the simple admission that they knew him, that he was a neighbour of
theirs. She was volubility incarnate about everything else
because it was such a treat to have somebody new to talk
to – Hansson was always there of course but after nearly
thirty years of marriage the novelty had worn off him and
even she had come to realise that some of the things she
told him had been said to him before. One had to make
the most of a visitor. She had progressed from a detailed
review of and commentary on the menus of the hotel in
the Algarve where they had spent their holiday last May
to the details of the operation so many years ago that had
made a childless woman of her – barren.

She had seated her visitor with her face to the window in
her pale functional sitting room with the cool blue woven
carpet so that she could inspect every detail of the face that
had so captured Hansson's attention. She wasn't suspicious
by nature, however, and it hadn't taken her long to get
round to treating Jenny Winblad as a confidante rather than
a threat.

'And a spiced biscuit,' she added, pointing towards the

pale brown pile of them on her best Orrefors dish.

Knowing how it would be, Hansson had refused her invitation to coffee – but without being brusque about it; he had things to do before the vet arrived, he affirmed vaguely. Much as he loved his wife, he couldn't face another account of her hysterectomy and its effects.

Jenny shifted in her chair, feeling impatience prickling through her. The signs were all there. This woman was going to keep her pinned down for at least another half an hour. Cushioned by the normality of the Hansson sitting room her worries about Ramsay's safety had subsided a little but she still didn't know where he was. She looked at Mrs Hansson with dislike, ready to jump up out of her chair, shake her by her plump shoulders and demand to know where she could find Johansson's place.

'Calm down,' she told herself, looking past the woman at the peaceful view from her living-room window, at the dark water of the lake beyond with its fringe of trees diminishing into the thinnest line of grey at its farther end.

'My husband never likes me talking about my inside plumbing,' Mrs Hansson confided after he had gone. 'You'd think being a farmer, having to see to the calving, castrating the young bulls and so on, it wouldn't bother him but he's just as squeamish as the rest. What they had to do, you see, was to tie those tubes, Fallopian tubes they call them . . .'

'Mrs Hansson,' Jenny Winblad broke in, 'I think that something is burning in the forest over there. Something is alight.'

In the distance, right at the other end of the lake a column of smoke – dark at the base but thinner and more transparent higher up – was fanning out against a backdrop of white fluffy clouds, climbing and coiling steadily in the still air.

Taken aback Ulla Hansson slewed round in her seat and looked where her visitor was pointing, her eyes adjusting to the distance – then she moved with an astonishing turn of speed.

'I'll get my man,' she said.

It felt as though they had been pushing through the forest all day but they couldn't have made as much as half a mile when they reached a broad reef of granite where nothing grew except lichens and one or two hopeful birch seedlings which had found a pocket of soil in the odd crevice. The forest around them blocked their view on all sides. Above them lay a wide patch of white sky soiled by the smoke of the blaze that Carl had set in train. At least they had outstripped the wall of smoke seeping through the woods. They had no idea where the two snipers who were hunting them had got to – whether they were still on the other side of it or had managed to work their way around it and were closing in now.

Carl was sitting on the edge of the rock, arms resting on his knees with his head bowed over them.

After a few seconds of respite Ramsay asked, 'What happens next?'

'We wait,' Carl said between laboured and asthmatic breaths although they hadn't travelled a taxing distance; it seemed to Ramsay as if it was his deformity that made the simple process of taking in air more difficult for him, especially air tainted by the smell of burning wood. How would he manage if the wind got up and the heavy pall of smoke drifting through the forest overtook them?

'Can't you go on?'

'Of course,' Carl grunted, unwilling to admit failure.

'Very well then let's move,' Ramsay commanded, jumping to his feet.

'We go no further,' Carl stated flatly, 'there is a hundred kilometres of forest in that direction. You can get lost in it if you want to but I don't see why I should.'

'If we stay here we shall get ourselves shot.'

'It's a calculated risk,' Carl answered, sounding as if he welcomed it.

It was then that they heard a sound which neither of them could identify at first. Part of it was a low drone which could have been made by the engine of a boat, Ramsay supposed, a large boat driving through the water rather than skimming over its surface. But it wasn't that because superimposed on that sound was a regular beat, slower and more deliberate – something turning, slapping the air.

They both looked upward at their limited patch of sky fringed by the branches of birch and fir; it had clouded over now and there was even a whisper of rain falling on their upturned faces. Because his head was fused into his shoulders, Carl was forced to lean backwards stiffly, supported by his bent elbows behind him.

They could see nothing – only hear the sound.

'A helicopter,' he said. 'I have seen them before, here in the valley.'

Had their attackers brought up a helicopter? They didn't need to go to that length just to make sure of two unarmed victims in the forest, thought Ramsay. Glancing at his watch he realised how long it was since they had started the fire. Fully an hour and a half; longer even than that. Perhaps the machine had been called out by the Forestry Service. There had been time enough.

They were tantalised. The sound of the machine's rotors grew closer but still it didn't invade the pale area of sky above them.

Should they stay where they were in partial safety or

return to the lakeside and risk being shot by one of the snipers before they could make contact with the crew?

Ramsay could hear the rotors slowing down because the machine was landing. He would go back and reconnoitre. 'Stay here,' he told Carl and getting to his feet he plunged back through the woods the way they had come.

The sour smell of charred timbers caught Jenny in the throat. Here and there attenuated spirals of bluish smoke rose into the still air. Behind her in the forest she could hear the curt commands of the leader of the fire-fighting team anxious to wrap up the operation. The walls of the house which had been impregnated with tar, the timbers of its roof and the wooden shingles that had covered them – the whole of that outside shell – had been burnt away, destroyed completely leaving only the remains of what had been inside – the half-burnt furniture, here a smouldering blanket, there a few books, still on their shelves except for one which lay open on the ground face up. A book about birds, its pages browned but still legible; one of them flipped over in a sudden breath of wind – a colour photograph of a Canada goose, she saw, printed on shiny paper. The floor with most of its carpet, such as it was, was still intact – the table and beds were still standing. It reminded her of the doll's house she had had as a child. One could take off the roof and slide the walls clear better to rearrange its interior.

She had known there would be trouble. She had told Ramsay before he had left. Standing next to her he said only, 'It's a good thing they've taken Smith's body away.'

'What has happened to the men who killed him? Where are they?'

'In the forest somewhere. They'll never find them,' he replied.

She looked sidelong at him and found herself kicking at a fragment of wood, trying to dislodge it – she couldn't think why. Realising that it looked a childish thing to do she stopped. Then the wind lifted and sent a puff of hot smoke in their direction which took her breath away for a moment. With her eyes watering she just managed to stop herself from sneezing.

Moving closer to Ramsay she detected no response from him – nothing to reassure her. Half-heartedly she tried to tell herself that his remoteness was only a reaction to his ordeal earlier in the day.

Charles Ramsay sensed her beside him by no means as fragile as she looked but vulnerable nevertheless. He knew exactly what she wanted from him, and why he had to withhold it from her – because it would lead nowhere. Gradually he had come to understand the effect on her of their encounter after the picnic on the island – that it was certainly not something that she could laugh off or pretend to have forgotten The truth was that it had kindled no equal fire in him, only regret. He was a man, no better and no worse than any other – and few men of his age would have refused the offer she had made him. Their coming together had marked the beginning of a truce between them but that was the most he could say.

He had hoped against hope that the great orgasmic cry she had given then didn't mean that the episode was going to have a significance for her which he couldn't support. When he realised that it had, that she wanted a relationship with him, he had cursed himself. The last thing he could afford to do now was to allow her to nurture any false hope. That would be to pile cruelty on cruelty.

They stood absolutely still for a moment each trying to cope with the truth in their own way. Then she walked away from him, taking great care to walk erect, not to stumble or falter at all. He didn't watch her – looked instead at the thin plumes of smoke, studied one or two small flames, transparent in the sunlight, which were still trying to stay alive. By the time he turned to look after her she was already in the woods, on his left, moving between the trees towards the edge of the lake. She didn't look back.

Of all the places available for bathing this was the best, Carl Johansson thought to himself as he lay back in the water and regarded the sky above him. He was loth to admit it but it was pleasant not to be dead, like Smith. For a moment he wondered what provision would have to be made for the man's dependents – anything within reason, the amount wasn't an issue. The difficulty might lie in finding his wife, finding a solicitor in England to ensure that the settlement was made in the most tax-effective way. He would remit the whole problem to the company's legal department, that would be easiest. Then he remembered that Smith had had the good sense not to get married, and felt grateful to his dead partner for relieving him of even that chore. There might be other relatives who needed support though. The legal men could see to it.

Besides the sweat and smoke of the day, this bathe had washed away much of the humiliation which the assassins sent by his father had inflicted on him but it was getting hellish cold in the water. He could see his hands and arms on either side of him, bloodless under the surface. Time to come out. He started to march heavily against the pressure of the water towards the small patch of sandy beach where his clothes were lying.

He had almost reached them when Jenny Winblad came through the trees and saw him standing there stark naked.

Instinctively he turned to face the open water showing the great troubled scar between his shoulder blades. He would have shrugged his shoulders had that been physically possible for him. He would have nodded his head if that had been his style. It wasn't, so he stood waiting for her to go away. She should have done – it wasn't fair to him to stay – but caught up in her own sadness she felt a sudden access of pity for him standing dumbly like an animal, a victim, it seemed to her, ready to put up patiently with whatever might befall him, the water streaming down the hard muscles of his thighs and calves. When she leaned forward, he shied away, aware of her although he hadn't glanced back. Instead he looked straight ahead like a horse resigned to a vet's examination. When nothing seemed to be happening he peered at her out of the corner of his eye before swivelling himself round to look at her full in the face. Suspiciously. Even though it was he who was naked – cold, wet and naked – and she was fully dressed he was aroused and she saw it; he had no means of hiding it. It couldn't add to his ugliness but it robbed him of his dignity. Turning away awkwardly he began to dress himself as quickly as he could. As he busied himself, pulling on his trousers, she approached and he stopped, hands on the buckle of his belt, waiting angrily for her touch. She didn't try to make any kind of soothing noise, merely allowed her hand to move slowly towards the great white blotch of scar tissue on his back. As she brushed it gently with her palm he shivered, then waited again, his eyes staring ahead. Still like an animal.

The lake was totally silent without even a bird's wing moving.

'Go away. Leave me alone.' He spoke fiercely in English, as though the foreign language would put some distance between them. He needed that distance. She had allowed herself to come too close to him – a woman, a soft unattainable woman.

Because she understood his feeling of rejection, because she shared it and wanted to bring him closer to her, she replied gently in their native language, 'There is no need now that you are decent, is there?'

He didn't need soothing, he needed respite. Didn't she realise how her sympathy was humiliating him?

'The Hunchback of Notre Dame. That is not a role which I have any wish to play.' Although he answered her in Swedish he made sure that the words sounded formal, that she couldn't interpret them in any other way. She was standing so close to him now that he could nearly feel her warmth, could smell her light feminine scent – he breathed it in like oxygen. His right hand shifted for a moment at his side and then was still. She was testing his moral sense to destruction.

'Please,' she said, laying a cool palm on his shoulder.

He could feel the gesture coming and he knew what effect it was going to have on him. He tried to avert it. Before it arrived he made an expostulation, began to pull his shoulders away, to dodge it. He was slow and too clumsy, perhaps deliberately so – perhaps he hadn't made the effort he should have done. When he felt her hand touch him he could no longer contain himself, nor the pent up and frustrated energy he had hoarded all those years. Still barechested, pigeon chested by his deformity, he scythed round with his long right arm and caught her by the waist, bringing his primitive triangular face close to hers. To make it worse he was only able to express the intense longing which had suddenly exploded inside him by giving out a dull moan which would have sounded laughable from the lips of anybody else but from his sounded frightening – his lips which now were not far from hers. Being quite unable to articulate his feelings – he had never learnt the language – he wrapped his arms around her as though to make her accept them by brute force. As she screamed he crushed her against him wanting, so she thought, to stifle the sound by squeezing the breath out of her body. Trying to pull away from him she stumbled and he fell on top of her, legs stretched out stiffly to either side, his naked back, still wet from his bathe, showing the livid marks where her hands had just clutched at him in panic.

That was the moment when Ramsay arrived, alerted by their voices. There was his benefactor, the man who had promised to save Bressemer, apparently raping the girl. Reaching Carl he dragged at his arm. That was no good so he clutched him round the chest and pulled him violently from side to side, this way and that, trying to dislodge him.

Jenny Winblad rolled clear and jumped to her feet.

'It is all right. Nothing wrong,' she insisted, 'We fell over, that is all.' She looked wildly round her for an explanation of any kind. Something that would do. 'I was trying to help him put on his shirt.'

The shirt which was four metres away from them. Heavily Carl went to pick it up, pulled it over his head, anyhow – the points of the collar sticking up awry against his cheeks. His back towards them he tucked it into his trousers as well as he could without loosening his belt and being forced into the humiliation of lowering them under the gaze of two human beings who were so much better equipped than he was, having necks, elegant necks, and heads that swivelled easily above well-moulded shoulders – whose appearance did not arouse pity or self-satisfaction in the eye of the beholder. The water which still soaked his hair was trickling down his face. Dumbly he picked up the rest of his clothes and went off towards the jetty.

Ramsay couldn't blame Jenny Winblad – it was scarcely

her fault. But her presence there hadn't done much good for the fortunes of the Ramsay family. If the situation had a redeeming feature he couldn't think of it. Taken all round it had been a bloody awful day. It could have been worse though. If things had gone differently two out of the three of them might not have been there to grumble at the end of it.

Then he remembered that the marksmen might still be hidden somewhere above them on the hillside. That was still a possibility.

Chapter Twenty-Three

It irked Johansson that he had to wear a dark suit today, any day, and he would have preferred the luxury of casual clothes to soften the occasion but one didn't wear slacks and a sweater to an execution and this was a termination of a kind . . . of hope, at least for him.

He looked round at his guests and mentally disparaged all of them. He was aware that his view of the people who dwelt in the grey hinterland outside his immediate circle was unconventional. He thought about them, when he could bring himself to think of them at all, much as an Australian sheep farmer thinks about rabbits – small, grey and very expendable furry animals – tolerable when taken one at a time but terrifying when seen in a large crawling mass devouring everything which a prudent family like his had built up, lifetime after lifetime. He was still sufficiently in touch with reality though to be aware that it didn't do to allow any of them to glimpse his feeling for them, to let it peek through. He assumed that other people, however small and furry, had emotions and concerns of their own – they must have – concerns which were doubtless important to them. Like that fellow Charles Ramsay over there whom Axel had invited to this reserved function for reasons which they both recognised as sound. The man who had been his son's companion throughout his recent and distant ordeal. It made an excellent story in the newssheets which had helped to restore the company's rather crumpled image all over the world. Yes, the man Ramsay presumably had emotions of some kind although being an Englishman he had hidden them deeper down than even a Swede would do. Johansson had to pretend to be sensitive to all that, to be correct in the manner of the day, particularly where his managers and business associates were concerned – not to tread on their fragile egos, or allow them to see how far he towered above them.

Hence the suit with its subtle pinstripe, tailored painstakingly in Jermyn Street like all his formal clothes. Axel who had organised everything had insisted on it. Had dictated what he should wear.

A tall blonde girl, a sound Aryan type, came over to him bearing on the bent hands of a supplicant a finely wrought glass plate with canapés on it. Small exotic titbits – tiny squares of smoked reindeer flesh or salmon, black Iranian caviar. He took a single one delicately from the plate and before he bit into it gave the bearer of the gift a smile every ounce as warm and sincere as her own. It tasted right – everything was as it should be. Axel had made a good job of the arrangements, had taken them under his personal control, anxious to make certain that if they were hauling down their flag the company would at least extract the maximum benefit from the occasion – all the juice. Sometimes Johansson admitted secretly he became bored at his deputy's efficiency – too predictable. Johansson would have been pleased to be able to find fault with something.

Bearing in mind that the room was filled with friends and associates of the company from the four corners of the earth, the girls had been well chosen, he had to admit. Stylish, and linguists all of them – students working their way through university or foreign *au pairs*, all of good family, typically taking a year out in Stockholm and glad of the opportunity to make a little spending money on a day off in the chic surroundings of the Villa Johansson. It was the kind of detail that made all the difference to the Johansson image. But his satisfaction at the handling of the event overlaid a leaden sense of defeat which brought up a taste of bile in his mouth when he remembered its purpose. A reception to mark his son's thirtieth birthday and his consequent entry into his inheritance under the terms of the 1874 deed drafted by old Arne's man of law.

The father's eyes swept the throng and lighted on the form of his detested heir, clothed formally too – no doubt he had his advisers too – in a suit of sober heavyweight worsted, dark blue, tailored by the same sycophantic man in London, so skilfully, with a wide shawl neck and a low waist, so that although it couldn't disguise Carl's deformity it made a strange and almost romantic virtue of it, creating a striking presence out of what he was forced to be. A pert Japanese girl was offering him a slim glass of champagne, flashing an effervescent smile at him to go with it. What thoughts about his son did that smile hide, Johansson wondered. Would she, for example, be willing to contemplate going to bed with the monster? Would any woman? Somebody could be bought he supposed, but not the sort of woman he would want to have as a mother for his grandchild. Certainly not a Japanese he thought inconsequentially, that he would *never* permit. In any case the chance that he would ever hold a grandson in his arms was becoming ever more remote. The dynasty which had sprung from the energetic loins of Arne Johansson was going to wither away now. The banality of that thought made him frown – and the sudden realisation which pervaded him, the realisation that if his son wanted to marry a Japanese helper at this family feast, and she, against all the odds were willing to endure sharing a bed with him, there was nothing, nothing at all, that he could do to prevent it. He had no say in the matter. Not any longer. His son had emerged victorious from the twilight into his inheritance and, by virtue of the public glare that would surround him for the rest of his life, had become invulnerable. He was beyond his reach.

Johansson forced himself to turn his gaze in the direction of his son again and found that the simple act took every ounce of willpower he possessed. He had to force himself to raise his eyes to look across the room. When the task had been accomplished though, he was puzzled to see the man his son was talking to, talking amicably, not as if it was an arms-length negotiation, smiling even, with that half-apologetic lop-sided smile of his. Young Engström, son of the shipping magnate. One of the Lloyd's members whom his son had ruined with his amateurish venture. That was unexpected and the sight of the two of them apparently reconciled – more than reconciled – unsettled him further, served to underline the fact that virtue had gone out of him; he was empty of half the power that he had enjoyed for forty years – ever since he had himself been invested with it at just such a function as this.

His eyes shifted to Quist, a guest whom he'd had good reason to invite despite all Axel's reservations. Subservient after his failure and anxious not to put a foot wrong the assassin had obeyed the summons and come. Now he was trying to ingratiate himself with one of the girls – his eyes scanning the shape underneath her kingfisher blue sheath of a dress, imagining the blood, how the two colours would blend into a pale magenta; imagining it as an artist would.

A tame technician who had been engaged to record the event for the Johansson archive was filming them, camcorder on his shoulder, and the girl was managing to be polite to Quist – just – because she was being filmed and you never knew what that might lead to. A dark statuesque girl with long fine hands.

A touch of the tarbrush there (too much of it in Stockholm these days), thought Johansson as he watched her. On another day he wouldn't have minded but this afternoon everything had to be exactly right, perfect, to bring it absolutely home to his son, that stunted mountain of imperfection over there, that his father didn't give a damn.

Johansson turned and caught sight of the Englishman, his honoured guest.

'Mr Ramsay,' he cried out, moving towards him with welcome lighting up his face. Stopping one of the slim helpers as she passed him carrying a silver tray of newly filled glasses he took one and handed it ceremoniously to him.

'Krug. Special *cuvée*.'

'Delicious,' agreed Ramsay, savouring a little of it. Of course it was good. Surely somebody with Johansson's money didn't need to underline the fact.

'You are an antique dealer, I understand.' The magnate spoke in a slightly mocking tone as though excusing such an eccentric choice of career in one who seemed to be a gentleman in every other way.

'For my sins.' Because he didn't care for the man Ramsay made his reply deliberately banal. Why bother? He stared at the bubbles rising in his glass, then over the brilliant edge of it he glanced towards Carl, so spruced up now, remembering how he had appeared a couple of days earlier, prone on top of Jenny beside the lake – and the blazing look he had given: despair mixed with humiliation. After that humiliation was he going to keep his promise to take care of Ernest Ramsay's obligations at Lloyd's?

Of course Carl had the resources now to fund the whole of

the syndicate's losses. A cynic might have observed that considering the size of his fortune the gesture wasn't going to be a painful one. Nor had it done the company's image any harm. The public's faith in the Johansson way of doing things would be fully restored by the time all the journalists who had been invited to this celebration had filed the reports which were expected of them. Perhaps it was all part of some settlement negotiated between Carl and his father brokered by the smooth Axel over there. But that didn't matter. The only thing that mattered was whether his father's name still figured on Carl's list of beneficiaries or not. That question nagged like an aching tooth. When he returned to England what was he going to tell the anxious old man? He wasn't certain – that was the simple fact – nor was he sure if he could bring himself to ask Carl the question. At a quieter time perhaps; when the party started to break up. Before the end of the afternoon he would . . .

'The clock, Mr Ramsay.'

The elder Johansson had been pointing at it and now he was chiding Ramsay because he wasn't looking at it. Pulling himself together he concentrated his professional gaze on it. A pretty thing. The golden goddess in her immobile drapery. Yes. The truth was though that he was more interested in the Molitor commode on which it rested. Not for sale of course because it was an investment in the future. Besides, people as rich as Johansson didn't bother to sell such things. If because of some whim it suddenly displeased him he would have it moved upstairs or to one of the houses which he didn't visit often.

'What do you think of it? I should be grateful for your opinion. I should draw your attention to one or two small blemishes. It had an accident at the hands of my son. Here, you see? I forgave him. He has much to bear.'

'The clock is charming. *Directoire*.' Obviously, but he was expected to say something. Worth about four thousand pounds even with the damage. They both knew that very well but that wasn't something to be mentioned in this company, in this room.

'Very fashionable in Sweden early in the last century because we imported a Frenchman as a king. Bernadotte. A foreigner,' Johansson added, wrinkling his nose a fraction.

'Yes. I know,' said Ramsay. He thought he did, vaguely. Bernadotte – one of Napoleon's marshals who'd found himself a good billet up here in chilly Stockholm and sidestepped the disaster which had overtaken his emperor. A shrewd man.

Johansson was watching Quist advancing behind Ramsay's back. The hireling had a half-questioning expression in his face as though he was seeking instructions or was it reassurance? Was it simply that the fellow was puzzled? It amused Johansson. He did sometimes enjoy keeping people less clever than himself in a state of uncertainty – not knowing quite what they had to do to please him and well aware that if they got it wrong they would suffer for it later in some way, some unexpected way. Much as dogs are sometimes treated by a master who isn't interested in correcting the fault when they have failed but merely wishes to assert his rights over them, who wants them to beg.

He changed tack. 'Your profession must involve you in some intriguing ethical choices from time to time, Mr Ramsay. To me that would be one of the most interesting aspects of being a dealer. Knowing what was right, and holding to that despite the handicap it gave you. Building up a profitable business without swerving away from that. It is a difficult thing.'

Probitas. It was a perceptive remark from someone whom Ramsay hadn't found congenial so far, and he felt himself warmed by a sudden empathy with the man. An understanding lay between them.

Johansson continued, 'In former times in Sweden standards of business morality were very high indeed. Even among dealers. Today though . . .' He shook his head and grimaced. 'Works of art are stolen, hidden, despatched to secret places abroad. The tide is changing – it is too strong and one cannot stand against it. To try to police the flood of goods coming just now from the East for example. An impossibility. Carpets from Central Asia, icons from the monasteries, imperial treasures hidden away by frightened people since the Revolution. Gold and malachite.' Keeping his blue-eyed gaze fixed on Ramsay's face, he went on, 'After so many years of turbulent and painful change who can say who is the rightful owner? So I stand back from all that and merely watch.'

He spoke like a judge or a commissioner of police because that was how he saw himself – someone who had the power to act and was conscious of the responsibility. Ramsay kept silent.

'Sometimes though it is not a trivial thing like the change of ownership of an oil painting, the re-allocation of some piece of furniture. Sometimes it is a matter of real wickedness. Wickedness, there is no other word. Say, for example, the sale of redundant nuclear warheads from the East to one of the dictatorships of the Middle East,' Johansson continued, lowering his voice, his gaze flickering towards the straight grey-suited back of their nearest neighbour, the ambassador of another Nordic state. The man caught the glance and returned a graceful nod of the head. 'The forces of government are always too feeble, too slow to move. So when that kind of wickedness happens I see it as my duty to act, to mete out correction to the evildoer in such a spectacular way that his collaborators will have no difficulty in understanding it and its implications for them.'

Like hurling people out of hot-air balloons or fitting them up with cement footwear thought Ramsay. It occurred to him that Johansson wouldn't have the slightest difficulty in arranging something just as exotic for him. His whereabouts, his place of business, was easy to establish. Johansson was probably raving but it would be politic to pretend that he were sane – at least until the end of the afternoon.

Johansson's voice broke in on his train of thought, once again with a shadow of reproof in it.

'. . . Are you interested in it, Mr Ramsay?' Charles looked blank. Interested in what? Of course, the clock. 'Perhaps you would like to buy it?' At that place and time the question was almost a joke. Johansson wasn't joking though. 'I don't know what it is worth – you would know. Shall we say ten thousand crowns?'

A trifling amount, about eight hundred pounds – barely a fifth of what it was worth, even with the damage. Careful not to show his distaste Ramsay regarded his host directly. Was this an attempt to make fun of him or to bribe him? Whatever it was it left a bad taste which his next sip of champagne couldn't remedy. Did this bloody man really think he could be bought off like that? Presumably yes. Wearily Ramsay decided that he couldn't allow himself the luxury of telling Johansson to find another home for his clock.

'That is much too little,' he managed to say. 'I think you should reconsider the figure.' The other man made a little shrug – ten thousand crowns was not a sum of any interest to him. It was about as much as the Johansson banks, industrial plant and ships had earned him in the few minutes since this conversation had started.

Ramsay reached for his traveller's cheques but was forestalled by Axel's voice behind him, a hand on his shoulder.

'I think you should forget that. The clock must be a present in recognition of your help in saving Carl's life.'

Axel picked up the clock in both hands. 'It should be presented to you properly and we must have a recording of the event,' he insisted, bustling to clear a space among the guests and beckoning to the cameraman. There was no point in being generous in secret.

It didn't take long. Johansson handed over the clock with a few neat phrases – even remembered a joke which was good enough to draw a laugh from the careful lips of the ambassador. Ramsay expressed his thanks in a modest English way. It was quite painless. Why had he bothered about it, he asked himself as an underling took charge of the timepiece. Ramsay saw its hard drapery of gilded bronze pressing into the flesh of the man's hands. When he looked back he discovered that Johansson had found somebody else to talk to. At least the little ceremony had relieved him of the need to be polite to him; now he was free to circulate. All at once he wished that Julia were beside him – this party was her style of thing. He needed her to talk to.

Quist looked uncertainly at Johansson, trying to guess what he wanted, regretting now that he had obeyed the magnate's summons to this celebration instead of making straight for Arlanda and taking the first flight out. Losing himself somewhere. In Africa or the Middle East.

Johansson took him by the elbow with a firm but apparently friendly grip which Quist took care to go along with. He found himself being led into an ante-room furnished in the same formal style as the big reception room, oak parquet underfoot relieved by boldly patterned Caucasian rugs, pale walls hung with immaculate Hiroshige woodcuts in matt grey frames – *The Hundred Views of Edo*. Because the curtains were drawn to protect them from the harsh midsummer light and the room was in semi-darkness he couldn't make out the expression on Johansson's face, but he knew how he was considered – as an underling of no account, on the periphery of things – so he waited without enthusiasm to hear what his next assignment might be. Carl was no longer a target, that much he had guessed. Perhaps Johansson had a down on the antique dealer and wanted him removed. You could never tell with him, his purposes were hidden, and Quist feared that he would be required to carry out this next task gratis to compensate for the failure of the other operation. If that meant he could get clear without any comeback so be it, he thought fatalistically. Let's get on with it.

Johansson closed the door to shut out the sound of voices making animated small talk in the other room. Performing the action as he did everything else, deliberately, almost placidly, because rarely in his life had he found himself forced to hurry. That was for others to do – people like Quist. They moved or stayed still, waiting, at his whim. After fifty years in command, his life moved at the pace he set for it.

Besides it amused him to keep the failure Quist on tenterhooks a little longer, to know his pleasure. He turned and faced the fellow silhouetted against the sunlit curtains which were decorated with the moving shadows of the branches of birch trees in his garden outside.

The elimination of Quist had been in Johansson's mind from the very beginning but only reluctantly had Axel arranged it. He had merely been required to lift a telephone. One telephone call, but he had demurred for a while because he couldn't see the necessity, because he realised that even that might implicate him. Nobody would ever be able to trace the transaction to Johansson himself – the order had been spoken softly, in their most private meeting place. What had been said had been elliptical and there hadn't been much of it. Finally Axel had capitulated with a frosty nod of agreement, knowing how quickly he could fall from favour and what a weight of power and money lay under Johansson's hand. It made no sense to hold out. He was unstoppable, omnipotent.

Johansson had made sure that he had no idea how much the imminent execution of Quist would cost but he doubted if it would amount to more than a couple of hundred thousand crowns, that was to say about as much as the company earned him in an afternoon. Four hours of his life would purchase the rest of Quist's – a man who looked healthy with a life-expectancy of about forty years. An hour of his life was equivalent in value to ten years of the assassin's. The idea fed his vanity – the proportion was as it should be.

Quist said edgily, having waited quite long enough in silence for a sign he felt, 'Why am I here? What else do you want from me?'

Johansson replied, 'Compensation.'

'For what?'

'You know very well.'

There was no reply from the shadows.

'You must be punished,' Johansson advised him in a pleasant voice. 'It is already arranged. Axel has seen to it. You had to be told of course and I am telling you now.'

He went on to explain candidly what was going to happen, that it was inevitable. There was no point in meting out retribution if the object of it didn't know he was being punished and why. Remote and judicial, he awaited Quist's reaction. He would plead for his life no doubt in a confused and illogical way, completely missing the point – the man was a fool. And his pleas would be fruitless. Johansson had already made that decision.

But there was still not a word from Quist – he hadn't

uttered. It was odd. Instead, he seemed to be bending forward, bending down as though to tie his shoelace. It was an unusual reaction but human beings reacted oddly under stress sometimes.

Out of the gloom an arm rose up and encircled Johansson, who was so astonished by the sudden touch of an inferior hand as it caught him in the small of the back that he didn't make a sound. Then he collected himself, opened his mouth to speak, just as Quist thrust his little friend easily between two of his ribs. The thin shaft of steel penetrated Johansson's chest with no more resistance than a skewer entering a rolled-up joint of pork so that he scarcely felt the thrust of it at all. It surprised him though, as well it might. He was about to cry out, had every intention of doing so, when the point of it reached his heart and put a stop to that – to everything.

Quist allowed the body, suddenly heavy, to fall noiselessly by stages to the floor. Then he withdrew his little stiletto, wiped it on his handkerchief – there was no great effusion of blood – and returned it to the sheath strapped to his ankle in case he needed it again. Without looking back at Johansson's body he made for the door and pressed down on the slim brass lever of a handle with his elbow. After leaving the room he moved as unobtrusively as he could through the chattering crowd, along the edge of the room, well away from the TV cameras, easing himself out of the Villa Johansson. He glanced at his watch. It would take at least twenty minutes for someone to notice that Carl's father was missing, another five to discover him, establish that he was beyond resuscitation and call for the police. By that time he would be halfway to the airport. The police had no photograph of him, nothing to go on. Once he reached Arlanda it would take him half an hour at most to get himself booked on a flight out to anywhere – he wasn't fussy. He couldn't lose. And if by some mischance there was something he had overlooked and they did catch him, a few years in a Swedish prison was a much better prospect than ending up dead. Quist was surprised that Johansson – with a mind so adept at the calculus of risk – had not worked that one out. Over-confidence, that was his weakness. Deluded by the barriers that his wealth had erected around him into believing that he couldn't be touched. Surely he knew that nobody was invulnerable. Nobody. Such a stupid man, thought Quist.

Chapter Twenty-Four

Jenny Winblad closed the front door behind the men with gloved hands removing the last green-painted crate – and the sight of Charles Ramsay giving her a last embarrassed wave because he knew that in taking these pieces he had deprived her of something of her home, a small part of herself. Leaving her with his large cheque stowed away in her bureau which was compensation of a kind. Enough there to keep the cold winds of real life from disturbing the artless calm of Alvarö until at least next spring. Lars and Gunilla would be able to continue with their inefficient fishing expeditions until the sound froze over for the winter. Uncle Henrik would be able to puff at his pipe and dispense advice gratis to anyone polite enough to listen, for a few months more. The deluge had been put off; time had been bought. She shook herself; it was nonsense to make such a tragedy of losing a few of her possessions.

She looked down at the place on the carpet where the feet of one of the wing armchairs had rested leaving four bleak depressions, as though it had merely become invisible and would still be there solid and secure as soon as the spell was lifted. She was a slut, she decided. There was dust there, she could see it, specks of white fluff because she had failed to vacuum underneath for days and now she had been found out. She went to find the cleaner, plugged it in, turned it on and in a moment had effaced the evidence, the four marks in the carpet, rubbing them away vigorously with the nozzle of the machine. There were other ghosts to be laid. The place where the Chinese Chippendale long-case clock had been and upstairs the marks of the bracket feet of the bachelor chest. All had to be erased before she could rest.

Above the din of the vacuum cleaner the single beat of the telephone erupted in the room.

'Winblad,' she said brightly, trying to lift her spirits.

A firm voice replied. 'Carl Johansson here.'

She remembered the scarred back, the look on his face as he had scrabbled to cover his white nakedness. Now he was composed, in control, apologising for troubling her, with no sign of any hang-ups, no inconvenient memories. Of course, with his father gone he was master of all the Johansson enterprises now. Monstrous or not the world had to accept him as he was – that was what she heard in his voice.

Her brother had held his own records of the syndicate's members, he said – their claims, the extent of their exposure, the calls that had been made on them. He wanted to have them crosschecked against his own files. Because Smith had been killed before the job had been finished everything needed to be done again, he explained. Pointless to settle the reckoning and find that someone's figures had been omitted or ignored. It would tarnish the whole exercise. Yes, she understood, and no, the request was not painful she assured him. It would not stir up any comfortless memories of her brother Bengt.

'Perhaps you could have the papers photocopied and then return them to me,' she added, remembering almost too late that the members of the action group would not want to lose control of them, conscious perhaps that she had gone further than she should in allowing him access to them. But his intentions were honest, praiseworthy, and she felt it impossible to refuse such a request from a man who was, she could think of no other word for his condition, disabled. Had he been otherwise she might have been more sceptical, readier to impose conditions. She told herself that you couldn't have guessed how he was, hearing his voice on the telephone, and immediately chided herself for such a child-ish thought. She realised that she thought of him as a lame dog, just like the others – Lars, Gunilla, Uncle Henrik, whose perfect manners had never got him anywhere.

'I'll send a car for them with somebody to make an inventory,' he insisted. Every detail would be attended to. Already she could feel his money beginning to take control of her. Such a simple thing to do – to lie back and let it take over.

Then the deep voice began on a new tack. 'I must apologise for the incident by the lake the other day. I hope that what occurred was not misunderstood. By you, I mean. I had become used to living alone out there – something of a recluse you know.'

Both of them alone, at either end of the telephone line. Rejection was their common problem. Wasn't that it? She wondered what it must be like to be cut off from everybody else by such ugliness, especially from the arms of women, enduring every day an involuntary vow of chastity imposed from the beginning of his life until the end. She pitied him – of course she did.

'One does let things slide in the country. I understand of course,' she replied. It was difficult to be unfriendly because that would seem so hard and now she had no idea how to bring the jerky, formal conversation to a close. It would be equally cruel to allow him to entertain any misconceptions about her. Wasn't that the lesson she had just learnt from the Englishman who had left only minutes earlier?

'Very well, I will send the man directly.' What already?

Now? She hadn't thought he had meant straight away.

'I need time, to get everything in order,' she complained.

'My personal assistant will see to that. He is competent and completely trustworthy. You need only show him your brother's room and where his records are kept.'

It was an intrusion and she wasn't to be taken for granted in this way – and yet she couldn't find it in her to tell him so.

'Just send the car,' she said, almost peremptorily because she was bothered. 'I'll find the papers myself and bring them to you.'

Wasn't that the best way? She wasn't going to have a supercilious stranger in her house looking at the gaps, not until she had been given a chance to put it to rights.

'I am grateful.' He even sounded as though he was – there was a warmth in his voice. 'Perhaps I might offer you dinner, here in the hotel, as a token of my thanks.' He meant in private so that she would not have to be seen with him as her escort, nor made the butt of the gossip columns posing the mute question to their female readers. 'How could she? Could you? Even if it meant access to that enormous wealth and life on a different plane from the rest of us? Could you, Beauty, bring yourself to embrace the Beast? In bed as well, you understand. In bed too? That is what we mean.' Something to give every housewife a *frisson* over her morning coffee. A pleasurable shiver of revulsion at the thought.

She would be spared the photographers – that was what he was trying to tell her. He spoke the words shortly, as though he was ready to disown them at once, to pretend that he hadn't said them, or at least to withdraw them instantly if they proved to be too much for her. He wasn't going to lay himself open any more than he had to.

Helpless because it was a wound that she couldn't bring herself to inflict on him, she heard herself accept the invitation not knowing where it would lead her. She had a weakness for lame dogs – Lars, Gunilla, her brother. But she wasn't at all sure that this man belonged in that category. Certainly he didn't have much in common with them. The newspapers were full of the story of the death of his father – of his accession to power, the changes he had forced through.

'The car will call in an hour,' he said with nothing like hope in his voice because he didn't believe in hope and he was strong enough now to do without it. Blessed are they that expect nothing for they shall be satisfied.

Chapter Twenty-Five

Charles Ramsay decided to go straight round to the showroom because that was where Julia would be and he would be wasting time if he went to the flat first. He had been away from her for too long. Besides, he was aware how much she resented his long stay in Sweden and he had to mend his fences straight away. All he needed was a quiet half an hour with her to calm her down and put the trip into perspective. Of course she would have to be told that he didn't know yet if it had been successful or not. There was still no word from Carl Johansson. Nothing. Which was one reason why, feeling himself balanced in limbo with nothing resolved, he had drunk too much on the flight. Coming back with her trolley from the rear of the aircraft, pushing it clattering gently up the aisle ahead of her, the stewardess had halted at his gesture and handed him, unsmiling, another two miniatures of whisky. She had left him to pour them out for himself. Then he had slept an uneasy sleep which had given him an awful taste in his mouth and a gritty irritation in the eyes; sleep never agreed with him in the afternoon. It had taken him fully an hour to wake up properly. If he had gone back to the flat he could have taken a shower and pulled on a clean shirt before this meeting but he couldn't wait that long.

The taxi stopped, the driver waiting impatiently while he worked out the tip and searched for English money in his wallet. That would do. Apparently satisfied, the man gave him a hand with his baggage into the showroom and there was Julia behind the desk.

'If you'd told me your flight number I'd have met you at the airport,' she cried out, running towards him, hugging him, giving his back an affectionate pat as she held him. That was better, a little better.

Then he caught sight of Ethelred Lewis behind her, watching them embrace with an avuncular look on his face, lolling on the sofa with his legs crossed, and he felt worse again. For once Lewis looked quite passable – less roly-poly, spruce even, although that made his presence at their reunion no more palatable. Him grinning there like an inverted Peeping Tom.

'Don't mind me, my dears,' he fluted.

It was then that Ramsay saw the easel – a serious Victorian easel closely jointed in mahogany. Where had it come from? The four-square kind, fitted out with solid brasswork, that might have come out of the studio of Millais or Watts. And sitting on it, in the glare of a spotlight, the picture of the town in Central Europe, Pirna, which he had last seen in the whitewashed showroom upstairs in Anders's shop in Gamla Stan.

'How did that get here?'

'We bought it,' said Ethelred, on the defensive immediately, 'Fair and square. Julia and I purchased it as a private speculation. Didn't we?'

'Absolutely,' she confirmed although she had the grace to look ashamed. Ramsay said nothing because there was nothing to say. Wasn't she his partner?

'What else have you been up to while I have been away?' he demanded, disturbed suddenly by the memory of what his solicitor had said to them both when the partnership had been set up. They were jointly and severally liable for its debts – something like that – and now it looked as though she had cut loose. His absence must have hit her hard but there was no way she could justify this, was there? It was he who had discovered the bloody painting, had sent her the photographs and told her where to get them checked out – and she had gone straight to Lewis with a proposition that excluded him. But that wasn't the problem.

'We meant you to have a share,' she said.

A share? Thanks.

'Don't look so morose,' purred Lewis, 'just because we beat you to it.'

There was silence.

Julia said, 'I couldn't get hold of you . . . We had to make a quick decision.'

We? What did she mean we? Ramsay wasn't prepared to have a row with her, not with Lewis there to savour it, but he wasn't going to let her off altogether.

'Let's just go over this step by step.' He ticked each of them off on his fingers. 'One, you are supposed to be my partner. Two, I found this picture in a back room in Stockholm, procured photographs of it and sent them to you. Three, I asked you to get an opinion on them . . .'

'Yes, yes and yes,' she interrupted, 'but that's only half the story. I was left here to mind the shop wasn't I, while you rushed off on this wild goose chase to Sweden? Twice I heard from you while you were there. Twice. What was I supposed to think? I assumed you'd lost interest in the business much as you had lost interest in me.' She paused. When he said nothing she went on, 'I couldn't get hold of you. I didn't know where you were. Ethelred had this buyer who wanted a decision the same day.'

'Buyer? Where?'

'France,' said Ethelred promptly – too promptly. 'Poitiers.'
'And his name?'

'My lips are sealed. A collector.' The light from the lamp above caught the ring on his finger and it flashed uncertainly, only half a spectrum of colours. He was lying of course. The buyer was mythical, just dreamt up to give Lewis time to scuttle around and find somebody. Ramsay wondered if, apart from anything else, Julia wasn't a touch too innocent for the antique business.

'We did get an opinion,' Julia said.

'So at least you did what I asked.'

'Your man couldn't place it,' Lewis asserted, dismissing him. That had to be false; they probably hadn't consulted him at all.

'My man could though,' Lewis went on. 'Unsigned. But the inscription on the back is characteristic. Unmistakeable. That's what he said.'

'And?' Ramsay enquired.

Ethelred pouted, wanting to tease. 'I paid for the advice. Why should I let you have it for free . . .'

'Tell him,' ordered Julia.

The dealer shrugged, made a brief sigh, and then capitulated. 'Bernardo Bellotto – and I bet you're no wiser.'

'The nephew of Antonio Canal. Known as Canaletto too. The nephew, I mean,' she put in awkwardly. 'He spent some time in England, then in Dresden as court painter to Augustus the Third of Saxony, which is when he painted this. Finished up as a pensioner of the King of Poland . . .'

'How much did you pay Anders?' Ramsay interrupted.

'I didn't use our joint money. My mother put up my half,' Julia explained. So Lewis had had to find half the price himself, which was a compensation.

'How much did you pay?' Ramsay insisted, beginning to enjoy himself.

'Twenty-five thousand . . . pounds,' she said.

'You could have done better. He asked me for only twenty.'

'A detail,' Lewis trumpeted, brushing that aside in his eagerness to show how smart they had been. 'Do you know what it's worth? Tell him Julia. Go on, tell him.'

'Two hundred thousand pounds,' she admitted, adding hastily, 'though we were going to share it with you. As I said.'

Perhaps she had meant to – but Lewis? Never.

'I don't want anything to do with it,' Ramsay answered.

'Cut off your nose to spite your face,' Lewis chattered. 'Don't be childish.'

'I can't afford to be involved.'

Julia was bothered. 'What do you mean?'

Ramsay said, 'That painting has to have been stolen.'

'Stolen. Where from?'

'Warsaw – Saxony. I don't know. I met Anders and he wasn't a novice. He wouldn't have sold you a Canaletto at an eighth of its value if it wasn't stolen.'

'You were interested yourself,' Julia pointed out.

'I didn't know what it was then.'

'Anyway it's here now and that's only supposition,' Lewis chimed in, trying to sound as though he was in charge.

'No,' said Julia. 'It'll have to be gone into.' She wasn't having her mother involved in anything which smelt of receiving, even if it meant confessing to her that she'd lost twelve and a half thousand pounds of her money.

Ramsay looked at her with affection and began to feel more cheerful. There would be no need for any confession. He would make sure that she was spared that. All she had to do was to tell her mother that the deal had fallen through after all. She could repay her from their joint account. The profit from the furniture he'd bought in Biskopstorget

309

would more than cover the loss. That was the least he could do.

It was the middle of the afternoon and the coast road was empty of traffic as Ramsay drove along with the sea beating on his right-hand side. Now and then patches of dark mirage appeared on the hot tarmacadam ahead of him, false pools of moisture. The shadow of a cloud passed over the scene making it dull, sullen.

He changed into a lower gear to turn into the avenue and as he did so he glanced away for a moment as if the image of Bressemer was going to be painful and he would have to force himself to look back through the two rows of heavy trees to catch his first sight of the house since his return. That was when he felt Julia's warning hand on his arm and braked.

There was his father. He was sauntering along by himself past one of the lime trees, lethargically, not striding out as he used to do, and the dog wasn't with him either. They had almost reached him before he heard the purr of the engine behind him and stood to one side, half stumbling against his walking stick.

He bent down to the window of the car, peering in.

'Good afternoon,' Julia called out cheerfully. 'May we give you a lift back to your house?'

The old man smiled to see them but his eyes seemed to be preoccupied with something else. 'I wasn't expecting you until later. It's all ready though.' He didn't say what was ready. Tea, Charles supposed – in Julia's honour. He would have laid out silver, porcelain cups and saucers in the drawing room.

'Where's Wellington?' Charles asked, solicitous.

'Oh he's all right. Didn't feel like a walk, that's all. Getting lazier by the day.'

Julia cleared a place for Ernest Ramsay on the back seat and he got in, his walking stick rattling against the door beside him as he tried to find a place to put it.

'I don't know why I bother with the thing. It only gets in the way.' He gave a bark of laughter which aimed to soften the impatience of the remark, then relapsed into silence as Ramsay drove the couple of hundred yards to the front door.

Ernest paused before shifting to get out of the car. 'I've got something to show you. I need your opinion.'

Julia went to give him a hand, reaching for his elbow. He waved her away and made his own way up the front steps. At the top of them he turned, the massive front door diminishing him, and threw his arms wide.

'Welcome to Bressemer,' he called out in a combative voice, that of a younger man, as if he were challenging somebody to gainsay him. He then led them inside, down the panelled hall with its Caucasian runner, to the study.

The big wing chair was in its usual place – so were the vivid armorials of the Ramsay family beside it. However the top of the bureau had been cleared of its usual mess of papers to make space for a tall bottle and three heavy wine glasses. Beside them was an envelope.

'This letter came this morning,' he announced. 'Here.' Picking it up he handed it to his son.

What was this about? Lloyd's again? Were they putting the screws on now?

Ramsay extracted the sheet of fine paper and unfolded it; at the top in pale blue Art Deco script – *Johansson AB*. He read it through line by line before saying a word to his father. Whatever the message was he had to make sure he got it right.

It was a circular letter addressed to all the members of the SJ Underwriting Syndicate, informing them that

Johansson AB would assume responsibility for the whole of the syndicate's liabilities, actual and potential, past and future. The signature was no more than a hasty curl of ink. There was a covering letter from one Kerstin Lindström – Carl Johansson's secretary no doubt – with other enclosures, instructions, a statement to be signed by the recipient. Ramsay flipped through the pages in case there was a personal message of some sort. A few scrawled words? No, nothing of that kind.

For a moment his father's forehead was clenched with anxiety. 'Is this straight? Do they really mean what they say there?' he asked.

'Yes. I'm certain they do.'

Ernest Ramsay still looked doubtful. 'All the losses, everything? It's a great deal of money. Are you sure it's not some gambit of theirs?'

Ramsay shook his head.

Julia had been standing back since strictly it wasn't her business. Now she felt free to give the old man the bottle and the corkscrew so that he could do the honours. Concentrating on his task, the neck of the bottle trembling a little, he filled the glasses and handed them round.

He made no comment nor did he offer a toast – somehow that was unnecessary, Ramsay agreed silently, taking his glass from the old man's hand, sensing that he had made it back to the shore, could feel the firm sand again beneath his feet.

A Rare Benedictine

The Advent of Brother Cadfael

Ellis Peters

'Brother Cadfael sprang to life suddenly and unexpectedly when he was already approaching sixty, mature, experienced, fully armed and seventeen years tonsured.' So writes Ellis Peters in her introduction to *A Rare Benedictine* – three vintage tales of intrigue and treachery, featuring the monastic sleuth who has become such a cult figure of crime fiction. The story of Cadfael's entry into the monastery at Shrewsbury has been known hitherto only to a few readers; now his myriad fans can discover the chain of events that led him into the Benedictine Order.

Lavishly adorned with Clifford Harper's beautiful illustrations, these three tales show Cadfael at the height of his sleuthing form, with all the complexities of plot, vividly evoked Shropshire backgrounds and warm understanding of the frailties of human nature that have made Ellis Peters an international bestseller.

'A must for Cadfael enthusiasts – quite magical' *Best*
'A beautifully illustrated gift book' *Daily Express*
'A book for all Cadfael fans to treasure' *Good Book Guide*
'Brother Cadfael has made Ellis Peters' historical whodunnits a cult series' *Daily Mail*

HISTORICAL FICTION / CRIME 0 7472 3420 5

A selection of bestsellers from Headline

APPOINTED TO DIE	Kate Charles	£4.99	☐
SIX FOOT UNDER	Katherine John	£4.99	☐
TAKEOUT DOUBLE	Susan Moody	£4.99	☐
POISON FOR THE PRINCE	Elizabeth Eyre	£4.99	☐
THE HORSE YOU CAME IN ON	Martina Grimes	£5.99	☐
DEADLY ADMIRER	Christine Green	£4.99	☐
A SUDDEN FEARFUL DEATH	Anne Perry	£5.99	☐
THE ASSASSIN IN THE GREENWOOD	P C Doherty	£4.99	☐
KATWALK	Karen Kijewski	£4.50	☐
THE ENVY OF THE STRANGER	Caroline Graham	£4.99	☐
WHERE OLD BONES LIE	Ann Granger	£4.99	☐
BONE IDLE	Staynes & Storey	£4.99	☐
MISSING PERSON	Frances Ferguson	£4.99	☐

All Headline books are available at your local bookshop or newsagent, or can be ordered direct from the publisher. Just tick the titles you want and fill in the form below. Prices and availability subject to change without notice.

Headline Book Publishing, Cash Sales Department, Bookpoint, 39 Milton Park, Abingdon, OXON, OX14 4TD, UK. If you have a credit card you may order by telephone – 01235 400400.

Please enclose a cheque or postal order made payable to Bookpoint Ltd to the value of the cover price and allow the following for postage and packing:

UK & BFPO: £1.00 for the first book, 50p for the second book and 30p for each additional book ordered up to a maximum charge of £3.00.

OVERSEAS & EIRE: £2.00 for the first book, £1.00 for the second book and 50p for each additional book.

Name ....

Address ....

....

....

If you would prefer to pay by credit card, please complete:
Please debit my Visa/Access/Diner's Card/American Express (delete as applicable) card no:

Signature .... Expiry Date ....